HIDDEN FATE

THE MARKED DRAGON PRINCE TRILOGY

JEN L. GREY

CHAPTER ONE

BLOOD TRICKLED from the mouth of the dragon king, and his legs wobbled. When he stumbled, two warriors grabbed his arms and helped him regain his balance.

A dagger protruded from his back.

"How could you?" his deep voice rasped as he gaped at his younger son. His blood soaked the bottom half of his lavender shirt, turning it crimson. His midnight-black irises lightened as death drew closer.

A mix of emotions swirled through Thorn's and my fated-mate bond as he watched his estranged father fade in front of his eyes, mortally wounded by none other than Thorn's younger brother, Drake.

Drake was born soon after his parents had tried to kill Thorn at the tender age of six. They'd nurtured the very son who'd grown into the exact thing they'd feared Thorn would become—evil. Not only had Drake stabbed his father, but he'd also hunted Thorn to kill him, and he'd tried to force me to marry him, even though Thorn and I were fated mates.

The cool breeze of late May from the Blue Ridge

Mountains shifted the tree branches in the small clearing and brushed across my naked skin, bringing the metallic stench of blood to my nose. I stepped closer to Thorn, needing his body heat and the jolt of our fated-mate connection. Our group was all naked. Drake had forced us to shift into our human forms, or else he would've hurt Tyson, who lay unconscious at his feet, naked with a tranq lodged in his side.

Drake's nose wrinkled as he lifted his head. "You're trying to prevent me from taking the throne...from making our race strong. You criticized me for choosing a wife and a breeder. I'm doing what's necessary to ensure our race doesn't die out."

Because his father had denounced his narcissistic ass as the true heir to the throne. This confrontation, though, was limited to the warriors here and our group, which no other thunder would trust, not yet. That had to be why Drake had stabbed his father.

To my right, Saphira straightened. The front section of her long, curly, dark brown hair cascaded over her shoulders, covering her breasts, and the other half fell to her midback. The color emphasized her gorgeous bronze skin. She narrowed her mocha eyes as she spat, "Like killing all the injured and old dragons? And forcing a human to be your breeder even though she might die?"

"I am keeping our bloodline pure." Drake clenched his hands. "If our race wants to survive and thrive, someone has to do the hard things." He waved a hand at his father. "*He* wasn't up to the task. He was going to hand over the throne to an *abomination*."

I snorted, unable to stay silent. I'd done that for too long with my stepdad, accepting the poor way he treated me, and I'd recently learned that he'd treated my brother and sister similarly while I'd been gone. "That's complete bullshit. Thorn is not an abomination. He's strong, caring, and can heal the injured. Having a permanent injury doesn't make anyone weak." Anyone who'd ever had to persevere and learn how to survive through adversities was stronger than Drake and all his loyal warriors combined. He was an entitled jerk who'd never had to struggle.

Drake's ice-cold ebony eyes drilled into me.

Bristling, Thorn fidgeted so that his naked body blocked most of mine from Drake's view. Thorn snarled, his anger palpable. Everyone must have felt it.

"Everly. Dear fiancée..." Drake sneered at me. Despite the breeze, his dark brown hair remained in perfect small spikes. "That is your *one* slip. Once we are married—"

Body shaking, Thorn stepped forward. My eyes locked on his mark, the very thing that had instigated this entire mess almost two decades ago. Spread over the base of his neck to the top of his back, the mark resembled a dragon tattoo. It denoted that he possessed magic, the kind that petrified the king and all the other dragons. Thorn could create new dragon shifters. He could also take a dragon shifter's magic away—a power Thorn's grandfather had possessed and abused for evil.

"She is *my mate* and *wife!*" Thorn bellowed. He tensed, every muscle in his back pronounced. He stepped over one of the ten unconscious warriors as the other forty surrounding us remained frozen in place. Everyone, including Vlad, Cassidy, Saphira, Tyson, Errol, and Brenton, was still reeling from what we'd witnessed—Drake stabbing his father, King Arman, in the back.

Drake laughed loudly. "Maybe now, but not for much longer. Once we get you back to the château, we'll record all of your deaths…except hers." He pointed at me. "Of course."

"Son, this isn't you." King Arman's voice came out garbled. Blood ran down his chin and onto the front of his shirt. "We raised you better than this."

The few times I'd met the king, power had radiated from him, enhanced by his dragon and his tall, muscular build. His salt-and-pepper hair and the crow's feet around his eyes gave him a wise air, although he'd made the foolish mistake of driving his older son—my mate—away. Now, even with two warriors attempting to hold him up, he dropped to his knees.

"Your Highness." Errol's face twisted with agony, and his chocolate-brown eyes darkened as he raced past his daughter, Saphira, and his brother, Brenton, toward his king. His short, dark brown hair ruffled as he squatted next to his friend and ruler. "Maybe Thorn can heal you."

"No!" Drake exclaimed. "There will be no healing him unless you want to rush your death. I have no problem killing you here if you push me."

My heartbeat quickened, and I moved closer to Thorn. He was now several feet in front of me, but as I stepped between Cassidy and Vlad, they each gripped my arms.

"Don't make yourself more of a target," Vlad murmured. His wavy caramel hair was wild, and I refused to look any lower than his cornflower blue eyes because he was as naked as I was.

"If Drake focuses on you again, Thorn might lose his ability to think straight," Cassidy added, her hazel eyes focused on Thorn, Drake, and the king. "We could get away if we time it perfectly."

My chest expanded. I hadn't considered trying to escape. Drake's warriors were distracted, but we couldn't walk away, not if Thorn could help his biological father. *Can you heal him?*

"I...I can't," he answered aloud, then connected with me, *It's a mortal wound.* Hurt and guilt slammed into me. *Your head wound was a slow bleed, not like this. There's no way to save him.*

Evil mirth darkened Drake's irises as he stepped toward his father on the side opposite Errol. Drake bent and chuckled menacingly while staring into King Arman's eyes. "What does it feel like, learning that the son you cast away and tried to bring back can't help you? Do you like knowing that even as you die, neither of your children can stand you?"

Thorn punched his brother in the face as a tear ran down King Arman's cheek. Drake stumbled back several feet, blood pouring from his nose.

The king's going to fall, I connected, as my lungs seized.

Drake wasn't focused on his father as he pinched his nose to get the bleeding to stop.

Agony ripped through Thorn, and he kneeled in front of King Arman and pulled the man into his arms. The blood from the king's mouth smeared across my mate's stomach, though everything inside me screamed at me to go to him, Cassidy and Vlad tightened their hold on my arms, keeping me back.

Drake snarled as blood trickled into his mouth, making my blood run cold. Thorn's back was turned to the asshole.

I yanked out of Cassidy's and Vlad's grip and rushed between Thorn and Drake, positioning myself so I could see both men.

"I'm...so...sorry." King Arman's words were nearly inaudible, even with my new dragon hearing. "I...was...wrong."

Thorn moved the king onto his side to look into his eyes.

I touched Thorn's arm, our jolt sizzling. I needed him to know I was there. At one time, the king had been a loving father to him.

"I forgive you," Thorn whispered, taking in a ragged breath.

A sad smile spread across the king's face. Then his already faint heartbeat stopped. The world seemed eerily quiet. The breeze slowed, and the only sounds were of everyone's pulse and breathing.

Two things the king would never experience again, all because of Drake.

Anger boiled inside me. I'd never held such rage before. Even though the king had done something horrible, he hadn't truly wanted Thorn to die. All of *this* was on Drake.

Drake wanted Thorn dead and me as his wife, so he'd ordered his warriors and all the other dragons to hunt us down.

Theron, Vlad's father's friend, had hidden us in his safe house near his thunder, and Thorn had healed his son to thank him because Drake was also hunting and killing injured dragons. Theron's second in command, Wyvern, had seen Thorn do it and, without knowing the true situation, alerted Drake to Thorn's presence. Drake had come here, willing to kill as many of Theron's thunder as needed to draw Thorn out. And now Drake had killed King Arman because the king had finally been poised to do what was right.

It all led back to the arrogant prince.

Tears trailed down my mate's face, stirring up that anger and hatred inside me. No one hurt my mate.

Errol, Saphira, and several warriors sniffled as they watched their king die. Every sound fed my hate.

Something moved in the corner of my vision, and I turned to see Drake pulling a tranq gun from a male warrior's side.

I jumped to my feet as Drake pointed the gun at Thorn's neck. There was no way in hell I'd allow him to shoot my mate. I connected, *Thorn, duck!*

My dragon surged forward in my mind, helping me move faster than normal. In a flash, I leapt the five feet to Drake and tackled him.

As I slammed into his chest, his arm lifted. I tried to stop my forward momentum, but Drake fell backward, and I tumbled right after him. At least he'd dropped the tranq gun.

A moment before my body would have pressed against Drake's, a strong arm wrapped around me and yanked me back against a hard, muscular chest. My skin buzzed.

Thorn.

Warm wetness hit the center of my back, and a lump formed in my throat.

I knew exactly what it was.

King Arman's blood.

White-hot fury blazed, but when Thorn's fingers pressed into my skin, I realized his anger was exacerbating mine.

"You will pay for *everything*," Thorn snarled, as he gently set me aside. "I'm going to tear you limb from limb."

"I'd like to see you try," Drake hissed as he stood. "I'm the acting king now that my father is dead."

That confirmed my worst fear. "King Arman said the throne doesn't go to you," I spat.

"He *never* said that. I don't know what you're talking about." Drake moved closer to me, and Thorn stepped back to keep the same amount of distance between us and him.

Drake smirked at me. "You'll be my wife and queen, especially with a body like that. I'll forgive that you allowed the abomination to touch you...just for *him*."

"You son of a bitch." Thorn pulled me behind him, blocking Drake's view, and connected, *Get out of the way.*

"Shoot him and detain the others!" Drake commanded his warriors. "We need to hurry back to the château. There are several executions to record and a coronation to plan."

Saliva filled my mouth. This time, we weren't getting out of this.

When none of the warriors moved, Thorn punched Drake in the jaw. Drake stumbled back, tripping over Tyson's unconscious body, which lay near five of Drake's guards.

Thorn rushed Drake again, but Drake snarled, "You know what will happen if you disobey."

The female warrior lifted her rifle with shaky hands, aiming it at Thorn.

No! Not this again.

As her finger touched the trigger, I connected with Thorn, *Get down!*

He dropped, and for a split second, my heartbeat steadied...until the dart barreled toward me. I ducked, too, and the dart sailed an inch over my head.

Thank goodness Thorn had over two feet on me, or that would've gone sideways.

Thorn stood, and one of the king's warriors lifted his weapon. His hands were steady as he fired...and the tranq soared past Thorn and into the woman who'd shot at my mate.

The warrior shouted, "Thorn is the future king! Protect him!"

Drake's eyes bulged, and his face reddened. "Take

down anyone who's against me, or your families will be *killed."*

Several of Drake's guards pivoted and aimed their guns at Thorn.

My breath caught, and I wasn't sure what to do.

"Protect Thorn!" another warrior yelled from the back, and two who were aiming at Thorn were hit with darts and fell to the ground.

Thorn, get out of the crossfire, I connected. Now that the warriors had moved back several feet, I rushed to Tyson and tossed the young shifter over my shoulder. Unfortunately, his penis hit my arm, but there was nothing I could do about it. We were all naked for this fight.

When I turned, Thorn was running, heading toward Theron's settlement, chasing after Drake.

A gentle hand touched my shoulder. I spun around, ready to defend myself and Tyson as best I could with one arm, but Cassidy's familiar face made me pause. She whispered, "We've got to leave. Get Thorn to listen. You're the only one who can do it." She took Tyson from me and ran back the way we'd come from, toward the safe house. Vlad helped Errol get away, and they rushed after her.

Glancing back, I marked Thorn as he was about to slip through the tree line after Drake. I connected to him with the only thing I could think of and prayed it would work.

Thorn, I need you!

CONCERN WASHED over me as Thorn responded, *What's wrong? Are you hurt?* Regret and guilt weighed down our bond as he spun around, his eyes narrowing.

The knot in my chest loosened. I hadn't been sure I could reach him, but thank goodness, his concern for me outweighed his hate for Drake. About a third of the king's warriors were fighting those loyal to Drake...though I wasn't sure if *loyal* was the right word since he'd threatened their families. Regardless, the outcome was the same. Eventually, they'd overtake the king's warriors and capture us. *We need to leave before—*

That asshole won't touch you. His irises darkened to cobalt. His pain and anger rushed through our connection. *Run. I'll get King Arman and be right behind you.*

My heart squeezed so tightly that it throbbed. I understood what losing a parent was like, but this had to be worse for him. This parent had abandoned him and tried to make things right moments before he died.

I stayed put, needing to make sure he wouldn't let his hate and anger take over again. Chaos unfolded around us.

The guards were focused on each other, and the ones who'd fought to protect Thorn were fleeing.

Luckily, Drake's guards were chasing them, leaving us alone, but they wouldn't for long.

Thorn lifted the king and rushed toward me.

Ev, go, he connected, his face twisted with concern.

A few of the remaining warriors paused, and a woman called, "Thorn and the girl are getting away!"

Tap into your dragon, Thorn connected and ran even faster. In a second, he caught up to me.

With no time to lose, I replicated what I'd done earlier. My dragon surged forward and connected with me, lending my legs extra strength.

My skin tingled as we rushed toward the thick line of oaks and red cedars.

Something whistled behind me. My breathing quickened, and I braced for the prick of the dart. My dragon surged, guiding me to zigzag instead of continuing in a straight line.

Fear squeezed my chest and the bond as my emotions and Thorn's melded together. He was moving in the same pattern, and neither of us was hit.

Footsteps sounded to our right, heading toward the clearing. Probably more warriors.

My knees wanted to buckle, but my dragon roared. If we fell, Thorn and I would be captured. I gritted my teeth and pushed through the discomfort.

The footsteps stopped.

Falkor asked, "What in the *hell* is going on?"

"Where is everyone?" Ladon piped in.

The two guards were awake. It felt like a lifetime ago since we'd knocked their asses out back where we'd found them with Theron, Sol, and Wyvern.

"Uh...the king is dead, and the warriors are fighting each other over who should be king," one answered quickly. "We're going after the girl and Thorn."

"What do you mean, warriors are fighting against Drake?" Falkor bellowed, a hint of hysteria in his tone.

Of course he wasn't focused on the king's death but on people acting against Drake. I wondered if that was because he was Drake's guard now or if there was more behind it.

We were gaining distance from them, and I was more than okay with that. Let Falkor and Ladon distract our pursuers.

Their voices grew fainter, and I almost cried with relief when Falkor commanded, "We can worry about the girl and Thorn later. With the king gone, it'll be easier to catch them. We have to make sure no one hurts Drake. *He* is the *future* and protecting him is our priority."

He was right. With the king deceased, there was no one left to keep Drake in check. All the injured and old dragons would be openly hunted, the same as we were. But that was a problem for later. Right now, we needed to get away.

Something was brewing in Thorn, but as the scents of Saphira, Errol, Brenton, Tyson, Vlad, Cassidy, Sol, Wyvern, and Theron thickened in the air, I didn't have time to decipher it. We were close.

A few minutes later, we ran around an oak tree and found them with Hydra. As soon as we came into view, Cassidy and Saphira let out huge breaths, their shoulders relaxing.

Cassidy murmured, "Thank gods. We were about to come looking for you."

Brenton held Tyson in his arms, and Saphira and Errol flanked him.

"Sorry," Thorn murmured as we stopped in front of the

others. That emotion I'd sensed had morphed into guilt and disgust, weighing heavily on our connection. He was struggling, and I *hated* that I wasn't sure how to help him. I didn't want to pry while we were still in danger.

I studied my mate for the first time since he'd picked up King Arman. Blood from the king's wound drizzled down his bare, muscular chest and streaked his body. Bile churned in my gut. Carrying his father's body was something he shouldn't have had to do.

Saphira looked toward my mate, and a growl emanated from my throat before I could stop myself. Her gaze was firmly on the king, but it was still way too close to my mate's naked body. I hated that he was exposed to another young, attractive, and very *unmated* female.

Surprisingly, Wyvern snarled as well, and Saphira glared at him.

We were all experiencing heightened emotions, and we needed clothes, *stat*.

"Let's leave." Vlad cleared his throat and glanced at the area behind Thorn, avoiding looking at me.

I kept my gaze set from everyone's shoulders up. There were some things you could never erase from your mind— like seeing your in-laws naked.

"I can't leave my thunder." Theron shook his head and turned to his mate and son. "You two go with Wyvern, and I'll meet up with you when I can."

My chest burned. Because of Drake, more people were being forced to run. This had to end.

"That's a bad idea." Wyvern raised his hands. Unlike us, Wyvern, Hydra, Sol, and Theron were dressed because they hadn't flown to get here. "I'm the one who reached out to Drake. He'll trust me more than you. Besides, you need to be with your family, and you might need to use your *resources* to find another safe location."

What is he talking about? I didn't want to ask out loud and delay us further, but I also wanted answers.

Thorn shook his head as he turned around, facing the direction we'd come from. *No clue.*

"Dad, he's right." Sol pursed his lips. "I'm pretty sure Drake knew we were lying."

"Yeah, but Wyvern attacked the warriors when the warriors were attacking them." Theron gestured at our naked group. "If something were to happen..."

Saphira nodded and stepped forward. "I agree. We can't risk Wyvern staying here. He needs to come with us."

"Dear." Errol touched her arm. "We shouldn't interfere with thunder politics. Unlike the king, they haven't asked for an advisor."

Wyvern smiled at Saphira. "Don't worry. I'll be fine, and I promise you'll see me soon. I can't stay away from you for long."

Yeah, they were definitely attracted to each other.

"If Theron and Wyvern know what they're doing, we *need* to go. Our scents need time to dilute." Vlad steepled his fingers. "Time is truly of the essence."

"We must bury the king," Brenton added, frowning deeply.

"Seriously, go." Wyvern gestured at the sky. "We were hidden by trees, so no one saw us attack the warriors. I'll keep you updated on everything I learn."

Huffing, Theron nodded and patted Wyvern on the arm. "You and Sol are the two I trust the most to lead the thunder in my absence. Just make sure you aren't in danger, and if something happens to you or the thunder—"

Wyvern lifted a hand. "We'll let you know. I get that I

fucked up by informing Drake that Thorn was here, but that was before I learned what he'd done for Sol. I'm sorry I caused this problem, not only for our thunder but for Thorn and the others as well." He nodded to us.

I nodded back. He had messed up, but I understood. I would've done the same thing if I'd thought people I loved were in danger. Hell, I'd handed myself over to Drake to save my sister, Eva, from a fate that happened anyway.

"Let's shift." Vlad stepped back, getting more room for his dragon form. "And Thorn, I'll carry the king from here. You've done enough." The last sentence was filled with emotion.

Everything was settled.

"Okay," I said. "We've all had enough naked time."

Everyone nodded, and we spread apart. Soon, every one of us, minus Wyvern, the king, and Tyson, was in dragon form. Theron gingerly grabbed his clothes, and I was confused until I noticed the lump of a cell phone in his back pocket. He'd need it to communicate with Wyvern.

"Go on." Wyvern waved us away, his gaze locked on Saphira. "I'll hold them off. Be safe."

I was certain those last two words were mainly directed at her. The butterscotch scales on her cheeks reddened, proving that dragons could blush.

Since it was still bright out, we bolted high into the sky, with Vlad carrying the king and Brenton carrying his son in their talons. I focused on our surroundings, making sure no aircraft were nearby. We flew as high as we could, and then Cassidy gestured in all different directions.

She's suggesting we split up, Thorn connected. *Let's go right. We can fly around the long way.*

I was more than okay with that. After the battle, I needed a release, and now wasn't the time to get it sexually from Thorn for so many reasons, so flying would have to do the trick.

The two of us peeled off, flying east with the sun at our backs. Summer was approaching, and the air was warm, even all the way up here. We flew in tandem, and I glanced back to see the others break off into groups. Sol stuck with Brenton and Tyson, leaving Hydra and Theron together.

After several long minutes, I couldn't take the silence. *I love you, and I'm here.*

Guilt and shame swirled inside him, and my dragon whimpered. Something strange was definitely going on with him.

I love you, too, and I'm so damn sorry, he replied, staring at me with those gorgeous eyes that matched the sky around us.

Something stirred inside me, making my scales crawl. *What do you mean?* I tried to keep my voice level, but I was confused.

When Drake killed my fath—King Arman, all I saw was red. He hung his head as we turned slightly, easing our way back toward the barn. *And I put you in danger.*

You didn't. He must have forgotten why we'd been there. It had been my influence, my suggestion, and now he felt awful about it? My lungs couldn't fill completely. *Remember, you didn't want to go. If I'd known—* I stopped. I didn't know what to say that wouldn't make it worse. No matter what we'd done, people would have died.

You were right to push us to go. Now we have someone Drake trusts who will alert us if something seems suspicious. We need more allies like that. But when King Arman died, I was so angry and fixated on Drake and everything he'd done that I left you behind. His eyes glistened. *Next time, that could easily be you.* I wanted to stop him. I *wanted to protect you, but instead, I left you exposed and vulnerable.*

My chest expanded so much that it hurt. I hated that I had put such a heavy burden on him. *You did nothing wrong. Your father died right in front of you while weapons were trained on us.*

Yeah, that sucked. Smoke trickled from his nose. *But if something had happened to you because I ran off to kill Drake, I wouldn't have survived that. Hell, I almost didn't survive you being stuck in that château with him. I sure couldn't handle not having you on this earth any longer.*

I've been training to protect myself. Remember? My heart skipped. Even through everything, his biggest concern had been me. I'd never had someone love me this much. He felt bad because he thought he'd abandoned me, though he'd chased after a threat to protect me. It would have been comical if it didn't burden him so much. *You have nothing to feel bad about. As soon as I said I needed you, you didn't hesitate. You came back to me.*

His dragon smiled. It was big, toothy, funny, and sexy all at the same time. *I've always been chasing after you. It started that night at the bar, the first time I saw you. I followed you home that night, albeit not with the best intentions, but I was drawn to you even when I thought I shouldn't be.*

The memory of that night crashed over me. I'd hunted Drake down to ask him to take me instead of Eva as payment for my stepfather's crime—before I'd learned about *all this.* It was the best bad decision I'd ever made and one I would never want to change. Yes, it had gotten me into this situation with Drake, but it had also led me to Thorn. *I remember seeing your eyes in the car from underneath the bill of your hat. I felt the pull, too.*

That was what we were—destined to be together. Fated mates.

All too soon, our flight came to an end. After looking around to make sure no one had followed us, we began our descent. The others dropped into the trees and started to shift back into human form, but before Thorn and I landed, I noticed something scrambling underneath us—something larger than the usual small forest animals. *Do you see that?*

Yeah, Thorn replied, and hot anger flared between us.

He swooped down, and I followed on his tail. A section of branches thinned, giving me a glimpse of what—no, *who* it was.

My stepfather. Peter.

And he was running for his life.

CHAPTER THREE

THE MOMENT he heard our wings, Peter's chestnut eyes narrowed as he scanned the area for something...most likely a place to hide.

His eyes widened, and he scurried toward some low brush between two sizable oaks and crawled under the branches. He clearly didn't think we could see him. His gray stood out starkly among the browns and greens shrouding his body.

Maybe this was comical, but not now. Not when there was so much at stake and with a man who thought only of himself, even over his own children.

Thorn didn't waste time. He landed and stuck his forelegs into the bush, then yanked my stepdad from his spot. Peter's face blanched as Thorn lifted him. In Thorn's talons, he looked tiny, despite standing at five-ten.

All dragons were gigantic, around four times the size of their human form, and Thorn was already huge for a human, coming in at seven and a half feet tall. Smoke flowed out of his nose as his chest heaved. The anger emanating from my mate was stronger than ever before. He needed time to decompress and mourn, but we didn't have that luxury.

"I...I'm sorry." Peter's bottom lip quivered. "I...I didn't—"

Part of me wanted to stand back and let Thorn do whatever he wanted, but if today had reminded me of anything, it was that I needed to protect my siblings. He was *their* father, and if something happened to him, they would be parentless...like me. *Babe, I know he's an asshole, but we have to remember Elliott and Eva. It would hurt them to lose him, even if he is a bad father.*

None of the anger ebbed, but Thorn replied, *I know. You don't want me to kill him. That's the only reason he's still breathing, but we can't trust the twins to watch him again. And if he doesn't stop putting you in danger, I don't know how long I can hold back.* He turned to me, his eyes full of concern.

The world tilted.

My siblings.

Peter must have done something to them to escape, and dammit, I couldn't ask him in this form. I had to get to them.

Thorn and I took off, flying over the treetops. The barn was in view, so we were isolated from any humans. We'd kept an eye out for hikers and campers before landing. None were around, which wasn't surprising. Theron's land was private property.

As we drew closer to the barn, Elliott and Eva ran out of the house with stony expressions.

They had to be looking for Peter.

The moment they noticed Thorn and me, shock registered on Elliott's face. His steel blue eyes widened as we landed in front of them. Thorn released Peter, who fell with a loud thud.

Peter winced and groaned as he reached behind to rub his tailbone.

"What the *hell?*" Elliott asked as he stalked to his father. "You ran away without bothering to tell your *kids?*"

Hissing, Peter jerked his head up. "Yes, I did. Because my *kids* are fine hanging around with fire-breathing dragons who knock out their only living parent!"

Elliott shrugged. "Can you blame us? If Thorn had tied you to that chair *and* knocked you out, you wouldn't have gotten away. If you're going to get mad at anyone, get mad at yourself. It's not our fault you're more pleasant when you're unconscious."

Your brother is strange, but he's growing on me, Thorn connected as he moved to stand beside me.

Brushing a loose strand of her dark brown hair from her face, Eva huffed. "El, I'm not sure you're helping."

Seeing them standing side by side in the sunlight reminded me of how similar they looked. The same shade of eyes and hair, the same nose and mouth, and the same fair skin tone. The only differences were that Elliott was taller and his hair was cut much shorter but long enough for his bangs to hang permanently in his eyes.

"Me?" Elliott puffed his chest. "I'm not the idiot who ran away, thinking I could get past badass dragons." His attention flicked to Thorn, and he rubbed his hands together. "Though that's about to change, since I'm ready to be one myself."

I sighed, and the sound was more dramatic in dragon form. We'd promised that Thorn would change him when we got back. We had a lot more problems now than when we'd left, so I'd completely forgotten.

Is he expecting me to do it now? Thorn connected, humor and annoyance washing away some of his anger.

While in dragon form and with Peter sitting right in front of me after he tried to escape?

Yes. My brother had a one-track mind that I firmly blamed on video games. He couldn't focus on anything other than what he wanted most in the moment, and right now, that was to become one of us. His need for instant gratification was why I'd forced him to take a few days to think about it.

The sounds of human footsteps caught my attention, and I glanced over my shoulder to find Saphira, Cassidy, Vlad, and Errol approaching. The others must still be shifting, but these four would want to know what was going on.

Vlad took in Peter as he slowly climbed to his feet, and then he looked at Thorn and me. "What happened?"

"Dear old Dad tried to run away." Elliott rolled his eyes. "I should've known he didn't actually want to watch Eva and me play video games. He's never wanted to before."

"You get engrossed in them." Peter scowled. "Both of you."

At least he hadn't done something horrible to them, such as knock them out, like I'd feared.

"You two go ahead and shift." Cassidy gestured toward the tree line where we'd shifted earlier. Our clothes would still be there. "We'll keep an eye on him."

Errol headed to the front door and glanced back. "I'll grab Sol, Theron, and Hydra some clothes while you three handle this."

"Maybe we could do more than just watch Peter." Saphira smacked the back of her hand against her palm. "I could do what Thorn's had the pleasure of doing several times now."

Peter grimaced. "My head just stopped hurting a few days ago. No need to knock me out again."

"Oh, but I think there is." She grinned, showing every one of her teeth. Saphira was a gorgeous and scary woman, and I loved seeing Peter shiver underneath her gaze.

Come on, Ev, Thorn connected, his wing brushing mine.

My head spun as our fated-mate bond thrummed between us. The bond was intense in both forms since we were two parts of the same soul.

As we headed for the trees, Brenton and Tyson stepped from between a red cedar and a sweetgum. My talons almost gave out when I saw that the younger dragon shifter was awake. His warm olive eyes locked on me, and he slurred faintly, "I heard that you picked up my ass and got me away from Drake." Dark circles lined his eyes, showing that the tranq was still affecting him.

My heart skipped a beat. I hadn't expected a thank you. I would have done that for anyone because it was the *right* thing to do. The fact that I liked him had made the risk more worth it. I blew out a breath, seeing as I couldn't speak in this form.

Brenton beamed, his emerald irises sparkling. "Come on, son. Let's go get you something to eat and drink to help you recover from the tranquilizer."

Thorn and I flew over the trees a little ways to where we'd left our clothes. We landed and pulled back our dragons, and I heard Errol giving Theron, Hydra, and Sol their clothes.

As soon as Thorn and I were dressed, he pulled me into his hard chest. His lips were on my neck, and he breathed me in deeply. My temperature rose.

I spun around in his arms and stared into his face. *Are you okay?*

Now I am. He lowered his forehead to mine, brushing a

finger across my cheek. *For a second back there, I didn't think we were getting out.*

In truth, I hadn't thought so, either. If King Arman hadn't shown up, we would probably be on our way back to the château, and not voluntarily. Cold tendrils of fear curled into my chest, and his eyes darkened as he sensed my emotions. I forced a smile to ease the tension in my body. "But we did." That was what we had to focus on. "And because of the king."

Pain lined his face, twisting a knife into my heart. Thorn had endured more than enough pain to last a lifetime.

"It was." He nodded and kissed me.

My lips sizzled from his touch, and I leaned into him. After what we'd gone through, I needed this moment as much as he did...alone and together.

"And for that, I'll have to let go of some of my hate. Because of him, I didn't lose you, and though I'd love to sneak away with you, we can't. We need to determine where to head next. It won't be safe here for much longer, and that's the only reason I can pull away right now." He moved back, frowning.

Heart racing, I wanted to change his mind, but that would be careless and stupid. "I fully plan to take you up on that offer once we finally get some alone time." I pouted and kissed him again.

His tongue slipped into my mouth, making my brain fuzzy as his faint vanilla taste and minty amber scent over-loaded my senses. This man looked like a god and tasted like happiness. I didn't know what I'd done to deserve him, but I would be thankful for him each and every day.

Eagerly, I responded to him, my hands fisting in his shirt. The urge to rip it from his body almost overwhelmed me, but then footsteps belonging to Theron, Hydra, and Sol filtered through my haze. I groaned and forced myself to pull away. Glancing into Thorn's eyes, I found his pupils were slits from his dragon peeking through. He smiled and kissed the top of my head before intertwining our fingers and pulling me back toward the barn and everyone else.

With each step closer to the barn house, I remembered how dire our situation was. Hydra, Theron, and Sol were about five hundred feet ahead of us, so Thorn and I picked up our pace and caught up to them as we stepped out of the tree line.

Everyone was outside, with Peter on the edge of the group between Cassidy and Saphira. Tyson was eating a sandwich and drinking a soda, while Vlad, Errol, and Brenton had found shovels and were digging a hole next to where the king lay underneath a beautiful dogwood. I could hear Saphira filling Elliott and Eva in on what had transpired back at Theron's thunder, but when Thorn's agony swirled into me, I focused on my mate.

He was staring at the king.

King Arman had been powerful, but he wasn't anymore. Though we couldn't see the wound where Drake had stabbed his father in the back, the king's lavender shirt was stained crimson except at the very top near his neck. His skin had been a dark olive, but now it was almost white—like the vampires I'd seen on television. The power he'd radiated was gone...extinguished, just like his soul.

Thorn squeezed my hand gently before releasing it and jogging to the grave. I wanted to go with him, but he needed time to grieve without me hovering. When he needed to lean on me, I'd be there.

The four of us reached Saphira, Elliott, Eva, Cassidy, and Peter just as Thorn took the shovel from Vlad and said,

"Why don't you go be part of that conversation, and I'll finish this?"

"Of course." Vlad nodded, the corners of his mouth tipping downward. Instead of saying anything more, he walked over to join us, giving Thorn the space he needed as he worked with Errol and Brenton.

Pulling my attention away from my mate was excruciating, but I turned so I could take part in the conversation.

Out of the corner of my eye, Eva stiffened. A chill ran through me as I followed her gaze, which had landed on Sol.

My muscles relaxed. From the way she'd reacted, I'd expected a warrior to be behind us, ready to attack. Still, her reaction was strange.

Sol tilted his head and took a hesitant step forward before stopping and swaying as if he were being tugged toward her.

Something curious stirred inside me. Could they be soulmates? Surely not. That would be too coincidental. From what I'd gathered, fated mates had been commonplace at one time, but as the dragon shifter population had plummeted, so had the number of fated-mate bond connections. What Thorn and I had was rare and must have been even more so since I'd been born human. I had to be reading the situation wrong.

Vlad jumped right in, addressing Theron. "Wyvern thinks you might have a connection that could hide us. Is that the case?"

Fidgeting, Theron rolled his shoulders. "It's possible. But it'll take time to set up. I have to make a post." He removed his phone from his back pocket, the one he'd taken the time to pick up gently in dragon form to bring with him.

I sucked in a breath. "Wait. No. You can't post that on the Dragonnet. Drake will track us."

"Wait." Elliott lifted a hand, his face radiating joy. "Did you fucking say *Dragonnet*? I don't know *what* that is, but it sounds *badass*, and I want to play it. I'm totally in!"

Sol's brows furrowed, and Hydra stepped back, placing a hand on her chest.

Of course Elliott had assumed it was a video game. "It's an intranet for all dragon shifter communications and where the royals can send out information and video speeches or whatever to their subjects." I still wasn't one hundred percent sure about that.

"Oh, don't forget weddings." Saphira wrinkled her nose. "They like to broadcast those as well."

If Thorn's parents hadn't been there, I would have given her the middle finger.

She smirked. "That's what you get for that comment back there."

She meant the brothel comment about her and Wyvern. I wanted to mouth off in return, but now wasn't the time. We had serious things to focus on. I'd get the brat later.

Scratching his head, Theron tried to regroup. "This isn't Dragonnet. It's a network for the thunders that have injured or differently abled dragons. It's a communication board on a private server that you have to be screened to enter. That's why I had to make sure I brought my phone."

"If you're sure Drake won't find out, then sure." Vlad lifted his hands. "It's not like we have many options."

"Okay." Theron swiped his screen and typed out a message.

After he was done, Errol rubbed his hands together. Our group turned in time to watch Thorn lift the king and carefully place him in the grave.

"I thought we might have a moment of silence to say our goodbyes before we finish the burial." Errol placed his shovel on the ground and rubbed his hands together. "We won't be able to take him back to the château where all the royals are usually buried. Mira can't even be here for the burial of her mate, but his loss is still felt here by all of us."

As Thorn stood, he wiped the dirt from his hands onto his jeans and reached out to me. He connected, *Will you come stand beside me?*

You never have to ask, I replied as I moved to his side. He wrapped an arm around me, using me as an anchor. His sadness, guilt, and resentment washed into me as he mourned the man who had at one time been his father and had become one again just moments before his death.

Our group surrounded the hole, each person deathly silent—even Eva, Elliott, and Peter. The birds chirped, and the breeze picked up as if the world wanted to say its good-byes as well.

I wasn't sure how long we stood there, but the sky had darkened to twilight, and tears still fell.

Then Theron's phone dinged.

He pulled it out, and everyone tensed. I'd forgotten that he'd put out that message a while ago.

"Did you find someone?" Saphira asked breathlessly.

Theron rolled his shoulders. "Yes...but there's a catch."

"OF COURSE THERE'S A CATCH." Elliott nodded, a slight smirk on his face. "This is like a motherfucking *movie*, and this is the sort of shit that happens. Let me guess...a battle to the death, and winner takes all?"

Sol's brows lifted, and Eva shook her head.

I hadn't seen Elliott this animated since before Mom got sick. It was odd that something like *this* was getting him back to being the spunky, weird kid I knew.

Thorn's annoyance flared through our bond.

"No." Theron shook his head. "It's—"

"Wait! Don't tell me." Elliott bounced on his feet. "Let me guess. How about—"

"Oh!" Tyson pointed both pointer fingers to the sky. "A race. Fastest dragon wins protection for a night."

"Fuck yeah!" Elliott bobbed his head. "That would require a nightly race. It would be nonstop preparation and adrenaline. Will we have shelter for another night? Who knows? Will Thorn motherfucking—" He paused and blinked. "Holy shit. What *is* your last name? I don't even know my sister's name anymore."

Does he even realize we're in danger? Thorn connected, his hand tightening on my waist.

There was no way to respond that wouldn't infuriate him further, so I kept my thoughts to myself.

"It's Hale," Tyson answered and patted Elliot on the arm.

I grimaced, my stomach roiling.

"Thanks, bruh," Elliott responded, and fist-bumped Tyson. "Will motherfuckin' Thorn Hale win us safety for yet—"

"Stop right there with this nonsense," Thorn growled. "And Everly's and my last name is *not* Hale."

My heart skipped, and my belly fluttered. I still thought of myself as Everly Woods, but we *were* married.

"Oh, gods." Saphira huffed. "Now they're at *bruh* level."

"What are you talking about?" Elliott lifted his chin, strolled to Tyson, then threw an arm around his shoulder. "He's been my bruh for *a week*. Between the video games and training, we already forged that bond."

Tyson snorted and winked at his cousin. "It's a true bruh-mance."

"Don't," Saphira deadpanned and lifted a hand. "I can't handle this."

Growling, Thorn stepped away from the king's grave and toward Theron, tugging me along beside him. He gritted out, "Ignore them and tell us grownups what's going on."

"Gladly." Theron tore his glare from the two young men and glanced around at everyone else. "A woman in the network offered shelter for a few days, but only if Thorn agrees to heal her daughter."

"What?" Thorn's pupils slitted. "You told them about

me?" Our bond heated, and it wasn't in the pleasant way that indicated desire.

Trying to ease my mate's mind, I squeezed his hands and connected, *If they trust one another, I can see why he wanted to be forthright about what they'd be getting into.*

He should've asked us first, he replied, tugging me against his side. *I'll be damned if I take you somewhere that warriors might be waiting to pounce on us.*

"I *had* to." Theron bit his bottom lip and stepped away from Hydra. "I can't just show up with you, and with Sol healed, they'd know. They're more willing to accept the risk by knowing their injured child or thunder member can be healed. Don't you understand how much we all *hate* Drake and what he stands for?"

He had a point. Anywhere we stayed, the thunder would eventually know we were there. Maybe it was better to give them a heads-up so they wouldn't feel tricked into helping us. But we were screwed in our current situation.

"Look, I told them that Drake killed the king and is putting his plans into action without any barriers. I also told them how you helped us instead of running off like you could have." Theron bit his bottom lip. "The king's death is making everyone panic. This particular thunder that reached out is in the Midwest. It's a two-hour flight from here."

That was farther away from Asheville and the royal dragon lands. The warriors would be focused on the internal uprising, and then they'd focus their efforts on looking for us here first, knowing we'd taken the king with us and wouldn't get far.

Vlad crossed his arms. "How do you know they won't make a deal with the guards? My dad vouched for you—

that's why we came here. What assurances do we have that this woman is trustworthy?"

"Everyone in this network knows that Drake is killing our people and is not to be trusted. Today's events solidified that decision for all of us. If Thorn is willing to heal the injured thunder members of the people who are willing to risk hiding us, then we have a better chance of resolving this situation." Theron placed a hand on his chest. "I would not be taking Sol and Hydra to a place with people I didn't trust. Drake now associates *us* with *you*. There's no getting out of that, and you all know it. If I'm willing to risk the lives of the two people I love most, I think I deserve the benefit of the doubt."

"Unless you allied with them to bring us in as a way to make up for *betraying* Drake." Errol rubbed his chin. "That's also an option."

"We know that wouldn't work even if we wanted it to." Hydra stood tall next to Theron. "Unlike my mate, I'm not afraid to admit that the thought crossed my mind, but to Drake, we're traitors. There's no way he'd forgive us even if he said he would."

Brenton kicked at the dirt left over from digging the grave. "If there is an injured dragon network, why didn't I know about it? Tyson would have benefited from that."

"We all found each other in passing, and one thing led to another." Sol shrugged, flicking his attention to Eva every chance he had. "We didn't know about Tyson. No one had seen him around."

Tyson's face fell. "That's because I barely ever left the house."

I swallowed around the lump in my throat and shivered, reminded of what it'd been like to be constrained. The panic of knowing I couldn't connect with my dragon had been damn near overwhelming.

"That doesn't matter." Thorn tapped his fingers against his leg. "We need to make a decision and move. If a few warriors aren't already searching for us, they will be soon, and more will join them. We need to leave while we can."

The sky was darkening, too, which would hide us from humans and aircraft.

I sighed. The hardest decision I'd had to make before all this was whether to go home after exams or work an extra shift at the coffee shop instead of studying. Now I and everyone I loved was being hunted.

"I don't think we have an option." I turned against Thorn's chest to look him in the eye. He was the one who would ultimately decide. "Theron has been on our side, even if begrudgingly, since we got here. If he trusts this woman, I say we should as well."

Peter sneered and glared at me. "Everly's always putting her nose in places—"

"Someone shut him up, or I'll do it myself." Thorn's jaw clenched, and his nostrils flared. "If I trusted myself not to cause permanent damage, I'd knock his ass out, but if he insults my mate and wife one more time, I won't care about the outcome."

Mouth snapping shut, Peter swallowed. Apparently, he didn't like to learn, but he remembered enough to know better.

A smile tugged at my lips, and I tried to keep my face neutral.

"My mate is *right*." He paused, shooting eye daggers at Peter. "We don't have much of a choice, so if everyone is agreed, we should pack some supplies and go."

Sol's shoulders drooped. "I promise Edna and Mindy

are solid. Mindy's dad died in the car crash that injured her five years ago."

This was the first time I'd heard of a dragon suffering a permanent injury while in human form.

"Let's split up and move." Vlad stared at the sky. "Get the bare essentials and load up the cars."

Hydra stilled. "We're not flying?"

"It's too risky." Vlad hurried to the door of the white barn house. "A warrior could come across our scents, and they'll have eyes in the sky. Traveling in vehicles will help us blend in better."

Raising a hand, Eva waved. "Let's not forget about the humans who can't fly."

"Or!" Elliott lifted a hand. "Just hear me out. You could change us, and *then* we could fly."

"Elliott Abbot," Peter rasped. "Shut your *mouth* right now and speak for yourself. I don't want to become *that*." He gestured at me.

Out of everyone here, he'd targeted me. At one time, that would've hurt, but now I rolled my eyes. He tried to blame me for anything he disliked.

Thorn released me, marched over to Peter, and got in his face. My stepdad stumbled back until he slammed into the side of the house. Thorn's face was red, and smoke trickled from his nose as Peter blanched.

Thorn punched him in the jaw.

My stepfather's head snapped back and bounced off the siding. His eyes watered, and he quickly covered the spot where he'd been hit.

"Clearly, you needed a reminder." Thorn's neck corded as he remained in my stepdad's space.

Eva and Elliott winced and closed their eyes. Even though Peter was difficult, he was still their dad, and I hated that this kept happening. However, Thorn couldn't handle his toxicity...especially toward me. I couldn't blame my mate. I'd be the same way, too.

"Just shut up," Elliott snarled. "For your own sake."

Wrapping an arm around Saphira and me, Cassidy nudged us toward Hydra, Theron, and Sol. She led most of us inside to get ready, while Vlad, Thorn, and Peter remained outside.

I wasn't sure what they were doing, but it wasn't my problem. I had Thorn to protect me, and even though I was certain I could do it myself, I no longer had to. I hurried inside to grab some things for both of us, leaving my stepdad to figure a way out of his own mess.

LUCKILY, we still had the two Suburbans, and Theron had his sizable older red truck, so we had enough vehicles to travel somewhat comfortably. We'd all packed a bag each, enough to have a few changes of clothes and toiletries to get us by.

Thorn drove one of the rentals, and I sat next to him on the passenger side. Eva sat right behind me in the middle row, with Saphira next to her. The two of them had been flipping through magazines they'd brought from the barn. In the very back, Peter sat behind Eva so Thorn could keep an eye on him in the rearview mirror, while Elliott sat in the center with Tyson beside him, the boys playing on Elliott's Switch. Every few minutes, one of the boys would yelp, and eventually, Eva drifted off to sleep.

Everyone else in our group was in the other Suburban in front of us, which Vlad was driving behind Theron's truck.

We'd been in the vehicle for over eight hours, and Thorn and I were struggling to stay awake. It was nearly four in the morning. Thorn yawned, and I reached across the center console and held his hand.

Do you need me to drive? I asked. We were in Indiana, and the surrounding woods gave my dragon a sense of peace. A reddish sign came into view with a drawing of a man sitting cross-legged that said, **Welcome Nashville Pioneer Art Colony Est. 1872**.

Glancing at me, Thorn smiled. *It looks like we're here.*

"You're going to die, asshole," Elliott snickered from the back of the Suburban.

Those two had been playing that game the entire time, and I wasn't sure how. I struggled to keep my eyes open, but they hadn't lost their enthusiasm.

The only things stopping me from falling asleep were keeping Thorn company and the odd emotion swirling through our bond. It was a strange mixture, and I wasn't sure what it meant, so I'd stayed awake, singing along to Soundgarden as we drove.

Soon, we were driving through downtown. There were several buildings side by side that weren't connected, and each one looked well-maintained. They weren't uniform in appearance, though, and the effect was welcoming. A few brick buildings mixed with aluminum-sided ones in various shades of yellow, green, and white made the place homey. Brown benches sat in front of a few shops, and one establishment's small porch was covered in birdhouses. It declared itself the General Store and Bakery.

This place would be so fun to paint, and I tried to burn each detail into memory so that I might be able to recreate it on a canvas one day. Mom would've loved to paint the picture with me like we had of the Asheville skyline in my attic room. Out of habit, I reached for the bracelet she'd given me before she died, but I came up empty-handed.

My throat dried. I had to remind myself it was in my bag, safe and sound. I'd stopped wearing it because of training and never knowing when I'd need to shift.

Hey. Thorn's mouth tightened. *What's wrong?*

Nothing.

He arched a brow and narrowed his eyes at me. He wouldn't let it go.

It's just...I was thinking about how Mom would've loved to paint a picture of this town with me, and then I reached for my bracelet... Emotion crowded uncomfortably in my chest. The last thing I wanted to do was cry, especially in front of Peter.

One day, you'll be able to wear it again. He nodded as if that settled everything, but my weird mix of emotions intensified, and I realized what it was: grief and a desperate need for calm. *I will make it safe for you to paint to your heart's content and wear whatever jewelry you want without hesitation ever again.*

Some of the discomfort ebbed as my heart fluttered. *Will that, by chance, include a wedding ring as well?*

His irises darkened. *Damn straight it will, and an engagement ring. I'll make everything right as soon as I kill Drake.*

Well, that had escalated quickly. Even though I preferred this version of Thorn, I was certain he hadn't thought of what it would mean if he followed through on that plan—that people would be looking to *him* as the new king.

I wouldn't bring that up until later, when we were closer to shutting Drake down.

We left the little downtown area and turned onto a dirt

road that led us deeper into the woods. It seemed like a perfect dragon location with privacy and space away from humans.

The moon was descending, and thick, fluffy clouds floated in the dark sky. After several miles, a red, one-lane covered bridge came into view. Luckily, with how early it was, we didn't have to worry about traffic. We slowed for each vehicle to cross alone, and then Theron picked up speed, leading us to our destination.

As we followed the dirt road, a shadow flew overhead, too large to be a bird.

My stomach clenched as my heart stopped. I connected, *Dragon.*

"SHIT," Thorn rasped, as he slammed on the brakes. The abrupt stop stirred up dust around us.

The large ebony dragon easily flew over the vehicles and landed on the road in front of Theron's truck. It opened its wings, making it appear larger. The road was too narrow to turn around.

I scanned the sky as my heart thundered. I expected to find more dragons rushing toward us, but none were visible from where I sat.

Thorn's and my connection squeezed tightly, melding our fear.

Slamming the Suburban into reverse, Thorn backed up hurriedly, just as Theron jumped from his truck.

What the *hell* was he doing? Did he have a death wish? Other warriors could arrive at any second, and he'd climbed out of his vehicle willingly. None of this added up.

Something dropped in the back seat, and Elliott yelped. Eva and Saphira groaned and stirred as the vehicle jerked and dramatically reversed.

"Wait," Theron shouted, turning toward us with his

back to the enemy. "It's Edna. I recognize the dragon. It's not the *others*."

Others.

Warriors.

I exhaled, and my shoulders slumped. I'd been so sure that the enemy had found us. Why would Edna do this when she knew we were coming to her house? Was this a warning or scare tactic to ensure we knew she was in control? As if we weren't already aware. That was the only possibility I could fathom.

Some of the tension in our connection ebbed, relieving the pressure in my chest. Thorn's scowl was firmly in place, and he swung his door open, marching past the hood of our vehicle right toward them.

We were all tired and stressed, and this scare had pushed Thorn over the edge. I hopped out, then looked back at Saphira.

She yawned and blinked, trying to get her bearings. "What happened?"

That was the question of the hour...literally. "Not sure. But I need to go with Thorn. Keep an eye on Peter, and make sure he doesn't do anything stupid."

Peter *hmph*ed, and I didn't need to see him to picture the scowl on his face.

"Dad, *come on*," Elliott chastised. "You've been knocked out twice, threatened more than I can count, and just got punched in the jaw. I'm with Everly. The possibility of you doing something stupid is high, and you accuse *me* of losing my short-term memory. All it would've taken was one punch for me to learn my lesson."

Mashing her lips together, Eva smiled timidly.

"I'll handle him." Saphira nodded, giving me the go-ahead to leave.

Pivoting on my heels, I hurried to catch up to Thorn. Vlad was beside him, and they both reached Theron.

"What the *hell* was that?" Thorn's chest heaved. "I thought the warriors had found us. Is this a sick game she's playing?"

Theron put his hands in his jeans pockets. "I'm sure it's not. She must have her reasons." He glanced at the dragon.

I followed his gaze, having to tilt my head all the way up to see her face. My eyes locked with her intelligent stormy gray ones. I paused by the passenger door of Vlad's Suburban. Her attention was on me, not Thorn.

A chill ran down my spine, and unease filtered through our bond as Thorn noticed.

Get back in the vehicle, he connected as he moved in front of me, blocking me from the dragon's view. His back pressed against my chest, and my skin sizzled.

I placed a hand against his back and replied, *No, we're in this together.*

His muscles tensed, but before he could say anything, Edna tapped the end of her long wing against her scaly chest, then flicked her head in the direction of the bridge.

"What?" Theron removed his cell phone from his back pocket and glanced at the screen. "I plugged in the address you gave me."

If he was expecting an answer, he'd be sorely disappointed. She was in dragon form. I opened my mouth to say that, then shut it. That comment was something Elliott would say, which meant I would be taken as a smartass. Now wasn't the time for that.

She fluttered her wings and flipped one back in that direction again.

"You do *trust* her, right?" Vlad raised his eyebrows. "I

just want to confirm. I'm with Thorn—this doesn't feel right."

Edna growled low and bared her teeth.

"That's not helping matters." Thorn puffed out his chest and reached behind him to place a hand on my waist.

Cursing, Theron put his phone back into his pocket. "Yes, I trust her. There has to be a reason for this."

The dragon nodded and hovered off the ground.

Everyone went back to their vehicles. Thorn and I buckled in, and he put the vehicle into reverse again.

Eva leaned forward and asked, "What's going on?"

"We aren't sure." Thorn clenched his jaw. "Saphira, Tyson, and Everly, I need you three to tap into your dragons and see if you sense any danger. This whole situation feels off."

Soon, we found an outlet to the dirt road with enough room for us to turn around. Thorn did so, the wheels squealing despite the dirt from how fast he was driving. My body jerked from side to side until we were heading back the way we'd come. Vlad and Theron followed suit, and I realized what had happened.

Thorn and I were in the lead. If there was an attack, we'd be the first ones hit. My stomach soured, and Thorn's hands tightened on the wheel, blanching his knuckles.

Nothing will happen to you, he connected and darted a look at me just as the red covered bridge came into view. *I swear. I'll die before I let anything happen.*

That's the problem. I was his weak spot, and I hated that. *I know you would, and just as much as you don't want something to happen to me, I feel the exact same way about you.* We would both gladly give our lives for each other. This was the sort of love that so many people coveted, but there was a reason I hadn't felt the sensations as strongly when I was human. I hadn't been strong enough to handle them. I was barely able to in dragon form. It was agonizing at times.

How about this? We stick beside each other and make sure neither of us gets into trouble.

My heart skipped a beat. Times like this reminded me that he saw us as equals. He was so protective because I was his fated mate and so precious to him. *I like the sound of that.*

He winked, though the usual warmth in his gorgeous eyes was missing. *Me, too.*

Edna took a right over the treetops just as a gravel road appeared.

Thorn slowed and coasted into the turn. "Do you sense anything?" His pupils slitted as his dragon surged forward.

My chest burned as my dragon surfaced and brushed against my mind. Though I couldn't sense things as well as when I was in full dragon form, my vision was enhanced. A mile away, a fox ran through the trees, and nearby, some bunnies were stirring. The only large things I could sense were Edna and a house two miles in the distance. "Nothing out of the ordinary."

"Same," Saphira answered.

"I do." Tyson coughed, and Thorn and I tensed. Tyson continued, "Elliott just farted, and it smells like rotten eggs."

The horrible stench hit me, and it was so strong, I could taste it. I gagged.

"Holy shit," Elliott gasped. "I swear, you smelled it before it even completely left my butthole. That is so fucking cool."

"Can I just say that I, for one, am glad I'm not a drag—"

Eva started, but then she wheezed. "Oh, my God. Let me roll my window down, *please.*"

Thorn growled as he pressed the child lock release button on the door handle. Both Saphira's and Eva's windows lowered, and they hung their heads out.

"Tyson, for the love of the gods," Thorn bit out as he glanced in the rearview mirror. "You know better than to pull that shit. I thought you saw something. You do realize, if this goes wrong, we're all going to be in danger?"

Begrudgingly, I rolled my window down as well. This car needed to air out, pronto.

A loud huff came from the backseat, and I didn't need to turn around to know who it was.

Peter.

I think something crawled up into your brother and died. Still scanning the area, Thorn lowered his window as well.

I mashed my lips together, but a small laugh escaped. Leave it to my brother to cause chaos when it was least convenient.

"This smells great." Elliott sniffed. "I don't know what your problem is."

"And you wonder why I didn't want you helping out with the company," Peter grumbled.

"El, I don't know how many times I have to tell you." Eva pinched her nose shut. "No one likes the smell, so just *stop.*"

Neck cording, Thorn gritted out, "Everyone focus. We'll be there soon."

That sobered everyone up, and I refocused on connecting with my dragon. I didn't sense anything other than the normal animals in the woods, which was a good thing. None of them sensed any danger.

A two-story light green house stood before us with a

beige stone chimney and a dark green slanted roof. The house sat in the center of a half acre of cleared land surrounded by thick trees.

We pulled right up to the red wooden front porch as Edna landed in the middle of the yard. Her eyes flicked to us before she turned and slid into the trees to shift back into human form.

Everyone climbed out of the vehicles and stood in front of the house. Three wicker chairs and a red wooden bench were placed in the yard, but as we'd been driving for so long, none of us sat.

"What is this place?" Thorn asked as he came around and took my hand, tugging me between Vlad and himself. He scanned our surroundings, his pupils slitting as he looked for something out of the norm.

Eva stood on Thorn's other side. Sol strolled up to take the spot beside her. Elliott and Tyson were between Sol and Saphira, but for once, they were silent. Errol and Brenton flanked Peter. Theron stood closest to where Edna had disappeared, with Hydra next to him.

"I don't know." Theron swiped his phone screen. "It's a thirty-minute drive from the main thunder, where we were heading."

Other than Edna flying at us out of nowhere, nothing seemed off.

"She's heading back, so we're about to find out." Cassidy faced the direction Edna had disappeared into the woods.

Silence descended.

Edna stepped into the yard, and my jaw almost dropped at her appearance. The same smoky gray eyes took in our entire group as she smiled warmly. Her hair was a caramel brown that hit a few inches past her shoulders, and she was only a few inches taller than me, coming in around six feet. The impression I'd gotten from the dragon was nothing like the kind woman standing before us.

She tugged her cyan button-down shirt over her jeans. "I'm so sorry I alarmed you. I'd planned on you all staying with Mindy and me, but the closer you got, the more restless I felt, so I went for a flight. Then I doubted my decision, but you guys were already close. The best option was to bring you here, a backup location I have for Mindy and a few of the older members in case..."

She didn't have to finish her sentence. Every single one of us knew what she meant: in case Drake came looking to kill her.

Thorn's jaw unclenched. "I'd rather your thunder not know we're here." He then connected, *We saw how well that went with Wyvern.*

Fair point. And Theron hadn't been very willing to help us until Thorn had healed Sol. Trust had to be earned, but hopefully, since Theron trusted us and the two of them had a connection, this would go more easily.

"Listen, I'm not comfortable hiding things from my thunder." She bit her bottom lip. "It doesn't feel right. They do know about this place, but we all avoid it so no one will tie us to it. Until I see that Thorn will follow through on his promise, I'm most comfortable with you staying here."

"Of course, Edna," Theron said and wrapped an arm around Hydra.

Edna took a moment to study each of us and frowned when her gaze landed on Peter, Eva, and Elliott. Her lips pursed. "And why did you bring humans? It's bad enough to have the marked one and Drake's missing fian—"

A menacing growl emanated from Thorn. "Do *not* finish that sentence. Everly is my fated mate and *wife.*

Drake took her, knowing she was *mine* and kidnapped her family to force her to surrender. That's why there are humans with us."

My heart skipped a beat at the word *mine*. I loved when he claimed me in front of others *and* behind closed doors.

Her eyes bulged. "Wait. Are you saying the humans with you are her family? That she was human and became your fated mate?"

He nodded, pulling me more tightly against him. "She was."

Edna stepped back and clutched her stomach.

She looked afraid, prompting me to say, "He did it to save me. I was going to die—it wasn't malicious. And I'm so glad he did." I glanced up lovingly at my mate.

Tilting her head, Edna observed me, and after a moment, her hands dropped to her sides. "That's good to know. But how is that possible? Mending a dragon doesn't make complete sense to me, but to create a new one from thin air?"

That was a good question and one that had a simple but complicated answer.

"When a dragon shifter dies, their magic is released and stays around us." Thorn narrowed his eyes as if he could see the magic hovering. "Healing and creating a dragon are pretty much the same. To heal a dragon's magic, I must remove the magic from its body and infuse it with our ancestors' magic to mend it. When I turned Everly, I filled her body with the magic of our ancestors, and it created her own unique dragon."

Edna tilted her head. "That's actually beautiful and makes sense."

I yawned. I couldn't help it. I'd been struggling to stay awake, and now the adrenaline from potentially being in danger had vanished, along with every last bit of energy I'd had.

Elliott snorted. "I've been up just as long as you, and I'm not falling over."

"That's because you're used to playing video games all night long." Eva placed a hand on her hip and shot him a glare. "And Everly fought the warriors."

Edna walked past our group and up the stairs to the front porch. She removed a key from her pants pocket and unlocked the front door. "I need to get back before the thunder wakes, and you all should get some rest." She opened the door wide. It almost hit the back of a heather-gray cloth couch in the living room.

"There are six bedrooms," she informed us as she handed the key to Thorn. "A master and another downstairs across the house from each other, three upstairs, and one in the attic. The attic bedroom actually has three full-size beds and a queen, so there should be plenty of room."

I waited for her to go inside, but she remained at the door and continued, "You all go in and get some rest. I'll bring Mindy by later today after lunch. If you need anything, feel free to call me. Just don't come to the thunder." She paused, glancing at all of us.

I forced a smile and murmured, "Thank you."

Wincing, she sighed. "I wish I could say I was doing this for you, but honestly, this is for Mindy. If Thorn can heal her, it'll be worth it."

Our bond pulsed with Thorn's trepidation. Each time he needed to use his magic, he grew uneasy. But his nervousness didn't seem as bad as before. I hoped he was beginning to realize that his abilities might not be a curse.

"It will be." Sol beamed as his arm brushed Eva's. "He made a difference for me."

"Good." Edna strolled past us, heading back toward the woods where she'd shifted.

She must have had clothes stowed away for when they came here, especially since she'd flown all this way, and it was at least a forty-five-minute drive back to the thunder.

Let's go inside, Thorn connected. His large hand pressed against the small of my back, buzzing against my skin and urging me in. A combination of grief and needing peace simmered in our bond.

I walked around the huge couch, which looked like two L-shaped pieces pushed together to form a U shape. There was a matching footstool in the center and a fireplace in front. A TV was perched over the mantel.

"We need to assign everyone a room," Vlad said as he entered the house after Thorn.

After a few seconds, we'd all crammed inside. Elliott flopped on the couch. If I sat down, I'd be asleep in seconds.

Saphira pointed at the couch. "I'll sleep here in front of the door. I'm tired of bunking with people." With a lifted brow, she glared at Elliott.

He rolled his eyes but moved down the couch, clearing a spot for Saphira. "Just wait until I'm a dragon."

"Everly and Thorn should have some privacy for at least a night, so Vlad and I can room with Peter." Cassidy walked over to the doorframe on the right. A hallway left of the stairs led to a bedroom. The stairs were directly in front of us, with some sort of table to the right, but the wall cut off most of my view.

"I guess that means Eva, Dad, and I are rooming with Cassidy and Vlad in the attic." Elliott pouted.

Sol bounced on his feet. "If you don't want to stay in a room with them, I can."

Cheeks flaming, Eva stared at the wooden floor but smiled shyly.

"What?" Theron shook his head. "No. They're family. They should stick together."

"Yeah, man." Elliott scowled and crossed his arms. "You sleeping in the same room as my sister? Not happening."

"We'll take a room down here," Thorn said and guided me to the hallway. "You all can figure out the rest. I need sleep." The pressing heat swirled harder between us, a desperate emotion taking hold.

The rest of the group continued to talk, but I couldn't focus on them. Thorn was struggling.

We headed down the hallway to the first door and stepped into the master bedroom. The wooden floor and beige color scheme matched the rest of the house, and a king-size bed sat against the far wall. Thorn locked the door and placed his head against the wood as those emotions he'd been holding back burst through him.

I stepped toward him and wrapped my arms around his waist. It was my turn to take care of him in whatever way he needed. *Just know I'm here.*

He spun around in my arms, his eyes darkening. *I know.* His lips touched mine as his tongue begged for entrance.

And just like that...all my exhaustion was gone.

CHAPTER SIX

AS HIS TONGUE stroked into my mouth, my body warmed. It had been over twenty-four hours since we'd had sex, which felt like forever. My stomach clenched with need, but I pushed it aside...for now.

My dragon roared in protest as I pulled back, breathless. Thorn countered my move to eliminate the distance I'd put between us.

Hands on his chest, I pushed him back hard enough for his eyes to open, allowing me to see his gorgeous sky blue irises. I'd already memorized every diamond fleck in them. They were one of my favorite parts of him and the first thing I'd noticed, even at night in a car.

His brow furrowed. *What's wrong?*

You're upset, and I want to make sure you're all right before we go further. I cupped his cheek, noticing his long lashes framing those eyes. *Don't get me wrong. I'm all for sex, but I don't want you to use that as a remedy to ignore what's going on inside you.*

Blowing out a breath, he frowned and clenched his jaw. *That's the last thing I'd ever want you to think I was doing.*

He lowered his forehead to mine and wrapped an arm around my waist, pulling me close.

In fairness, I didn't think it was intentional. I smiled sadly. *But you did just lose your biological father, and you've been a mess of emotions since we left the barn.* I kissed his cheek. *I don't want to push, but I also don't want to taint our bond, even accidentally.*

He nodded and took my hand, leading me to the bed. We sat on the mattress, my hand running along the gray paisley comforter as we scooted up to lie back on the two oversized pillows.

Lifting our joined hands, Thorn stared at the wood-paneled ceiling. "You're right. I've been struggling. I hated him for *so long*, and then for him to denounce Drake and apologize to me, only to die right after..." His pain and guilt flared through our bond. "I...I don't know how to feel. On the one hand, I'm still angry. It took all of *this* for him to finally see the truth? But then I feel guilty for being mad." His voice cracked, and I turned to him as his eyes glistened.

"You have *every* right to be hurt, angry, and confused. The king screwed you over, and even after he realized what he'd done was wrong, he wasn't willing to stand up to Drake...until it was too late. He doesn't get a pass just because he's dead."

The thing was, I understood how Thorn felt...somewhat. My heart clenched over the loss we shared. "Mom was an amazing mother to me, but when she died, not only did I lose her, but I got left with Peter. I was so angry about it, but I didn't have anywhere else to go or anyone else to help me. Though I wasn't mad *at her*, I felt guilty about being angry at all because she was gone. It took me a while to realize it's okay to be upset and that sometimes, life hands us crap, and we have to figure out a way to move on."

"I'm so damn sorry you had to go through that." Thorn's face twisted in agony. "I wish I could've been there to help you. That you could've leaned on me."

"I've come to believe that everything happens for a reason." A tear trickled down my cheek, my vision clouding. "But the point is, I felt guilty for being mad. If she hadn't married Peter, Elliott and Eva wouldn't be here, and though we weren't close then, I still loved them and couldn't imagine a world without them."

A smile tugged at the corners of his mouth. "I could've gone without smelling your brother's fart tonight. It was pretty rank."

I giggled, my chest expanding. I'd never told anyone how I'd felt when Mom died, and I was glad I'd told Thorn. He knew exactly what to say. "True, but—" I placed a hand over his heart. "I want you to know that I believe your biological parents loved you, and at least King Arman realized his mistake and was able to apologize. If he hadn't, you'd have gone on thinking he never loved you. And Thorn, I think that could've hurt the man I know you're going to become. So grieve, scream, and flip off the world all you need, but know that through it all, I will be standing right beside you."

Warmth soared through me, and Thorn purred, the sound enthralling.

"With you by my side, I know we'll conquer the world." He scanned my face and whispered, "You own me."

My breath caught, and desire pooled inside me, causing a deep ache in my core. I needed him so desperately, but I had to make sure he was okay.

When his lips landed on mine, I had to say something else before I lost myself in him. Unable to speak, I connected, *Maybe we should sleep.*

In a little while. His hand slipped under my shirt, and he unbuttoned my jeans. *I promise, I just want to make love to you, my mate. There is nothing else on my mind other than wanting to merge with you and show you exactly how I feel.*

As his hand slid under my panties, all I could focus on was his touch, his scent, and my longing to taste him again.

His fingers circled between my lips, and he lowered his head, kissing me again. This time, I had no thoughts of stopping. His emotions were searing hot from his love for me, confirming I was the *only* thing on his mind.

Our tongues collided, and his faint minty taste turned me on even more.

Desperate, I clutched his shirt, pulling him on top of me. His hands didn't miss a beat, shifting the pressure that had my head arching back. His lips moved down my face to my neck, and when his teeth grazed my skin, ecstasy exploded within me as he took me over the edge.

He raised his head, watching me melt into him. *So damn beautiful,* he connected as his irises darkened to cobalt.

Crazed, I yanked at his shirt, and he chuckled. The dark, throaty sound had need soaring through me again. His fingers weren't enough. I needed him inside me.

Removing his hands, he rolled to the side and tossed his shirt to the floor as I lifted, stripping my shirt and bra off. Within seconds, we were naked and ogling each other.

I took in every curve of his muscles. My favorite part was the V that pointed down the one part of him that could satisfy me. Though I hadn't touched him, he was ready.

When I reached for him, he caught my wrist and held it by my head as he settled between my legs. He whispered, "If you touch me, we might not get to do this. I'm already close. You're so damn sexy."

"Well, that would be a shame," I breathed, loving how he'd restrained me. A shiver of anticipation ran through me.

He entered me slowly, our gazes locked. His pupils slitted, fueling me further. I bucked my hips underneath him, and with his free hand, he grabbed my waist.

Sex with him before had always been mind-blowing. In fact, each time we came together, it was better than the time before. But this time was completely different.

Lips on mine, he moved at a slow pace, slipping deeper inside me than ever. The emotions between us were intense, the build of sensation slow and powerful. My body arched against his, and he groaned.

Nipping my ear, he connected, *You're driving me crazy.*

The words made me feel loved and sexy. Our connection opened wider, each of us feeling the other's emotions. I treasured the moment as we pleasured each other, and our souls merged like they'd been meant to do.

Sweat slicked our bodies, and the friction increased until I couldn't contain myself. I pushed on his shoulder and moved on top of him. I was tired of him having all the control, and he didn't resist.

I grabbed the headboard as his hands cupped my breasts, fingers gently rolling my nipples. Somehow, I kept the pace slow, and then I glanced down at his body. His muscles flexed as he thrust into me in sync with my movements, his eyes dark and heavy with desire.

His beauty and the love he had for me made my chest ache painfully. He was perfect for me. *You own me, too,* I connected, because sometimes, *I love you* just didn't cut it.

His dragon roared, and an orgasm ripped between us. His pleasure merged with mine, and his hands continued to do delicious things to my body. Our bodies convulsed, and I grew dizzy.

I wasn't sure how long the ecstasy lasted, but when I crumpled onto him, fatigue hit me hard. He turned, curling his body around me, and within seconds, I fell asleep, content and happy in the best place in the world—his arms.

AN ALARM BEEPED, and my eyes fluttered open. Sun shone through the closed blinds of the window next to my bed, the light hitting Thorn's arm, which was threaded underneath my head. His other heavy, warm arm was slung over me, and my body buzzed intensely. It took me a second to realize that we'd fallen asleep naked after having mind-blowing sex. My dragon purred at the memory, and heat flared between my legs again.

The only thing dampening my desire was the buzzing of the damn alarm.

I groaned. "When did you set that?"

He grumbled. "I didn't. It's coming from down the hall."

Footsteps approached from down the hallway.

Where we were and why flooded back into me. "What time is it?"

"Time for you assholes to get up," Saphira said from the other side of the door. "Edna will be here within the hour, and we need to be ready."

I exhaled and snuggled deeper into Thorn's chest. I called out, "Just a little more sleep." Though I had no intention of sleeping. My body was ready for round two.

"Uh, no. Get out here." Saphira gagged. "I can smell your intent, and hearing the two of you last night was more than enough. You kept my ass up for an hour while you *violated* each other."

Thorn chuckled and propped himself up on his elbow.

He nuzzled my neck, a hand brushing down my body. "We did not violate each other. However, if that's what you want to hear, we can do that—" His hand slipped between my legs, and I gasped as that familiar clench of desire slammed into me.

"Ew. No." Saphira banged on the door. "If you start, I'll make sure to get Cassidy and Vlad down here immediately. I know Everly would *really* appreciate that."

That was the equivalent of a cold shower, and I scooted away from Thorn, already missing the touch of his hands.

"That was low," Thorn hissed, but he smirked. "But don't worry. I can make her forget that she cares."

"Oh, really?" Saphira bit out. "We'll see about that. The *brothel* smell is already cut in half. I'm assuming what's left is from Thorn."

I snarled. The idea of her purposely smelling him almost made my dragon come unglued.

"Girl, I was teasing," Saphira said warily. "For all I know, it's you. Believe me, I don't want to sniff your man. I have someone else I'd much rather be sniffing."

Wyvern.

Something had jolted between them when they'd seen each other while confronting the warriors. I hadn't had the opportunity to ask her about it. Some of my anger ebbed, allowing me to think rationally again.

"Don't listen to her." A wicked glint sparkled in Thorn's eye. "You should ravish me to make sure Saphira knows I'm yours. Maybe even stake your claim against my neck again."

My dragon roared, urging me to do just that. Damn the consequences.

"That's it. I'm going. Just remember, someone's coming who could rat us out or kick us out on our asses." Saphira stomped away, and as promised, she clomped up the stairs.

Inching closer to him again, I kissed him, lingering on his lips. I connected, *Though I love seeing you smile, we do have to get ready. We need to grab something to eat so you can focus on healing Mindy.*

His smile fell, and I hated that I was the reason for it. He nodded. *You're right in every way. If we want to be able to be like this always*—he gestured to the room and how we were lying naked together—*we have to eliminate the threat. I'm just not sure how we do that.*

My body sagged against his. I'd been pushing him to do the right thing. I knew his reluctance wasn't because he didn't want to but because he'd been through so much trauma. Though I wished the king hadn't died, maybe his death wouldn't be in vain if Thorn finally saw the light. I just wished it hadn't taken losing his biological father to accept himself. But I couldn't deny that being on the same page as my mate was nice. *We start out by helping whoever we can, finding allies, and training them. With everyone's help, we'll figure out the rest from there.*

He pecked my lips and climbed out of bed.

I scanned his naked body. Every inch of him was hard and solid...every single one. My body flared back to life.

Grinning, he grabbed his jeans. *Too bad you turned me down.*

Damn shame. I licked my lips and forced myself to get up. My dragon spurred me on, knowing he'd let me devour him if I insisted, but my logical side screamed at me to stay the course. If we wanted a life where we didn't have to worry and could just be together, we had to stay focused...at least during the day, when we had things to accomplish.

With every ounce of willpower I had, I strutted past him, copping a feel along the way. His sensual groan turned into one of frustration when I moved my hand away. I scooped up my clothes and dressed quickly while he watched.

He shook his head and laughed. "That was just dirty. You'll pay for that tonight."

Just like that, he had a knot forming in my stomach all over again.

* * *

EDNA AND MINDY would be here any minute. Elliott, Peter, Tyson, and Brenton stayed in the house, while the rest of our group stood in the front yard, waiting for their arrival.

Sol and Eva sat on the red bench swing, talking about some game that Eva liked. They leaned in closely to each other as if the world around them had ceased to exist.

The rest of us stood in a semicircle. I looped my arm through Thorn's and laid my head on his shoulder as Saphira stepped forward beside me to look at Theron on Thorn's other side. She asked, "Have you heard anything from Wyvern? Is he—er—the thunder doing okay?"

My eyebrows quirked. That was more than normal interest. I had to talk to her sooner rather than later about what was going on between them.

Nodding, Theron pressed his lips into a line. "I talked to him a little while ago. The thunder is fine. Drake threatened them, but as Wyvern suspected, the thunder was left to him to rule since he showed loyalty by alerting Drake to us. He's supposed to notify Drake if he hears or sees us again."

At least that hadn't blown up in our faces.

"Wyvern asked about you," Hydra said, placing a hand

on her mate's arm. "He wanted to make sure you, specifically, were okay."

Saphira's face reddened, and she beamed.

"Why would he..." Errol's words died as he studied his daughter. His forehead lined, and his mouth gaped.

An engine that had been rumbling faintly in the background grew louder.

"Are they coming by vehicle?" Vlad moved further into the yard and near the dirt driveway.

Staying close to her mate, Cassidy followed. "It would make sense if they did, in case warriors are searching the area."

"She didn't say either way." Theron crossed his arms. "But we're about to find out."

Our group fell silent as a burnt orange Mazda CX-5 pulled up. In the driver's seat was none other than Edna.

The woman in the passenger seat was a few years younger than me, close to Eva and Elliott's age. Her hair was a little shorter than her mother's and dyed a vibrant burgundy that made her chardonnay-gold eyes glow. As soon as the car was parked, Mindy opened her door and got out. Her eyes immediately focused on Thorn.

They hurried toward us, Edna rubbing her hands together.

Mindy just smiled at Thorn like he held all the answers. "I hear you're going to heal me."

Our fated-mate bond constricted from the pressure she'd put on him.

Thorn rolled his shoulders, and his body tensed. "I'll try."

Her expression faltered, but Theron stepped in and introduced everyone to Mindy.

"We don't have long." Edna glanced at her car. "The

news of the king's death hit the Dragonnet, as did the warriors' preparations to search for your group. Our thunder is concerned. Mindy isn't the only one at risk, so we'd like to bring some of the older members here for safety. I need to tell them about you before that can happen. Fear has a way of causing chaos, and I need to head back and get things moving...if only for their peace of mind."

The anxiety rolling off Thorn amped up even higher.

You've done this twice, now. You've got this. I squeezed his arm comfortingly.

Thorn nodded. "Okay. Where is your injury located?"

I remembered she'd been injured while in human form.

"My back," she whispered.

He turned to me, kissed my cheek, and connected, *I can't risk you touching me.*

Let me know if you need me. I stepped far enough away to give him the space to not feel like he'd impact me accidentally.

Theron and the others followed suit.

Now I have an audience, Thorn connected as he placed his hands on Mindy's shoulders. "I'm going to channel magic inside you. If I can fill in the missing magic, your dragon will feel a little different until you shift and fly."

Mindy bit her bottom lip as Sol stood on the porch and called out, "He's right. After flying, you'll reconnect with your slightly different dragon. It'll be okay."

I asked, *Do you want me to ask them to go inside?*

No, it'll make everyone uncomfortable. He closed his eyes. *I'll be okay.*

"I'm going to remove your dragon for a moment and give it back," he informed her as his hands glowed. "Don't be afraid."

The magic churned through him, and I watched as

everyone's mouths dropped open. Only Theron, Hydra, and I had seen him use the magic before, and it was amazing.

His hands lit up the area around him despite the sun shining high in the sky.

I smiled as my chest swelled. He hadn't even hesitated or needed my help. He was getting control of his magic and not struggling to connect with it anymore.

As the friction vibrated through our bond, I knew he was already working. The moment he took her dragon, Mindy whimpered, "It's gone."

Then a different tension filled our bond...an emotion I'd felt from him only one another time—when he'd realized Drake had captured me.

Terror.

I can't heal her, he connected. *Her dragon isn't injured.*

Fear strangled me. If he couldn't heal Mindy, we weren't safe anymore.

CHAPTER SEVEN

MY MOUTH SOURED as his words replayed in my mind. Our group was in horrible trouble. The deal had been clear: Edna would help hide us if we healed her daughter. If Thorn couldn't heal Mindy, she might inform Drake that we were here.

Mindy whimpered, I assumed due to her missing dragon. From the friction swirling through our bond, I knew Thorn was holding on to it.

His fear strangled our bond, making it seem half its normal size. The warmth of our usual connection cooled in my chest.

I'm going to give it back to her, he connected. *Her dragon is about to dissipate. I can feel it.*

Do it. He needed to hear me say it. *The only thing worse than not healing her would be taking her dragon away.*

Tension roiled from his body. I didn't have to be connected to him to sense it. Out of the corner of my eye, I saw Vlad inch toward Cassidy. His jaw clenched. He sensed something was amiss. Of course they could read Thorn. He was their son, after all.

The friction in our connection intensified as Thorn gave Mindy her dragon back. The moment the transfer was complete, our bond returned to normal. His hands stopped glowing, and he removed them from her shoulders.

Mindy gasped and opened her eyes.

"Well?" Edna asked as she scurried over to her daughter. "How do you feel?"

She bent down toward her toes...and groaned. "My back still hurts. It doesn't feel any different."

"What?" Theron shook his head. "That's impossible. He healed Sol and Tyson."

"The agreement was that he heal her." Edna's eyes hardened. "And he didn't." She turned to my mate and scowled. "Why? Is it because she's a female?"

My mate's jaw slackened. "What? Gods, no. That has nothing to do with it."

Anger sparked through me, and my hands fisted. I didn't like her insinuation. He'd risked his life for my sister and me.

My breath caught, and my attention settled back on Mindy. "Wait. You were hurt in human form, right?"

She arched a brow but nodded.

"Sol and Tyson *weren't*. They were injured in *dragon* form." I bit the inside of my cheek, letting my hypothesis settle over me. I was premed, so though I didn't understand magic, I understood the human body. "When you were injured, did you go to the hospital for care?"

Edna scoffed. "Of course not. It's forbidden. Her dragon healing kicked in within a day, and we were focused on burying my mate—her father."

That was the answer. "She might have healed, but her back wasn't in proper alignment. Just like a broken bone, it has to be set in a brace so the bones can heal *properly*. It's not an issue with her dragon."

"She's right." Errol stepped forward. "Thorn's power is to create or take a dragon. He can fill in gaps in their magic, which is how he healed Tyson and Sol. Mindy's magic isn't missing anything, so he can't heal her. It's impossible."

Mindy hung her head, a tear trailing down her face. "So...I'll always be broken."

My heart ached. Drake had made these people feel as if there was something wrong with them, as if they weren't whole, just because they were different. The same thing had happened to Mom when the disease had been killing her.

What they didn't see was that they were stronger than the rest of us. They kept moving forward when others might have given up. "You are not *broken*," I insisted. "You are strong. Stronger than Drake and his idiotic notions. Do not let someone like *him* define how you see yourself."

Flicking her gaze to me, Mindy sniffed. "You don't know anything about me. You don't know if I'm strong or not."

"I don't have to know you to see your strength." That was the thing about being broken the way I had been for so long. There was something in a person's gaze...a lifelessness that she, Sol, and Tyson hadn't shown. I gestured to Edna. "And there's no way her daughter wouldn't be as strong as she is. She wouldn't allow it."

Mindy snorted and wiped away a tear. "Okay. You've got me there." She blew out a breath and placed a hand on her stomach. Her gaze went over my shoulder to my mate. "Thank you for trying."

Some of the tension in our connection eased as Thorn came to me and placed an arm around my waist. He murmured, "I'm sorry I couldn't heal you, but my mate is right—don't let a douchebag like Drake define you. If I'd done that, I'd have handed myself over to him for execution, believing I didn't deserve to live because of my powers."

Pride swelled in my chest. That was exactly what Mindy needed to hear. "And I would've been mar—"

Fingers digging into my side, Thorn snarled. The white-hot anger seared through our bond, eliminating the fear from moments ago. "Do *not* finish that sentence, *please.*"

I shut my mouth. *Sorry. I was trying to help.*

Remorse floated through as he connected, *I know. You have nothing to be sorry for, but remembering that and knowing he's hunting you...I just want to rip his throat out. The only reason I haven't rushed off to do it is because you're here beside me, keeping me grounded.*

My heart ached from how much I loved him.

Cassidy cleared her throat. "We'll pack up and leave. Please at least let us get out of here before you notify Drake."

"I'll pack our things," Hydra said and turned toward the house.

The swing squeaked as Eva's feet hit the wooden porch. She'd been listening in the whole time. I glanced over my shoulder to see Sol easing in front of her, blocking her from Mindy's and Edna's view.

"Will you hold off until we leave?" Vlad asked as Cassidy and Hydra rushed through the front door.

"Yes, of course." Edna's face crumpled. "I don't want harm to come to any of you. I just need to protect my daughter and thunder the best way I can."

"That's bullshit," Saphira snapped and marched over to stand beside me. She placed her hands on her hips.

"Honey..." Errol warned. I didn't have to turn around to know he was trying to rein Saphira in.

"This isn't fair. Thorn tried." Saphira waved a hand at my mate.

"Saphy," Brenton hissed.

Saphira didn't flinch, her attention on Edna and Mindy. "We held up our end of the bargain. It's not Thorn's fault that she can't be healed. He *tried*."

But that wasn't how it worked. Life wasn't fair. I'd learned that six years ago when Mom died, and Thorn had learned that at the tender age of six. Shit happened, and we had to deal with it. Having a meltdown would accomplish nothing...other than, perhaps, Edna not waiting until we were gone to contact Drake.

I placed a hand on Saphira's arm, and her breathing calmed. "We need to get ready and leave. This is their decision, and it's final."

She huffed, some smoke trickling from her nose. I tugged on her arm and almost cried when she relented. I'd expected her to fight more.

Thorn's hand fell from my waist, and I was surprised that he didn't follow us—until he said softly and full of regret, "I'm sorry I couldn't help. I wish there was something I could do to keep you off Drake's radar, but my mate's right. Do not let one person define you when everyone else sees who you really are."

"Mom, maybe—" Mindy started.

"They have to go," Edna said firmly. "They *have* to. If Drake and his warriors come here and learn about your back issues, that will be bad enough, but if they find *them* here as well, he'll kill us. We can't risk it."

Saphira spun around, lurching toward the two women, but I held tightly to her arm and dragged her up the stairs.

I got that leaving wasn't ideal, but we had no other choice. "If we force them to allow us to stay, we'll be no better than *him*."

That knocked the wind out of Saphira and gave Errol and Brenton a chance to reach us and take her from me.

A moment of silence descended before Theron rubbed his hands together. "How long do we have until you warn Drake and the warriors?"

"I'll give you one more night." Edna sighed. "Like Saphira said, Thorn tried, and the reason he couldn't heal her makes sense. I don't think you guys are lying, but our people have to come here and hide, and I don't have a good enough reason for you all to be here, putting them more in danger. I wish things were different, but that's not our world. Not anymore. I need you out by dawn."

Dawn.

That was more time than I'd expected. That would give us a night to figure out where to go.

"Thank you." I held each woman's gaze. "For giving us shelter, even for two nights."

Frowning, Edna nodded. "I truly wish I could do more. If the warriors come through and we're certain they won't come back, I'll message Theron."

As the two of them headed back to their car, Thorn marched toward me, a scowl on his face and his shoulders hunched. Vlad and Theron stayed put, watching the two women pull away.

You did the right thing, I connected. I needed him to know how much he meant to me. When he reached me, I cupped his cheeks with both hands. *You own me.*

He smiled sadly. *You make me into the sort of man I never expected to become,* he replied, the warmth of his love spreading through the bond. *I wish I could save you from all of this, because you know you own me, too.*

I pressed a soft kiss against his lips. *As long as you and I are together, that's all I need.*

Intertwining our fingers, Thorn tugged me to the porch just as Saphira, Errol, Brenton, and Sol went inside. We would figure out our next steps and survive. We had to.

There was no other option.

THAT NIGHT, we all hung out in the living room in silence. Elliott and Tyson didn't even play video games.

No one had volunteered to let us into the injured dragon network, as I was calling it. After learning that Thorn couldn't help Mindy, everyone feared allowing us near.

That wasn't the main problem. Even though Cassidy, Vlad, and Thorn had saved money in case of an emergency, it wasn't that much. We could find a place to rent somewhere, but we'd have to find a source of income, which was a huge problem since a dragon shifter could pass by at any second and give away our location to Drake. We also couldn't go too far— not if we wanted to stop Drake from hurting more people.

One thing at a time. I thought about painting for money, but I couldn't risk going back into Asheville to sell my work through the gallery, and I didn't have a client list of my own to contact.

"The safest bet would be allowing me to get back to my *job*," Peter grumbled from where he stood in the corner of the room, a deep sneer on his face.

No one responded. Vlad sat on the far end of the couch,

searching on his phone for a house to rent, and Theron swiped his phone every few seconds from where he sat between his mate and son. Of course, Eva was crammed in beside Sol, next to Cassidy. Saphira sat on the other end of the couch, with Errol between her and Brenton. Elliott and Tyson sat on the footstool in the center.

Thorn and I leaned against the wall perpendicular to Peter, too restless to sit down. He didn't want to wait until the morning to leave in case Edna decided to call Drake early.

When Theron glanced at his phone, he blanched.

I wasn't the only one who'd noticed, because Sol asked, "Dad, what's wrong?"

"Just got a text from Wyvern." Theron closed his eyes and lowered his head. "There's a huge problem."

Saphira's head jerked toward him so quickly I feared it might fall off. She rasped, "Is he okay?" Her mocha eyes darkened as she jumped to her feet like she was prepared to leave.

"Yes, he's fine." Theron looked at Peter, Eva, Elliott, then me as he said, "We've got another issue."

Stomach souring, I asked, "What now?"

"You four have been reported missing." Theron dropped his phone into his lap. "Every dragon shifter will now link Everly's family to us. We aren't just hiding from dragon shifters anymore—humans will be able to recognize us as well."

My breathing seized. This had Drake's name all over it.

Peter snickered. "I told you that you should've left Elliott and me out of this. I figured this would happen."

"Yes, because if we had, you'd have been far better off in Drake's *prison*." In a way, I wished we had left Peter there, but we'd be in a worse situation if we had. Eva and Elliott would have been beside themselves, and Drake would have made sure to hurt him to get the reaction he wanted from them. This way, the four of us were safe.

Thorn wrapped an arm around my waist and glowered at Peter. "You should be thankful you're here with us, especially since Drake already hates you."

A phone rang, and Theron cursed. "It's Edna."

Something heavy weighed my limbs. If the news was out nationwide, that had to be the reason she was calling.

"Answer it." Hydra pressed her lips into a line. "There's no point in holding off. She might tell you that the warriors are on their way."

"Tell her I found a place and I'm about to book it." Vlad removed his wallet from his back pocket and pulled out a credit card.

Theron answered the phone. "I know why you're calling. Vlad's booking—"

"We need Thorn." Edna sounded desperate.

I leaned into Thorn's side as my heart hammered. Something was wrong.

No one responded. I looked up at my mate.

"If he doesn't come here, someone will die." She sighed. "I'm not sure if he can save her, but he's here. I hope he's willing to try."

Everyone stared at Thorn, waiting for his answer.

This could be a trap, he connected, pivoting toward me.

It could. We couldn't be foolish. Edna might turn us over to the warriors to protect her daughter, especially since you couldn't tell Mindy was injured by glancing at her. But there was one issue. *What if it's not?* Could we let someone die because we let fear dictate our response?

"If this is a trick, I will take every one of your dragons," Thorn rasped, his pupils slanting.

"Understood," she replied. "Theron, I'll send you the address so you can come straight to the house. Please hurry." She hung up, and a second later, his phone dinged.

Vlad and Theron jumped to their feet as Thorn and I headed for the door. When I reached the edge of the couch, Thorn spun around to face me and said, "Stay here. This could be a trap. I can't risk you going."

I laughed. The idea of staying behind was absurd. I glared at him and prepared for war.

CHAPTER EIGHT

HURT SWIRLED THROUGH ME, stealing my breath. I knew he didn't want me to go out of fear and not because he thought I couldn't handle myself, but that didn't lessen the sting. "I'm going."

He huffed and touched my arms as he rasped, "Please. Stay. If something were to happen to you—"

"Oh, *hell*, no." I stabbed my finger into his chest, hitting rock-hard muscle. "If *I* were leaving, there would be no way you'd stay behind. That goes the same way for *both* of us."

"If it were the other way around, there's no way I'd allow you to leave." Thorn's jaw clenched.

Elliott snorted, and Saphira muttered, "And here I was beginning to believe he wasn't stupid."

"Stay out of it," Thorn barked as his nostrils flared, but his gaze didn't leave mine.

"Thorn..." Cassidy's voice held warning. "You're in the wrong, and we don't have time for this. Hydra and I are staying for our own reasons, but you're the true heir, and Everly is your mate."

"That's my point." Thorn lifted his chin, his irises darkening. "That's why Everly needs to stay here with you and Hydra."

He listed the two other mated women, making his point clear—they weren't demanding to go, so why was I?

I swallowed my anger. If I didn't calm down, we'd fight each other even longer. All my years of swallowing my anger around Peter were coming in handy. *I get that you want to protect me, but you didn't want to go in the first place. You're going because of me, and I need to be there. I trust Edna. They seem like good people. So if this is a trap, it's because they're in trouble, and I couldn't live with myself or you if something happened and you made me stay here alone. Remember how you felt when I left you to turn myself over to Drake?*

He lowered his head, touching his forehead to mine. I could feel the change in our connection. *Thinking something could happen to you makes me damn crazy.*

I feel the same about you, but other than my stupid moment when we first connected, I haven't asked something like that of you. I leaned back and softly kissed his lips. *Please don't keep doing the same to me.*

You fight dirty. He frowned, but defeat darkened his gorgeous sky blue eyes.

I chuckled and laid my palm against his chest. *I don't mean to, but it's only fair that we respect each other. I want us to be a team, and this is something we should do together.*

You're right. He huffed. *I'm sorry.* He took my hand and tugged me toward the door.

"It's a damn good thing he came to his senses, or I'd be helping Everly with the smackdown." Saphira stood and marched to the door. "I'm going with you four."

Errol's mouth opened, and he turned around in his seat. "Saphy, no."

"I have to. This is getting worse because people like me ignored Drake's horribleness and let it get out of control." Saphira crossed her arms. "You can stay here and plan our next steps while I go with my bestie."

I grinned. She'd called me her best friend. No one had called me that before, and I realized I felt the same way about her. Even when I'd met her when she'd come to take me to Drake, something about her had been comforting.

"We'll watch her." Vlad nodded. "But we've got to get going."

"Be safe." Errol frowned as he watched us walk out the door.

The five of us were in the yard. My dragon stirred inside, ready to fly. It hadn't been terribly long, but I'd learned that anytime I got anxious, she inched forward, wanting to help. "Saph, let me run in and get a duffel bag so we can carry our clothes there in dragon form."

"No." Theron removed the keys to his truck. "We can't risk it. If the warriors are on their way, they could be nearby. The last thing we need is our scents in the air."

Thorn stopped in his tracks, pulling me to stand beside him. Vlad and Saphira paused, following his lead. Thorn said, "You're right, but before we pull into their neighborhood, we need to get out of the vehicle and make sure we don't sense anything strange. Since we won't be in our dragon forms, it'll be harder to detect threats."

"That's fine." Theron didn't break stride to his vehicle.

The rest of us hurried toward the car again. Theron was already inside with the engine started when the four of us reached it. Vlad took the front passenger seat as Thorn climbed in behind Theron. Of course, I got stuck in the middle, with Saphira scooting in next to me a second after I was settled.

As soon as the last door closed, Theron reversed and quickly turned the car around, then barreled away from the safe house. He tossed his phone to Vlad. "Can you plug in the address? I think she put in the exact house. I have a general idea of how to get to where Edna cut us off."

"Yeah." Vlad swiped the phone and tapped.

Thorn's unease swirled between us, and I took his hand. I understood what was going on. He didn't want to do this, but for a different reason this time. It wasn't about wanting to run. Rather, he was petrified that this was a trap and Drake was taking advantage of our good nature. I couldn't blame him, but Edna didn't strike me as a dishonest person.

"I hate to agree with Thorn's attitude toward Everly, but he has a point." Saphira sighed. "Theron, are you sure she wouldn't lead us into a trap to save her daughter? Think about you and Sol. We need to be on the same page, and I feel like you're the one who's rushing in blindly...and you're driving the truck."

I loved how she'd put all that out there. She clearly had grown up watching her father, the advisor to the king.

"That's fair." Theron's hands tightened on the steering wheel. "But every parent on the injured network cares about the others. It's not just about saving their family members but everyone. If this were a trap, I firmly believe she would've warned me somehow. I get that you're all suspicious. I would be, too, if I hadn't been involved in this network for the past year. We take risks to get resources to other people's hiding spots and address needs such as financing and contacts. A few of us have shared our addresses with other families in the network when they were compromised and warriors were getting close to them. If one of us betrayed another, it would ruin everything our network stands for."

The tightening sensation lessened from Thorn, but his body was still tense, and he kept a death grip on my hand.

"I got the same read from her." Vlad turned toward us. "That's the only reason I didn't push not going. But that doesn't mean we just throw caution to the wind. Someone could be pressuring her and watching her so she can't warn us."

That was true. If warriors were there, they'd be watching her every move. But I still believed she would try to notify us somehow.

The GPS started talking in that horrible nasally voice, and the truck became silent. We drove over the red covered bridge again and past where Edna had stopped us. With each mile, my heart pounded harder as we kept watch, tapping into our dragons.

"Roll down the windows," Vlad said, lowering his.

All four windows went down, and the cool night wind of early June swirled around us. We could hear and smell everything this way.

I asked my dragon to amplify my hearing and vision, not enough to begin the shift but better than my normal human form. Though I couldn't sense the surroundings from miles away like I could as a complete dragon, I could sense things nearby, which wasn't much. Just a few foxes and some raccoons scurrying around in search of food. Between them being out and the lack of dragon scents, my lungs worked more easily.

A few minutes later, some houses peeked through the tree branches. The GPS began talking, guiding us toward the area. Several two-story buildings came into view, the bottoms in brick and the top halves sided in various colors. Each house sat on an acre of land that backed up to the woods. Of course, if an entire thunder lived here, they wouldn't need more room since they wouldn't have to constantly hide their existence from their neighbors.

Theron stopped on the right edge of the dirt road and turned off the vehicle. None of us climbed out, remaining quiet and listening.

A door opened, and a man ran out into the yard of the fifth house down on the left. "Mindy! Your mom said she needs you." His voice broke. "Emily needs CPR!" The guy dropped to his knees. "I can't...I just can't see her that way."

There was no way this was a setup.

"We need to go." Pain ripped through my chest as memories of Mom's death swirled around me. I touched my wrist but came up empty. The bracelet was still safely in our bag.

No one moved, and I gritted my teeth, ready to explode.

"You heard my mate. Now go." Thorn wrapped his arms around me, pulling me to his chest. *Baby, what's wrong?*

That heartbreak. A tear rolled down my cheek. *Someone he loves is dying.*

Theron punched the gas, and as we pulled up in front of the dark gray house with the man on the ground, Mindy rushed toward us from across the street.

My medical training surged through my mind, and I reached past Thorn and shoved the door open, then rolled over him and onto my feet. I knew CPR, and I had to get in there to help.

"Thank gods you're here." Mindy ran toward us. "We need you to come inside."

"I heard CPR is needed." I rushed to the door. "I can help with that."

Mindy's eyes bulged, and her shoulders sagged. "Good, because I have no clue what to do, and she's gotten worse."

The man straightened when he saw Thorn and me. He appeared to be in his thirties, with short dark blond hair and olive skin. His slate gray eyes narrowed. "What are *they* doing here? Will he take the baby's dragon? Will that even save her?"

I flinched, but I was pretty sure I was caught up. "Someone is having complications from having a baby?" There were so many scenarios running through my brain. She could be having a heart attack, which Thorn couldn't fix.

"She's human." Mindy wrung her hands and glanced at Thorn. "We were hoping he could change her."

"Mindy!" Edna screamed from inside.

We were running out of time.

Mindy raced to the door and waved us in.

"Wait." The man pointed at Thorn. "He can make someone into a dragon shifter? All I saw on the wedding footage was him taking dragons."

Thorn growled. The man wasn't helping his wife, friend, or lover by delaying Thorn.

"Yes! He changed me," I answered and took Thorn's arm. "Let's go. If her heart stops, we won't have much chance of keeping her alive."

The man paled. "Then go! Help her. *Please.* Save my wife and our baby."

"Theron and I will stay out here and keep watch," Vlad said and pointed at Saphira. "Go inside and help. I'm thinking your style of help will be better than ours."

"That's for sure." Saphira didn't hesitate, rushing after us.

The stairwell split the foyer. Mindy ran up the dark beige carpeted stairs to the top level. A flimsy plastic gate sat to the right of the top floor, blocking the opening to the stairway. A navy cloth couch butted up against it, with a flatscreen TV on a stand across from it, but when someone screamed in pure agony, the surroundings blurred, and that became the only thing I could focus on. We turned left, rushing down a hallway into the first bedroom.

Then the nightmare truly began. A woman I assumed was Emily lay in a king bed on what had once been white sheets. Half of the fitted sheet was now stained crimson. Her heart was barely a flutter, telling more of the story. Her body was wearing out.

The little bit of training I had kicked into gear as soon as I saw Edna standing helplessly between Emily's legs. The baby's head wasn't showing, and Emily's legs hung lifelessly. The baby couldn't get out that way.

This was bad. *Really* bad.

I jumped into action.

"Oh, my gods," Mindy squeaked. "She's far worse than when I left."

That didn't help matters. "Saphira and Mindy, lift her legs the way you have to when you go to a gynecologist appointment." I examined Emily. "Thorn, if you can, change her. We need shifter healing to kick in. Her body is overstressed."

Mindy and Saphira ran to the woman's legs on either side of Edna, but they just stood there, staring at each other. Mindy murmured, "Do you have any idea what she's talking about?"

"No dragon shifter I know goes to a gynecologist."

Ugh. Of course they didn't. They wouldn't want a human doctor working on them.

Thorn went to Emily's shoulders and placed his hands on her. I felt the moment he tapped into his magic. The thrumming started in our connection, and his hands glowed.

I was again in awe of his growing confidence in his magic, and I was certain he hadn't noticed that he was getting attuned to it.

Emily's heart sputtered, and I moved from between her legs and rushed around Mindy to her other side, across from Thorn. His magic pulsed into her, and as I watched, her pale, blotchy skin smoothed into a beautiful complexion, but the color didn't darken. The thrumming stopped, and he removed his hands. Her heart still fluttered, and she was gasping for air.

Next came the hard part. I'd have to monitor her and be ready to administer CPR since the baby was still coming and her new magic couldn't focus only on healing. I pivoted and snatched one of Emily's legs, bending it up toward her chest. "This is what you need to do." I nodded to the leg by Saphira.

To her credit, she didn't hesitate and followed my example.

"Mindy, take my spot."

The young shifter listened, but when she took the leg, her face twisted in agony.

Shit. Her back.

"Here, I'll do it." I took the leg.

She hung her head.

I didn't need to be able to mind speak to know what she was thinking. I hadn't meant to make her feel inadequate, but I didn't want her in pain. However, this was probably for the best. "She knows you, so she'll be more comfortable if you're next to her head, talking and guiding her through the process."

Mindy's face lifted, some of the pain easing from her eyes. "Oh, yeah. That makes sense."

"See if you can wake her up," I suggested, pulling the leg back.

"I see the head," Edna said with relief. "Finally. I was worried."

That had to be partly due to Emily's new dragon growing stronger.

"Uh..." Thorn cleared his throat and stared across the room at the window, making sure to keep his head north of her stomach. "What do you need me to do?"

If Emily hadn't been so close to death, I would've laughed at him. Such a typical male. "Go keep an eye out with Vlad and Theron."

"And leave you?" His brows pulled together, and he flinched.

"You'll be on the other side of this wall." I smiled reassuringly. "I'll let you know if I need you. Ask her husband to come back in."

"Okay," he said and eagerly left the room.

Saphira laughed. "He couldn't get out of here fast enough."

"Can you blame him?" Mindy quipped and placed a hand against the woman's face. "Emily. Can you hear me?"

She moaned quietly in response, and that was enough to make me feel better. Emily was coming around. Now we had to focus on the task at hand.

I WASN'T sure how long we were in the bedroom, but eventually, the guys came inside the house and waited in the living room. About thirty minutes ago, Emily had given birth to a boy, and I'd stayed with her longer to make sure she didn't go into cardiac arrest. During that time, her heartbeat had grown stronger, her dragon magic swirling inside and healing her. Even though she was healing, her husband had scooted a chair next to the bed, where Emily could see the baby while he held him.

That had been one hard labor.

The front door opened and shut, and Thorn's discomfort flowed into our bond. Someone must have come in.

Glancing at Emily and her mate, whose name I'd learned was Mikah, I said, "I'm going to check on things out there."

Before they could respond, a woman shouted, "What in the *hell* are they doing here, Edna?"

Thorn connected, *We've got to go. Now.*

Dazed, I hurried out the bedroom door, the irony not lost on me.

Even when you did something nice, sometimes...it didn't matter.

CHAPTER NINE

AS I STEPPED into the hallway, I found a middle-aged man and woman standing at the top of the stairs, their attention on the living room. The woman's indigo eyes were locked on my mate, who was standing in front of the television, with Vlad and Theron flanking him and Saphira moving to stand in front of him.

The woman's reddish-brown hair was pulled into a haphazard bun with several tendrils curling around her face. Her white shirt was wrinkled, and her jeans had a coffee stain on them despite the early hour.

The man beside her was similarly disheveled. His ice-blue eyes had dark circles under them, and his dark blond hair was unkempt. Though the woman was the one who'd asked the question, the man seemed even unhappier.

Edna strolled out of the kitchen and squeezed past the couple into the living room. She lifted her hands. "Katla, I need you and Volos to calm down. If it weren't—"

"Calm *down*?" Katla scoffed, a vein bulging in her neck. "You have the very man who steals dragons in this house with my son and his wife! How the hell am I not supposed to be frightened? My sweet daughter-in-law is in there, near death after giving birth. We came here to check on her, and we find this instead?" Her voice trembled.

Theron and Vlad inched closer to Thorn protectively.

No one had updated them. Maybe telling Katla that everyone was okay would calm her. I said, "The baby was born safely, and Emily's going to be okay."

Volos and Katla jerked their heads toward me, the man's face blanching further. He rasped, "That's the king's heir's kidnapped fiancée. She's here with the dragon thief?"

Thorn snarled, his jaw clenching. "She is *not* his." His anger soared between us, so powerful that it was palpable to everyone.

Yeah, that plan hadn't worked. If anything, I'd made the situation worse.

"You took all the dragons and kidnapped her because you wanted her for your own." Katla shook her head, taking a few steps away from Thorn and bumping into her mate. "And now you're going to take all our dragons."

Smoke trickled from Thorn's nose as his pupils slitted.

"Son," Vlad whispered, placing a hand on his shoulder. "You have to remember that Drake will twist the story in his favor and pit others against you."

"Not everyone is privy to what you did for my son," Theron added, trying to ease the tension.

Saphira snorted and rolled her eyes, not bothering to hide her disgust. "If that were the case, do you think he would've been sitting here in the living room when you arrived? Or standing here now, letting you run your mouth? Seriously?"

I mashed my lips together to hold in my laugh. Leave it to her to spell out their stupidity.

"Maybe he just got here." Katla crossed her arms, but her words lacked conviction. "He hasn't started."

"Thorn and Everly"—Edna gestured at us—"are the only reason that Emily and your grandson are alive."

Some of Thorn's anger ebbed. *Though Edna is backing us, you need to be ready to go. We can't risk someone bringing the warriors here. Not after everything we've been through.*

I hated that he was right. I wanted to keep an eye on Emily a little while longer, but we'd already stayed too long, especially since Edna had informed us that the warriors were heading this way. Further, Edna had set the strict condition yesterday that we needed to leave by dawn.

"Grandson?" Katla whispered dreamily.

Beaming, Edna nodded. "Yes. You have a *grandson*."

Glancing at Volos, Katla touched her chest. "How did they prevent a different story from happening?"

Mindy appeared at the threshold between the kitchen and the hallway. "Thorn changed Emily. She's a dragon now, and because of that, her body could handle the birth."

"As things were, Emily was struggling with the labor. Everly came in, knowing what needed to be done." Edna smiled and rubbed a hand down her face. "I've helped deliver a baby before, but I've never handled a birth with such complications. Things would have ended differently if they hadn't answered my desperate call...even after I told them they couldn't stay in the safe house."

Surprise filtered through our connection.

"Wait." Volos's face scrunched. "Is that the real reason you ran us out of here earlier? Emily was near death, and you asked these people to come and didn't tell us anything until it was over?"

"No." Edna cut a hand in the air. "When I asked you to

leave, it was before Emily took a turn for the worse. Emily said she needed silence so she could concentrate. She was in so much pain, and her labor wasn't progressing. It wasn't until her body started to shut down that I called Theron and begged for Thorn to come."

Katla's bottom lip quivered. "We heard Mikah yelling last night, and we tried calling so many times. No one answered, but thankfully, Mikah texted us, saying the labor was progressing and Emily was doing better. We waited as long as we could stand before coming here. We were so scared that something horrible happened and that's why we weren't hearing from anyone."

"That's my fault." I could tell the past several hours had been hard on them. "I wanted to monitor Emily's heartbeat. Even though she was changed into a dragon shifter, her pulse wasn't strong. I didn't want her to be more stimulated until I was comfortable she was out of danger."

Volos's breath caught. "Is she still in danger?"

In a way, this was my dream—to be the person who told family members that their loved one was all right and going to survive. It had been the message I'd prayed to hear about my mom so many times, and though it had never come, the doctors had been amazing until the end. But this was the kind of news every doctor hoped to give. "She's fine and going to make a full recovery."

The couple hugged each other as Katla whimpered, "Oh, thank gods."

Something warm coursed through our bond, and I glanced at Thorn to find a proud grin on his face. He connected, *You really are meant to be a doctor. You're glowing.* Then something dampened the warmth. *And because of me, you might never get to become one.*

I despised how he always put the burden on his shoulders and never anyone else's. *No, it's because of Drake, remember? And being with you, well...life has changed, and new priorities have emerged.* I opened myself up more to our connection, wanting him to feel the magnitude of my truth.

"*None* of this was Everly's fault. I took the coward's way out, not wanting to call and tell you not to come." Edna frowned. "If that had been Mindy, there's no way in hell I wouldn't have headed over. I just thought it might be easier to inform you after Everly gave me the okay. That was the wrong call. I should've realized you would've heard Mikah last night and needed a good update. I was so preoccupied that the thought didn't occur to me, and I'm sorry for that."

The door to the bedroom creaked open, and Mikah stuck his head into the hallway. My heart pounded until I noticed his smile and the baby swaddled in blankets in his arms. He tiptoed out and quietly shut the door behind him.

All the hurt and anger vanished from Katla's and Volos's eyes, which twinkled with excitement. Even Thorn's emotions became light and happy as all of us focused on the new life.

Katla took a tentative step forward. "Is that *him?*"

My cheeks hurt, and I realized I was smiling. I'd never been part of something like this before, and my heart felt full to bursting. Moments like these were why I'd wanted to become a doctor—knowing that in some small way, I'd made a positive impact in someone's life. And the icing on the cake was that Thorn was here, seeing what his magic had done. *Yes, I may have helped with the labor, but if it wasn't for your magic—what only you can do—Emily and the baby would've died. If that's not proof that your magic isn't a curse, I don't know what is.* None of us had surgical experience, and many people didn't realize there was an art to a

C-section. You had to cut precisely in order for the child to survive.

"It is." Mikah hurried next to me to stand before his parents and pulled the blanket down from the sweet baby's face. "I'd like for you two to meet your grandson, Thorn."

My heart ached with such happiness. My attention drifted to my mate, whose mouth had dropped open. He moved toward the hallway, his arms wrapped around his body as a mixture of emotions swirled through him. *You're right. My magic can be used for good. It can be used to help people instead of hurting them.*

A sob built in my chest, but not from sadness. I was so damn glad he was finally seeing himself in a different light.

Vlad and Theron were right behind him, and Saphira remained in place. The corners of her mouth tipped upward as she rocked back on her heels. "Seriously, you're going to give the guy a big head, and it doesn't need to get any bigger."

I gave her a look of warning as I watched my mate experience something unique.

"You don't have to name him that." Thorn's voice was deep and emotional.

"I know we don't." Mikah stared at his son in his arms. "But we want to. My wife and child wouldn't be here if it wasn't for you and Everly. It was a no-brainer which name to choose when we realized he was a boy. Emily and I agreed it would be one of your names for doing what you did for us, especially when you didn't have to."

"Hey!" Saphira winked. "I held one of her legs, so you should've considered naming the baby Saphira, even for a moment."

Everyone chuckled, and for an instant, Thorn and I felt content...as if we truly belonged.

Then Theron cleared his throat. "I hate to ruin this, but our group should get going. The sun is rising, and we need to get back to the others so we can head out."

That reminder had my stomach hardening. Even when we felt like we belonged, we didn't. Not only that, but the warriors could show up at any time without any notice.

Vlad nodded. "Congratulations on your new addition. Having a child, especially now, is truly a gift."

"It'll be best for Emily to shift into her dragon when she can," I said. I remembered how disconnected I'd been with my dragon until we'd merged. "She shouldn't rush it, but if she starts feeling antsy, that will help her connect with her dragon."

Come on, babe. Thorn reached a hand toward me, waiting for me on the steps.

"Let me go check on Emily one last time." I pivoted back to the room. "I just need a sec." I quietly opened the bedroom door and heard that Emily's heartbeat was stronger. She was asleep, lying on the bed with a fresh, clean white comforter surrounding her. She was going to be fine.

I shut the door again and made my way to my mate. As we got ready to leave, Mikah, baby Thorn, Katla, and Volos sat on the couch in the living room.

When I took Thorn's hand, Edna said, "Don't leave. Head back to the house and stay. After what you've done for us, that's the least we can do to repay you."

Hope sprang to life in my chest. We didn't have anywhere to go. Allowing us to stay would help us more than she realized.

"Are you sure?" Theron asked carefully. "We don't want you to do something you aren't comfortable with."

"Not only that, but the later we leave, the more thunder

members will see us." Vlad chewed on his lip. "We can't risk word getting back to Drake and the warriors."

"No one should be up if you leave now, but that will change soon." Edna patted Theron's arm. "But after we learned what happened to your thunder, no one will be tempted to say anything. We don't want the warriors here. Though most people know we have a safe house, they have no clue where it is. I did tell them it exists because fear for Mindy and two older couples was taking hold of our thunder. When I confirmed we had a backup in place, some semblance of control replaced the fear. They won't risk our thunder, not after Mikah, Mindy, and I tell them everything you've done. They'll want you to stay, and it's my call."

"And we'll back them." Katla now had the baby in her arms. "I'm so sorry for the way we reacted. But Mikah, Mindy, and Edna wouldn't lie, and because of you, we have a grandbaby."

Vlad and Thorn looked at each other, uncertainty lining their faces.

"If anything seems off, I'll let you know." Edna placed a hand on her heart. "Please trust me like I trusted your group when I opened our safe house to you."

She had us there. Though she trusted Theron, we could've been forcing him to use his resources. Having us here was a leap of faith.

I think we should trust her, I connected with Thorn. *I believe she would tell us if something didn't seem right. Besides, can we risk not having a safe place to stay? Leaving could be worse.*

Thorn pursed his lips. "Okay. But if even one person isn't behind it..."

"We'll let you know." Edna crossed her heart. "I promise. Our community is tight, and I can read my people. I just need to sleep after being up all night. Then I'll talk to them before bringing over the couples and Mindy to stay with you."

The house would be full, but it was worth the crowd if we got to stay. I smiled. "Thank you."

"Now go on, before more people get up." Edna pointed at the front door. "I'll visit you later, after the conversation happens."

That was all we needed.

As we walked down the stairs, Mikah popped up, looking over the banister. "Thank you all again. It was an honor to meet you, Your Highness."

"You're welcome," Thorn growled, though surprise swirled between us as we hurried outside and climbed back into the truck.

As soon as the truck pulled away from the neighborhood, my eyelids grew heavy. I laid my head on Thorn's shoulder, and he wrapped his muscular arm around me. I closed my eyes, enjoying the sounds of his breath and heartbeat while his scent hung around me.

You know...after we handle Drake and save our people, maybe you and I can live near your university so you can get back to school and become a doctor. Watching you tonight was damn sexy, and you made me so proud. His fingers stroked my arm, and both my skin and heart tingled.

I lifted my head as the world tilted. *Wait. No more running away? You actually want to stay?*

Let's just say I finally see that you're right. He kissed my forehead. *Our people don't deserve to live in fear and under constant threat. They deserve to have full lives, happiness, and a leader who will fight for them. If we run, it wouldn't be right. All these dragons are being killed because Drake doesn't understand their worth. We have to fix this, for them and for the two of us to have the kind of life we deserve with each other.*

I cupped his face, afraid my chest might crack open from all the happiness swirling through me. My mate was amazing, and he was finally seeing his worth and what was right for us all. Plus, combining my dreams would be fantastic. I nestled back into his side. *I'd like that future. You could rub my feet as I studied all night.*

I'd do more than rub your feet. His chest rumbled with desire.

I smiled.

"Ew," Saphira gasped. "I don't know what you two are saying, but quit it. I can smell the effect. You are not *alone* in the backseat."

I laughed, but it cut off as I fell asleep quickly.

DARKNESS DESCENDED with no word from Edna. None of us knew how to take it, and Theron had sent several text messages that had gone unanswered.

I was worried that something had changed with Emily, but I believed Mindy or Edna would've contacted us by now. We'd all been exhausted, but Thorn and I had woken up a couple of hours ago, hungry and horny, and not necessarily in that order.

Thorn, Vlad, Theron, Hydra, Sol, Eva, Cassidy, Errol, Brenton, and I were sitting in the den. Tyson and Elliott were upstairs in the room with Peter, playing their video game, while Saphira was still sleeping.

Errol sat on the far end of the couch next to his brother. "If you keep helping dragons, word will get around."

Brenton scowled. "But so will our location. We all know how Drake is about that."

"Has your thunder heard anything?" Cassidy asked Theron from her spot between Brenton and Vlad.

"Nothing." Theron blew out a breath from his spot on the far end of the couch, opposite Errol. "They haven't even heard from Drake since it all went down."

"That's because the warriors are focusing on those who oppose him." Vlad rubbed his forehead, his elbow brushing me. "Which is good. That's one reason they haven't gotten further with their search, but Drake will want to solidify his hold on the throne as quickly as possible."

Eva's forehead lined as she asked, "How would he do that?"

"The coronation." Sol slid an arm over the back of the couch behind her.

"This is insane." Hydra pouted, but her irises twinkled at what her son had done to Eva. "I don't know how we're going to fight this."

"It'd be a whole lot easier if we had someone on the inside," Thorn said as he placed a hand on my thigh.

Theron's phone beeped. He glanced at the screen and raised his eyebrows. "Well, this just got interesting."

My lungs seized. Who could be messaging him now?

CHAPTER TEN

I RUBBED my hands on my legs, trying to calm the ringing in my ears. We always seemed to be running toward or away from something, but Theron's body language was one of puzzlement, not danger.

Thorn tensed, his jaw twitching. "What's going on?"

"I just received a text from Wyvern." Theron swiped his finger over the phone again.

Saphira's head snapped toward him, her eyes bright.

Chuckling, Sol rolled his eyes. "That's not interesting. You two message each other constantly. I'm surprised Mom hasn't gotten jealous yet. You run to your phone every time it dings, wondering if it's him."

"Not all the time." Hydra wrinkled her nose at her son. "When it matters, his attention doesn't stray, so I'm not worried."

His smile disappeared as he grimaced. "I don't want to hear stuff like that."

"Oh, I'm pretty sure I'll be hearing and smelling stuff like that from you soon enough." Hydra's smile was blinding.

Eva dropped her head, her cheeks reddening, and her hair fell across her face as she used it as a barrier.

I wasn't the only one who'd noticed how they revolved around each other, but I understood my sister was more on the private side and didn't like the attention. I could relate to that, though I'd overcome it recently. "What was interesting about the text?"

"A warrior is at our thunder, asking Wyvern to contact us on his behalf. Apparently, he's been talking to Vlad's parents as well, and there's no telling who else." Theron placed the phone on his lap. "He wants to schedule a time and place for all of us to meet."

My head tilted back, and a lump formed in my throat. I hadn't expected *that*.

"Obviously, that's not going to happen." Cassidy chuckled hard. "I get that there were warriors fighting against Drake when the king died, but we know he's putting them in their place. We can't trust anyone."

She had a point, but I still believed that most people wanted to do the right thing. Of course, there were exceptions—there always were—but I couldn't bring myself to think most people were bad. That was too black and white when the world was full of gray. Everyone was a villain in someone else's story. By teaching me my love of painting, my mom had also helped me to understand that the world was more complex than right and wrong, and to capture an image perfectly, you had to see it from all angles.

"Who is it?" I doubted I knew them, but I had to ask.

"A warrior named Uther." Theron mashed his lips into a line.

Uther? Now my head really jerked back. Out of every warrior possible, it would be him.

"I don't know him," Theron continued. "But he's been

poking around. Vlad's parents informed Wyvern that someone was asking about us discreetly, and now this person is doing the same thing. It can't be a coincidence."

"I heard of him recently." Errol leaned forward, resting his elbows on his knees. "He moved to the château grounds the week Everly was taken, but he wasn't assigned to the king and me, so I'm sure his allegiance is with Drake. I wouldn't trust him."

Drake had hand-picked him, and I wondered where he'd pulled Uther from.

I swallowed to get rid of the uneasy feeling. "I wouldn't be so sure about that."

Vlad's attention landed on me. "What makes you say that?"

"He was one of the guards assigned to watch over Eva and me while we were there."

A menacing growl vibrated deep within Thorn's chest as his anger boiled through our connection.

I placed a hand on his arm, hoping to provide comfort. "He was nice—kind and regretful. Drake made it clear on multiple occasions that if Uther did something he didn't like, his young daughter would pay the price. Despite that, Uther treated us kindly and looked out for us the best he could. Even when we were at Theron's thunder and the warriors attacked, he didn't want to hurt us."

"Which means Drake could be using Uther's daughter against him now to set us up." Thorn's body quivered. "For all we know, Drake told him to be like that to earn some level of trust."

The urge to pull away from Thorn surged through me, but I remained still. He was upset, and his words held merit. If I were him, I would possibly be thinking the same thing.

I took his hand and squeezed it, pushing down the frustration fluttering inside me. "I get it, but you weren't there."

His face twisted in agony. "You don't have to remind me. I was living each one of those hellacious moments away from you and losing my damn mind the entire time."

"Thorn," Vlad warned. "That was hard on her as well. You need to remember that."

We didn't need to keep rehashing this. We *all* knew it had been a horrible time for everyone. But I was surprised when Eva spoke up.

"It was a horrible time for Everly, too. Despite her puking all night and tossing and turning, she protected me every step of the way. And Uther *is* kind. Whenever Everly was forced to go with Drake, he'd stay behind to make sure another guard wasn't cruel to me."

A deep scowl settled over Sol's face. Though he hadn't been around when all this had gone down, he obviously didn't like hearing about the time the woman he had a crush on had been forced into captivity and mistreated.

I was beginning to think my hunch that he and Eva were soulmates, like Thorn and I had been before he'd changed me, wasn't so far off after all.

Still, I had to focus on what she'd said, and that information was good to hear. I'd suspected that Uther had protected her since Eva had never fallen apart while I'd been gone. But Thorn was still a bundle of nerves beside me.

"Look, I'm not saying we trust him completely." I couldn't be blind to Thorn's point. Drake could have realized that Uther had an amicable relationship with us and be exploiting his daughter. "But I think it's worth considering."

"And let me add"—Brenton patted his chest—"when someone threatens your kid, it doesn't leave you feeling warm and fuzzy toward them. Based on what Everly and Eva are saying, this isn't something he'd *want* to do, which could be to our advantage."

Hydra leaned into her mate. "What did Wyvern think? Did they talk on the phone?"

"No, he showed up at the thunder with a handful of other guards. They said they came back to see if they'd missed any clues, but after they split up to search the area, Uther circled back." Theron ran a hand through his hair. "He said he didn't have a lot of time but that Drake was settings things in motion, and if we wanted to stop them, we had to act soon. He also said he needed to get in touch with us and asked if Wyvern knew of a way. Of course, Wyvern said no, but he asked us if we needed him to say something else."

"Are they still there?" Vlad asked as he and Cassidy met each other's eyes, using their fated-mate connection to communicate.

I don't like this, Thorn connected, his grip tightening on me. *There are so many ways meeting him could go wrong. It's not worth the risk.*

I inhaled, trying to think clearly. *What if he's sincere? What if we could have someone on the inside? You want to fight Drake, and I agree. We should. We have to. But right now, we're running and hiding without many allies. This could swing things in our favor.*

"They are." Theron crossed his arms. "But I'm not sure for how long. They came at nightfall so they could fly over the area without worrying about humans seeing them as easily."

Thorn sighed and leaned his head back on the couch.

We were all tired...so damn tired.

Standing, Vlad paced around the footstool in front of

the television. "Everly and Eva know him better than any of us. He wasn't the king's hire, so Drake would have something to leverage over Uther to force him to remain loyal. Maybe he wants to be free, and we should meet him."

Releasing my hand, Thorn straightened. "Dad, you can't be serious. If it's a trap, we'll be handing ourselves over to them!"

Arching a brow, Vlad leveled his gaze on Thorn. "You should know I wouldn't go in blindly. Nor do I think Everly and Eva would. We'd have to assume it *is* a trap."

"That's good." Errol bobbed his head. "We'll need to make sure no one is hiding at the meeting place and that he's not followed."

"We need to set up a location where we don't plan on staying." Vlad rubbed his hands together. "We'll be ready at the real location and watch when he arrives. There'll be no chance for others to get into position ahead of us."

Thorn rolled his shoulders. "I could get behind that plan."

"Wait." They were missing something, or I'd lost my mind and wasn't following. "We have one problem to figure out before we can get to the meeting logistics."

Narrowing his eyes, Brenton focused on me. Then he snapped, "How to get the meeting scheduled without putting Wyvern and the thunder at risk."

Exactly. "Even though I trust Uther, you all are right. Drake could be pulling his strings, so if Wyvern schedules the meeting, it'll prove that he's in contact with us, putting them all in danger."

"Shit," Thorn growled, and lowered his head. "You're right. It doesn't even matter if he's trustworthy. We can't risk it, which is more than fine with me. I didn't like the thought to begin with."

There had to be a way to fix this. "Errol, Brenton. Do you have any friends you trust at the château?"

"I do." Errol rubbed a hand along his chin. "A maid who cleans my house, the château, and the house the guards live in on the grounds. I've known her since she was a child, and when her parents passed, I got her a job on the premises. I made sure she was provided for as best I could, and I know the type of person she is. She told me Drake was up to no good, but she refused to tell me specifics, and I thought it was his usual shenanigans like when he was younger. When I realized what Drake had done to Saphira, her warnings made more sense, but it was too late. Then the king asked me for help, and I knew it would get me back to my daughter. There was no question where my priorities lie."

"Is there a way she could leave a message for Uther that no one else would find?" That might be impossible, but it could work.

Some of the worry ebbed from the connection as Thorn connected, *You're brilliant. Have I ever told you that?*

My face heated. He actually hadn't, but he'd complimented me several other ways.

Taking my hand, Thorn leaned toward me and said, "When I lived in the château, I remember the guards having their own lockers in the house where they log their weapons upon returning them into inventory. While the other maids are working, she should be able to slip a note into his locker undetected. Then they wouldn't be able to guess who left the note. We just need a way of communicating with her."

"Errol and I can drive several towns over and find a phone to call her." Vlad grabbed a set of keys. "If they trace the call, it won't compromise our location, and if they somehow get wind of the meeting, we'll have it set up in a way that doesn't lead them here."

The plan was shaky at best, but it was the only option I could think of to get a message to Uther. We couldn't risk giving away our location or proximity to Edna's thunder.

"Now?" Errol's mouth dropped. "I thought we were waiting on Edna."

"We should leave the message as soon as possible if Drake has imminent plans we need to know about." Vlad headed to the door. "The good thing is they won't be sure who is connected to us, which will give the warriors pause before the meeting. We'll schedule something for tomorrow night so they don't have too much time to get things ready." As he opened the door, I heard the faint sound of engines.

Someone was headed this way. It had to be Edna and the others they were bringing.

We headed into the yard as Vlad and Errol reached one of the Suburbans.

Edna's car and a Ford Escape SUV pulled in a few yards back so Vlad and Errol could leave.

Edna climbed out of the car, frowning. "What's going on?"

"We received some news, and Errol and I are going to drive several towns over to make a phone call." Vlad opened the front door. "I promise we'll go far enough that it won't be traced back here."

Edna's forehead wrinkled, but all she did was nod as two older couples got out of the Ford, and Mindy shut the passenger door. The two older men stepped to the back and removed a pair of large suitcases as Mindy reached into the back seat and pulled out a duffel bag. This was the group who'd come to stay here.

The two women stared at us. The taller of them had thick gray streaks in her black hair and crow's feet set deep around her pale brown eyes. She was about Saphira's height, so she had several inches on me. The other lady was all gray, but her face was less wrinkled. Her baby blue eyes had a layer of white over the top like cataracts.

The shorter one smiled as her gaze settled on my mate. "Belinda, that's him. The prince who saved Emily and our precious new baby."

Belinda beamed. "Tia, he's nothing like the angry man we saw on the net of dragons." She hurried toward us and threw her arms around my mate, hugging him tightly.

For a split second, Thorn stiffened, and his shock pummeled through our connection before he relaxed and wrapped his arms around the woman, giving her a small hug in return. The emotions rolling off him had tears burning my eyes. He was moved by the gesture.

Mindy snorted. "Belinda, it's called Dragonnet. How many times do we have to tell you?"

"Eh." She waved a dismissive hand. "Close enough."

"Honey..." The man with short white hair chuckled as he carried their bag. "Leave the poor prince alone. You can't just go hugging everybody. Besides, he's young and muscular. Don't make my dragon more jealous, especially when I know you'll be lying next to my feeble old body tonight." His emerald eyes twinkling, the man's smile didn't break as he marched to his mate. When she pulled back, he patted Thorn on the shoulder.

"Oh, please, Merlin. There is nothing feeble about that body." She winked and nestled into his side.

Heart swelling, I didn't want to look away from this lovely couple. Maybe having them around wouldn't be as awkward as Thorn had feared.

"See, Tia knows better than to go hug on a young'un." The other man laughed as he came near. He and Merlin were about the same height, coming in at around seven feet.

This man had salt-and-pepper hair, though it was more salt than pepper, and a matching beard. His dark brown eyes held a similar twinkle of mischief.

Tia placed her hands on her hips. "Maybe I should just so you don't think I'm fully trained, Ryu."

At least now we knew their names.

"I bet when I said two older couples, you thought you'd need to behave for their sake," Edna said. She laughed and patted Ryu on the back. "You'll soon learn they're worse than teenagers." She launched into introductions.

We gave them our background and story along with why we had humans with us. They handled everything with grace and seemed genuine in their desire to share the house.

When it was clear everything would be fine, Edna left, and our group headed inside, minus Vlad and Errol.

As soon as the front door shut, Brenton called out, "Tyson, Elliott, Peter, and Saphira, come on down so you can meet our new roommates."

"Oh, great. More dragons," Peter ground out as they thumped downstairs.

"I take it that's the disgruntled human we can't trust." Tia waggled her brows. "This will be fun. Being old gives me an excuse to run my mouth without apology."

Elliott led the way downstairs, pouting—until he glanced at our group. His eyes bulged, and he missed a step and tumbled down the rest of the stairs. He landed at the bottom, his head smacking the floor with a sickening thud.

I rushed to him, fearing the worst.

CHAPTER ELEVEN

AS SOON AS I kneeled by Elliott, Thorn was across from me, assessing the situation. The bottom half of Elliott's body lay on the stairs, while his torso was on the ground. He was lying face down, but I could hear his heart beating wildly.

"Elliott," I whispered brokenly. If I lost him, I didn't know what I'd do. I wanted to flip him over, but I had to fight the instinct. It could make his injury worse.

He groaned and groggily said, "What the *fuck* happened? I saw an angel. Then all of a sudden, I was falling. I think it was for her."

I had no clue what he was talking about. "There's no angel here."

Thorn snickered. "Speak for yourself."

Cutting my eyes at Thorn, I couldn't help but grin. Elliott wasn't necessarily okay, but talking coherently was a good sign.

"Is he all right?" Mindy asked, and I noticed she'd pushed through the group to kneel at his head. Her fore-

The entire group wore similar expressions...except Peter, who shook his head with a scowl.

Wow. He was showing some real fatherly concern.

"I don't know yet." I touched his legs. "El, can you feel my touch?"

"Dude! That tickles." He jerked and winced. "Stop."

A laugh bubbled out of me. "Okay, I knew you were ticklish as a toddler, but I thought you would've grown out of it *some*."

Tyson nodded while pumping a fist. "Heck, yeah. Next all-night marathon, I'm going to use that to my advantage."

"Oh, *hell*, no." Elliott lifted himself off the floor and glared at Tyson. "That's cheating. And only losers cheat. You just don't like that I can beat your ass, but suck it! You're a fucking dragon. You aren't getting any sympathy from me."

Belinda *tsked*. "Language."

Usually, I'd agree, but his choice of words was not my concern right now. "Elliott, stay still. We need to make sure nothing's wrong, or you could hurt yourself worse." One side effect of a brain injury was loss of balance.

"Uh, sorry." He swung his head toward Belinda but stopped short when his gaze settled on Mindy. His body jerked as his mouth dropped. "She's really here."

I was so confused. "What are you talking about?"

"The angel," he said simply, then clamped his hands over his mouth as his cheeks turned red.

"Oh, I think our little human here has a crush on Mindy." Tia chuckled.

"Uh...I mean, she's cute." Elliott glanced at Mindy. "You're cute." He looked away and shrugged, though his face was the same shade as a tomato. He tugged on his borrowed navy shirt, which was two sizes too big on him.

Our options here were limited, and he was stuck wearing dragon-sized clothing.

Tyson hung his head. "Not smooth, and can you move? I'm trapped on these stairs, and I swear, your dad is literally breathing down my neck."

I didn't want Elliott to move more, but when I noticed he wasn't struggling more than usual and had control of his limbs, some of my worry eased.

He's okay, Thorn connected and took my hand, pulling me into the living room beside him.

The comforting buzz of our connection washed away the rest of my concern.

"I'll get him some ice," Mindy said, and she hurried past the stairs to the kitchen.

When she returned, Saphira joined us, and while Elliott iced his face, we hung around the living room and chatted. We'd learned that both couples were close to five hundred years old, which was pushing the older end of a dragon's lifespan. They'd been born in this thunder, had lived here most of their lives, and had all been best friends since birth. They told us about Edna's conversation with the others and how the thunder had unanimously voted to allow our group to stay here.

In return, we answered their questions. What I hadn't expected was the information they provided about Thorn's grandfather.

As Thorn listened, his brows pulled together. Taking after Vlad, he paced in front of the television. His apprehension blanketed me, making my skin crawl. I also had to stand, but I leaned against the wall, knowing he needed to expend his nervous energy.

"You knew my grandfather personally?" Thorn wrung his hands.

"I wouldn't say *personally*." Merlin shook his head and placed an arm around his mate. They were sitting on one end of the long couch. "Back then, we didn't have the..." His face wrinkled.

Mindy chuckled. "Dragonnet."

"Oh," Elliott mumbled next to her, and Mindy focused on him, adjusting the position of the ice on his head.

Biting her thumb, Saphira blinked from her spot on the stairs. She'd missed the debacle, and she'd been side-eyeing them since she'd come down.

"Dude, that's so sad." Tyson snorted and shook his head.

Luckily, Cassidy and Hydra were sitting between him and Elliott, or Elliott probably would've elbowed him in the side.

My gaze landed on Eva and Sol, who were sitting on the footstool in the middle of the room. I couldn't help but notice they were now holding hands. Their relationship had started off with a reaction similar to Mindy's and Elliott's, and I wondered if it was coincidence or if all three of us were destined to be with dragons. But that was impossible.

"Let the lad get the attention the only way he knows how." Tia giggled.

Merlin patted her leg. "Now, honey. Behave."

"Ha. You know better than to waste your breath telling *her* that." Belinda wiggled a finger.

Thorn's anxiety was palpable, and Brenton must have noticed, because he pushed off the wall on the other side of the room where he'd been standing next to Peter, close to the front door, and spoke.

"From what I remember, before the internet, every ten to fifteen years, the king would make rounds to visit the thunders and update them personally." Brenton steepled his fingers. "Each year, the king focused on a different region, and if there was an announcement everyone needed to hear at once, he would have warriors help spread the message worldwide. The more thunders heard the news, the faster it traveled."

Sort of like the rumor mill of the modern world for things people didn't want documented. The more people who knew, the quicker word spread.

Merlin scowled. "The last time we saw your grandfather was near the end of his life. His health was failing, which made him even angrier. The last time he visited our thunder, our leader told us all to stay inside. We'd heard stories of his cruelty and how just looking at him the wrong way could make him strip you of your dragon. When the king came and saw none of us waiting for his arrival, he assumed we were hiding something. He stripped our leader of his dragon, killing him. He was close to four hundred— too old for a human to survive. Then he stripped several more of the oldest members of their dragons. After someone finally confessed to why we hadn't greeted him, he began to calm down, but then he took ten more dragons to be sure."

"Of course he did." Thorn rubbed the back of his neck, where his mark lay, and grimaced. Discomfort and shame coursed through our bond as they always did when anyone talked about his mark and its history. He did everything he could to hide the mark, even from me, and it had taken me seeing the birthmark while we were naked and vulnerable in front of Drake to realize it. Even when we showered together, he kept his front side turned to me.

You are not him, I connected, pushing my love toward him. His father had destroyed the way Thorn saw himself, and though he was getting more comfortable with his magic, the baggage wasn't gone. I had faith it would go—he just needed time to process everything.

I wondered if his grandfather had been mentally ill. "Something must have caused him to become like that."

"Abusing his power did." Belinda frowned and shook her head. "When a person from the royal line is blessed with the magic, it's intended to restore the balance of dragonkind."

That stopped Thorn in his tracks. "What do you mean?"

"You don't know?" Tia tilted her head, examining him.

"Would I be asking if I did?" Thorn countered gruffly. He crossed his arms, which molded his white shirt to his muscular chest more than normal.

My body warmed, and saliva pooled in my mouth while my dragon inched forward. He was so damn sexy, and for a moment, I forgot where we were.

"Thorn Wight," Cassidy scolded. "I taught you better than that."

And that was exactly what I'd needed to get my head on straight. This moment, this conversation, was not the time for me to want to pleasure our bodies. My dragon huffed as she settled back inside me.

"No, I deserved that." Tia crossed her legs, nestling into Merlin. "I did ask a stupid question. I get on to young'uns for doing that, but here I am, doing the same damn thing."

"Hey!" Elliott shook a finger at her. "Language."

An adoring expression crossed Merlin's face as he stared at his mate. "You have a knack for doing the exact thing you scold others for."

"I'm old." She tapped her head. "I can't be held liable for my actions."

"Please." Belinda snickered as she smacked Tia's arm. "Your memory is fit as a fiddle. Don't let her fool you."

I was pretty sure we'd all figured that out. But Thorn needed answers. Since he was no longer pacing, I moved beside him and took his hand. He squeezed my hand tightly.

I cleared my throat, hoping they'd get the message.

Bowing his head slightly, Merlin answered, "It makes sense that you don't know. Most everyone around now is too young to remember the stories from before your grandfather's reign, and he left a mark. Fear has a way of molding the present and concealing the good others did previously."

"You're talking about other royals who had the same gift." Hydra's brows furrowed. "Now that I think about it, I do remember hearing some of the history. The mark is associated with King Arthur."

"King Arthur?" I hadn't heard that name before.

"Arthur was my grandfather's name." Thorn swallowed.

"I've never heard him called that before." Now that I thought about it, that was strange.

Eva inched closer to Sol. "It's like Lord Voldemort from *Harry Potter*. No one wants to say his name."

"Huh. If he's the villain in the movies, it's a good comparison." Sol wrapped an arm around her.

Eva's mouth dropped. "You've never seen the movies?"

Sol scratched his head. "I don't watch much television."

Elliott moaned, and Mindy dropped the ice and gently touched the knot on his forehead. "Are you okay?"

"No!" Elliott shook his head hard, proving he was milking his injury for her attention, and gestured at Sol. "I'm not okay. He doesn't play video games, and he hasn't watched the *Harry Potter* movies? The next thing we'll learn is that he doesn't like *Star Wars*!"

Sol flinched.

"Oh, my God." Elliott turned back to Mindy. "I'm feeling faint again. This can't be real life. The guy my sister likes doesn't know *anything*."

Face scrunching, Mindy blew out a breath. "I don't, either, so maybe you don't want my help after all."

Elliott's eyes bulged out of his head. He whipped around to look at Tyson. "Dude, please, if our bruh-mance is going to survive, tell me you aren't like them. They get a pass, but for you, dude, there's no coming back from that."

Tyson scoffed. "Please. Do I look like some uncultured swine?" Then *he* flinched and glanced at Mindy and Sol. "No offense."

Lifting both hands, Sol tipped his head back. "Offense taken."

"Don't worry." Elliott waved him off. "He'll be fine. But apologize to Mindy."

"Fine. Sorry, Mindy." Tyson placed a hand over his heart. "I didn't intend for my truth bomb to be taken so harshly, but being the bigger person, I'm willing to help you out for my bruh. We can watch *all* the things."

Peter grunted from his place against the wall. "I thought the two of them were bad, and now it's like they're multiplying."

This conversation had been completely derailed. There was only one solution. "Go upstairs, take Peter, and watch *Star Wars*," I ordered. "Educate these underprivileged individuals so they'll be on your level."

Snapping, Elliott pointed at me. "Now you're talking my jam. I get the gist of the story. King Arthur was bad and made people think his power was bad, and Thorn here is going to remind them that it's not the case. Noted and filed." He stood and pulled Mindy to her feet. "And I have my friend Jared's password to his Disney+ account, so *Star Wars* marathon, here we come!"

"He's going to kill you." Eva laughed as she and Sol stood with them.

"Eh, he's human, and we'll probably never see him again," Elliott answered as he grabbed his father's hand and tugged him toward the stairs. "We're going to be dragon shifters soon!"

They continued talking as they clomped up the stairs, and when the door shut, Thorn connected, *Finally. I love our brother and sister, but damn, sometimes, they make things so convoluted. I have a feeling that tomorrow, Elliott will go back to harassing me to change him.*

My stomach cartwheeled. I loved the fact he'd called them *our* siblings. He thought of them like family. *Yes, he will.*

"To be young and falling in love." Tia snorted and laid her head on Merlin's chest.

"You were saying?" Thorn prompted, guiding the conversation back to his grandfather.

"Before King Arthur, two other royals had the same magic. From what I heard as a little boy, they were the ones who saved dragonkind when our numbers were dwindling." Ryu yawned. "But King Arthur destroyed their memories and instilled fear in his people, which is what you have to overcome."

Something swirled inside my mate—warring emotions of hope and dread.

"Listen, I hate to end this chat, but we're up later than normal." Belinda stretched. "I'm about to fall asleep over here."

Brenton grabbed the new couples' luggage, and Cassidy

jumped to her feet. She said, "There's a room upstairs with two queen beds, if that's okay."

"That's more than perfect." Tia stood. "We can do the old sock on the doorknob thing when one of us is busy. I saw that on some show a while back."

Saphira laughed loudly. "Oh, gods. I needed that."

As the others meandered away, Saphira sat next to Hydra. The two of them began talking about Wyvern and things going on back at Hydra and Theron's thunder.

Thorn led me toward our room. When the door shut behind us, he pulled me into his arms, and a mixture of his emotions overwhelmed me. I wasn't sure what to do other than hold him.

An emotion settled over him as if he'd made a decision. He pulled back, and I saw something in his expression that I hadn't expected.

I froze.

CHAPTER TWELVE

THE ENTIRE TIME I'd been with Thorn, a heaviness had shrouded him, even when he was happy. Over the past week, that sensation had lightened, but not by much. I'd come to realize what it was—scars. Scars from his magic, his past, and his family. I was pretty sure that ever since I'd rolled into the picture, I'd made it worse because now he feared losing me. Granted, running off while he'd slept to turn myself over to Drake, thinking it would save our loved ones, hadn't helped.

Now, a look and lightness like hope filled him and stole my breath. His sky blue irises were brighter, the flecks of diamond standing out more, and his face didn't show the lines of worry that were usually there unless we were making love.

My heart expanded. He'd always been gorgeous, but this version of him was transcendent. "What's going on? I've never seen you like this." My smile was reflected in my voice.

"I..." He blew out a breath, grinning. "I understand

what you've been trying to tell me. That this magic isn't a curse. That was only how I'd been taught to feel about it."

"Really?" I arched a brow, my heart fluttering. I didn't care how he'd gotten here, just that he had. I could only hope that his eyes were truly opening to the amazing man he was and was still becoming. "Just *now?*"

He snickered and tucked a piece of hair behind my ear, the sizzle of our connection thrumming between us. He murmured, "I know. I should've believed you, since what you think is most important to me. In fairness, it's the only reason I've come as far as I have." His smile drooped. "But to hear the history that people either didn't bother to tell me or didn't know confirmed what you were saying all along. My magic *is* a gift, and it's about keeping the balance and ensuring our race doesn't die off. Helping to heal injured dragons and create new ones so they don't have to endure what Emily did is also a blessing."

Balance. Sacrifice. Two words that always seemed to circle magic. "Well, the bad always seems to outweigh the good and instill fear."

"It does. It has." He settled his hands on my hips. "And I have a mate standing beside me who never knew about my past, yet she still tried to convince me that my magic could be used for good."

His love poured into the bond, and I felt as if I could combust from happiness. I cupped his cheek and connected, *It's because I know you. Even before we became what we are now, when everything indicated I shouldn't trust you, I knew you weren't bad. You are a pure soul who was misunderstood for far too long, and a fundamental change won't happen overnight. You have to believe that yourself—I can only get you so far. And I'm happy that the conversation tonight changed that for you. You deserve to be happy and not hate your reflection in the mirror or the mark on your back.*

You own me, Everly Woods. His pupils slitted as his dragon peeked through. *You have my heart, my body, my soul, and my trust. I don't know what I did to deserve you, but I won't give you up. No matter what, I need you by my side.*

Warmth flooded me, and my stomach clenched with desire. *You own me, too. No matter what. When things settle, I plan to have Errol sign our marriage certificate so I can take your last name.*

That would make me so happy, he replied and kissed me hungrily.

His tongue swooped into my mouth, and I answered each stroke with my own pent-up desire. I bit his lower lip. Growling, he placed his hands on my ass and lifted me to settle against him. He was already hardening as I wrapped my legs around his waist.

He moved forward, his hands kneading my cheeks, and had me tumbling back onto the bed. My hair fanned out around me as he leaned over and paused.

"So damn beautiful," he murmured, and his lips landed back on mine.

My hands slipped under his shirt, tracing the curves of his hard muscles. His stomach quivered with each brush, showing the power I had over him.

His hands moved under my shirt and slid underneath my bra, caressing my nipples. I moaned, not even trying to hide the effect he had on me. His deep, sexy chuckle had me writhing inside.

Pulling away from my lips, he whispered, "I love how you respond to me."

"I feel the same way." I winked and dropped my hand to his crotch, touching his hard outline.

He growled as he kissed his way down my neck, his teeth scraping the skin where my pulse pounded. My dragon roared inside, thrilled by the attention. I unfastened his jeans, tired of the barrier between him and my hands, as he continued to suck on my neck.

His jeans dropped on the floor, and he shifted his weight as he continued to stroke my breast. With his other hand, he pushed his boxers down, giving me the best view of the entire day. The only way it would be better was if he were shirtless, too.

My hand wrapped around him, and I stroked him. He groaned as he dropped to his side and removed his hand, leaving me bereft. Within seconds, he was removing my jeans and panties. Then he lifted up, pointing to my shirt, and grinned. "That's kind of in the way."

I bit my bottom lip. "Oh, is it?"

"Very much so," he responded as his hand slid between my legs. I sucked in a breath, eager for him to continue. But his hand disappeared.

My eyes popped open, and I glared. *What the hell?*

Shirt and bra off. He narrowed his eyes. *If you want me to continue.*

The spicy scent of arousal swirled between us. I loved it when he got bossy. He was never over the top with me, just the right amount without being disrespectful. *Only if you do the same.* I quirked a brow.

He beamed and quickly removed his shirt, then tossed it to the floor. *Your turn.*

I laughed. His eagerness was so endearing and made me feel desperately wanted. As I rose to remove my shirt and bra, I took in his body. Hard and tanned, it was better than any painting I'd ever seen, which was saying something. Just looking at him had me pulsing with a need that wouldn't be satisfied until he was inside me.

His eyes reflected the same hunger, and the world tilted. From what I'd heard through my school acquaintances, the undying love you felt for someone and the thirsty need for their body faded with time, but so far, that wasn't the case with us. In fact, it was the opposite. Every day, every touch, and every time we had sex had me jonesing for my next hit of Thorn. The thought of having any sort of life that didn't include him next to me was so devastating, I couldn't consider it.

Hand sliding back between my legs, Thorn moved his mouth to my breast. His tongue rolled over my nipple as he teased the spot that already had friction building inside me. My hand circled him again, and I stroked in time with what he was doing to my body.

Pleasure washed over me as we opened our bond to each other. There was no doubt he loved me as much as I did him, but love didn't fully express what we felt for each other. It was otherworldly, something that couldn't be explained...all-encompassing.

As I neared ecstasy, I pulled away.

He reached for me again, frowning. "Uh...where the hell do you think you're going?"

But there was one thing I needed to do before we connected. Something I'd been wanting to do our entire time together. "Turn over."

His irises sparkled as he flopped onto his back, and he held his hands out to his sides, ready to grasp my legs when I straddled him. He grinned wickedly, and I laughed. I couldn't help it. "Now turn around."

Face falling, he tilted his head. "Uh...what?" He glanced at the mattress as if that would explain everything.

"Turn around?" I laughed and swirled my finger.

He mashed his lips together. "I'm down for almost anything you want to try." He moved as if to see if I had something behind my back. "But I'd like to discuss it first, especially if it might involve my exit."

I smacked his leg, chuckling. "I am all about every inch of your body, except that one place. So don't worry. Nothing will get near your butthole unless we discuss it first."

"Just so we're clear." He rolled onto his stomach.

Once he was settled, I crawled up the bed next to him and ran a hand over his back to the bottom edge of his mark. He tensed, sensing where my fingers stilled.

I waited for a second. If he told me to stop, I would, but when he didn't say anything, I traced the outline of the dragon's body, its wings extended. A shiver coursed through him, and his dragon purred as I traced the image from the top of the wing to the dragon's head. I connected, *It's gorgeous. With the level of detail, it's hard to believe it's not a tattoo.*

Believe it or not, it's like I can feel you touching my dragon. I'm exposed to you. It's so intimate. His breath caught, and something shifted between us, drawing us closer.

You don't have to hide from me. I continued to trace it, my dragon inching forward. She was as excited as I was to finally touch his entire body, and more need pooled between my legs. *I would rather die than hurt you.* The truth of my words had the air whooshing out of me. But it was true. Everything inside me lived to keep him safe and happy.

A deep purr escaped my man as well. *I know that, and I can't take it anymore.*

He flipped over, and I almost complained until I saw the expression on his face. His eyes darkened with desire as he grabbed my waist and pulled me onto his lap. He placed a hand on the back of my neck and brought my head down so he could kiss me.

Our mouths melded together, and I shifted my hips while he guided himself inside me. As he filled me, my body rocked ever so slowly against his. The movement was sensual and all-consuming.

I pulled my mouth from his, wanting him deeper so I could ride him. He groaned as his hands cupped my breasts, his fingers caressing my nipples. He rocked underneath me, and our bodies moved in sync.

Pleasure soared through me as we quickened our pace. Our emotions intermingled, both of us feeling the other person completely. As my ecstasy increased, his did in tandem, proving our souls were interconnected.

He thrust underneath me, and I swiveled my hips, sensation taking over my body.

Sitting up, he repositioned me on his lap, grabbing my waist while his mouth covered my breast. As his fingers dug into my skin, I moved faster, both of us desperately racing toward our climax.

I cupped his head, pulling him away from my breast, and kissed him again. I wanted to taste, smell, and feel him. As his tongue swept into my mouth, my orgasm rocked through my body. I responded eagerly to the kiss, and he shuddered through his own climax.

After who-knew-how long, our bodies stilled, both of us completely satiated. I rolled off him and cuddled into his arms.

As my eyes began to close, a knock sounded at our door. Cassidy called out, "They were able to get hold of the woman, and she's going to deliver the message. They're on their way back. I just wanted to let you know all is well so you two can get some sleep. We can talk more in the morning. Good night."

Any remaining tension ebbed from Thorn, and we fell fast asleep in each other's arms.

THE NEXT MORNING, Thorn's weight left the bed, stirring me. I opened my eyes to find him dressing his gorgeous body.

I pouted. *What are you doing? You're taking away my eye candy.*

His brows lifted. *There's still some eye candy left.* He gestured to his face and tilted his head.

Sure. I rolled my eyes, fighting to keep the corners of my mouth from tipping upward. *I'll pretend to agree.*

His mouth dropped open, and he patted his chest. *Are you saying you only find my body attractive?*

Your face isn't bad. The smile broke through. *I mean...it'll do.*

It'll do? He gasped and jumped on the bed, his fingers digging into my sides.

I giggled, jerking away. My sides were the ticklish part of my body. He straddled me, locking me in place.

Tears streamed down my face from my laughter. *Please stop. I can't take much more.*

Just like that, he stilled. "I guess, but just so you know, I won't be putting out for a while. Not until you begin appreciating this face."

"Lies." I squinched my nose. "You can't hold out on me." I lowered my hand and grabbed his crotch, which was already hard from him being on top of me.

"Fine," he scoffed, then kissed me. "But I'll have you know I love every part of you, including your foul breath."

I slapped my hands over my mouth, my face burning. I blew out and sniffed. "*Fine*, I'll go brush my teeth."

"I was just teasing." Chuckling, he pulled my hands away from my face and kissed me again. *I had to get you back somehow.*

Unable to refuse, I kissed him. *And I was teasing, too. Your eyes were the first thing that drew me to you.*

He winked. *I know.*

"Where were you sneaking off to?" I wiggled out from underneath him. Though he was aroused, he had something else on his mind.

"To find Vlad and Errol and learn the details." He stood and helped me out of the bed. "I felt bad not waiting up, but having time with you was more important."

My heart swelled. "Let me go with you." I hurried to my feet, threw on my clothes, and ran my fingers through my hair. "I'm hungry, anyway."

Taking my hand, he led me into the kitchen. The cheery shamrock cabinets greeted me. The kitchen was spotless, but the smell of bacon and eggs lingered, indicating Cassidy had already cooked and cleaned up breakfast. I glanced at the time and noticed it was after ten.

"They're finally awake." Elliott sighed and placed a hand to his forehead. "It's been days."

"Are you having a *Gone with the Wind* moment?" I teased as I opened the refrigerator in search of something for Thorn and me to eat.

"Sis, I didn't fart." Elliott dropped his hand on the wooden table. "I would own it if I did."

Thorn broke into a fit of laughter. *Your brother doesn't know much beyond video games and random gross facts, like peeing on fires.*

Don't remind me. I grabbed some bacon and two cold biscuits.

"She meant the movie, dumbass," Eva deadpanned. "I swear, I love video games as much as you do, but I still know the romance classics."

"Says the person who thought *Super Mario Kart* was the best game ever." Elliott crossed his arms. "So I don't take offense."

"I was *six*." She grabbed a napkin from the middle of the table and tossed it at him. "You thought *Donkey Kong* was an epic game!"

"Fuck, it *is* epic." He lifted a hand. "Two badass gorillas or some stupid cart that slides on bananas. Please, you make me sick."

Where were Sol and Mindy? I needed them to distract Eva and Elliott from their bickering. "Where is everyone?"

"Outside, training with the oldies." Elliott smirked.

"Elliot!" I slammed the door shut and glared. "They are your elders."

"Please. Tia is an instigator, and Belinda pretends to be offended but eggs her on. Let's not even talk about Merlin and Ryu. Those two are worse than me. They took over my gaming system this morning until Vlad and Theron came upstairs and told them they needed to train with the others." Elliott rubbed his hands together. "And calling them oldies riles Tia up, which serves her right for telling Mindy I was staring at her all morning."

Oh, dear goodness. I opened a cabinet and pulled out two plates, which I covered with biscuits and tons of bacon.

"Why aren't you two with them, and where's Peter?" Thorn asked as he placed a hand on my back, our connection buzzing.

"Vlad and Theron made Peter go with them, and El and I stayed behind because we wanted to talk to you." Eva stood, running her hands down her legs. "I've made my decision about becoming a dragon."

My heart hammered. This was it. And I wasn't sure whether I wanted her to say yes or no.

CHAPTER THIRTEEN

THORN BRUSHED his fingers against my back. A *zing* flowed through me, and calm settled into my heart, slowing it to a normal pace. No matter what she decided, I'd respect it as long as she was making the decision for the right reasons.

"Oh, my gosh," Elliot gritted out. "Just come out with it. She wants to change, so, like, let's do this thing." He stood and patted her shoulders while waggling his brows. "Thorn, lay your glowy hands on me. I've been ready for weeks."

"Uh…" Thorn's nose wrinkled. "I don't even know how to respond to that. For one, I'm certain you're trying to make this pervy. And two, I'm not changing you until your sister gives me the final okay, and we'll do it *outside*. I have a feeling that as soon as you feel your dragon, you'll try to shift, and we're not messing up this house."

Leave it to Elliott to speak on Eva's behalf. I rolled my eyes and focused on my sister. Before I could say anything, Elliott started up again. He placed a hand on his heart, and his bottom lip shook way too hard, like he was being overly dramatic. "I must say, I thought Everly and I shared *everything.*"

I groaned, while Thorn's mouth dropped open. I was certain Thorn hadn't thought Elliott would take this further, but my brother loved pushing the envelope.

Wanting to save my mate, I pointed a finger at my brother and popped our biscuits into the microwave. "Sure. I'll share everything with you once I play a round under your profile on the PS."

"You bish." His eyes bulged. "You wouldn't."

"Sharing everything would also include your gamer profile and stats so I can play the higher levels I can't get to on my own." I pressed the buttons on the microwave and hit start, my stomach grumbling for breakfast.

You play dirty, Thorn connected as his humor wafted between us. *I love it. Don't ever change...not even with me.* He walked behind me, wrapped his arms around my waist, and kissed the tender spot on my neck, causing goosebumps to rush over me.

"Fine." Elliott scoffed. "Just take me outside and change me. I was teasing, but Everly ruined *all* my fun."

With Elliott deflated, I'd chat with Eva before he started back up again. One thing about my brother—he rebounded quickly. "Is it true?" Needing to see my sister, I begrudgingly pulled away from Thorn. Every tic, every eye flicker, every...well...everything.

She rubbed her lips and nodded. "Yeah, I've decided to become a dragon. I just wanted to think everything through."

Smart. That was what I'd wanted them to do, but I had to make sure she wanted to change for the right reasons. "May I ask why?"

"It would be easier." She spread out her arms and

gestured around the room. "We can help you fight, and we won't need as much protection."

Those were good reasons but temporary ones. Something must have triggered her to take the plunge. The microwave beeped, and I opened the door and handed Thorn the plate while I grabbed the other biscuit. *I'm going to talk to her alone. I need to make sure Elliott isn't pressuring her into this.* I didn't think my brother would, not on purpose, but his enthusiasm could be overwhelming.

I'll keep him entertained, but you owe me. I'll take payment in sexual favors, he replied and kissed my cheek before speaking out loud. "I don't know, man. I was thinking *Super Mario Kart* is a pretty badass game. You race other people and get a trophy at the end of it."

Elliott's jaw almost hit the table. "Are you *fucking* serious? If you are, there is something fundamentally wrong with you." He proceeded to launch into a dissertation about why my mate was horribly wrong about everything in life, how the games he viewed as badass hindered his ability to think through other things properly and he needed to fix the error of his ways.

I took a bite out of my biscuit, wanting to do something other than laugh and make this situation worse. I glanced at Eva, who rubbed her temples as if Elliott were giving her a headache. When I caught her eye, I nodded toward the door leading out back. She stood and hurried to the door. As we walked outside, I glanced over my shoulder and saw Elliott gesturing everywhere and Thorn's eyes glazing over.

Yeah, I owed him for this, but I had to admit, I was surprised he knew as much as he did about *Super Mario Kart.* There was still so much I didn't know about him, even though I felt like we'd never been apart.

Outside, we could see the group about two hundred

yards away in the open field, training. Eva's eyes darted to Sol immediately. Everyone had paired off, including Vlad with Peter. They were all sparring in human form.

Eva must have felt me watching her because she cleared her throat and put her hands in her jeans pockets. "Is something wrong?"

That was a loaded question. An easier question would be what was right. "I wanted to talk to you where Elliott couldn't answer on your behalf." I took another bite of my biscuit and went to lean against the trunk of a white dogwood tree. "I want to make sure you really do want to change. Once you get a dragon, Thorn might not be able to take it back. He couldn't with me." Which still didn't make sense, since he had no trouble removing a born dragon shifter's magic. Maybe he couldn't remove a dragon he'd created.

"Yeah, I'm sure." She nodded. "This is right for me."

"What made you change your mind?" I wondered if it was because of a certain dragon shifter. If they weren't fated mates, he could stumble upon his and crush Eva. From what Thorn had said, fated mates were rare and something to be treasured, but given the people around us, I was beginning to think they were less rare than anyone thought.

Her cheeks reddened, giving me the answer without her saying anything.

"Look, I get you think Sol is cute, but changing for *him* isn't the answer." My appetite vanished. I didn't want to discourage her, but I had to protect her. "We've all seen how you hold hands, look at each other, and sneak away, and that's all fine. I want to see you smile, but if you take it to the next level, and you two don't work out, I don't want to see you hurt."

"I know." She closed her eyes, then opened them and focused on me. "I get it. That's one reason I didn't say yes right away when I met Sol—I still took time to think about it. Maybe it's not a good reason, but Ev, each day I'm around him, something inside me becomes more desperate for him. Hell, the first time I saw him, his eyes captivated me. It's like he can see right into my soul."

I froze. That was *exactly* how I'd felt when I'd first seen Thorn. "Eva—"

"Let me finish," she said forcibly, then winced. "Please."

That was why we'd come outside—for me to listen. I nodded and forced myself to eat.

She huffed, pushing her long hair over her shoulders. "I get your concern, and I'll be the first to admit that if this were you, I'd be asking the same questions. But I don't want to lie. Yes, a major reason is Sol. He helped me get there. I don't want to have a life he isn't in, but it's more than that. I knew the answer wasn't a flat yes or no even before I met Sol." She wrung her hands as grunts from the group's training sounded in the background. "When Drake took us, I'd never felt so helpless, even more so than when Mom died. Not only could I not save you, but I couldn't even help myself."

She shivered, and though I itched to hug her, I forced myself to remain in place, knowing she needed to get it all out.

"I didn't say yes immediately like Elliott did because that level of change scares me. Will I even recognize myself afterward? That question keeps circling my head, despite everything else screaming I should do it. But as I've watched you become a stronger, more confident version of yourself, and after Sol came into the picture, that question lost its impact. So, am I saying yes today because of Sol? Maybe. But I *swear* I've known for a while that my answer would be yes all along. I needed time to accept it. He just got me there faster."

I exhaled. "Okay. I just need you to understand that even if you change, there's no guarantee the two of you will wind up together." Until she turned into a dragon, we wouldn't know if they were fated mates. I didn't want to make any false promises just because I suspected the answer was yes.

She wrapped her arms around herself. "Is that even close to what it was like between you and Thorn when you were human?"

"Yes." I wouldn't lie to her. I couldn't. That wouldn't be right. "It was like I could sense the type of person he was, even though he'd kidnapped Saphira and me. I wanted to be around him even while fearing him at the same time. I thought I was getting Stockholm syndrome, but it was our souls reaching out to each other. But Eva, that's supposed to be rare, so I don't want to get your hopes up in case—"

"In case it's not." She exhaled and dropped her arms. "I get that, and thank you for not lying. I promise I would've come to this decision regardless. I wouldn't do it just for a man."

I took the last bite of my biscuit and pulled her into a hug. "I believe you." My eyes burned as my vision clouded. I was going to cry if I didn't pull myself together, and that was the last thing I wanted to do. I was happy she'd confided in me, something I didn't think she would've done before Drake took us. "We'd better get in there and save Thorn. He was distracting Elliott so we could talk."

"Oh, yes. That man is a saint." Eva's irises twinkled.

"Just for the record, I'm so glad he's my brother-in-law. He is completely in love with you, and that's why he puts up with Elliott. He deserves a medal."

Laughing hard, I said, "Maybe, but he did call you and Elliott his family earlier, and he meant it. So yeah, he's a keeper."

Before going in, I scanned the group again and grinned when I saw Peter sitting on the ground, refusing to stand and continue to fight. For some reason, our decision not to change him brought me comfort. At least I knew what to expect from him.

The two of us entered the house to find Elliott still talking. Thorn was staring at the table, his empty plate and two steaming cups of coffee in front of him.

My heart fluttered. *Is one of those for me?* I desperately needed a cup.

Yes. Although I'm contemplating drinking it if you don't hurry. He took a sip from his blue mug, leaving the purple one for me. *Your brother has almost put me back to sleep.*

I know one way to distract him—if you're willing to change them while the others are preoccupied. I grabbed my cup.

Let's do it. Thorn nodded. *Honestly, I'll be more comfortable when they're dragons. And they'll need time to acclimate.*

Another good point. They'd need to learn how to fly and get comfortable with their dragons. "Who wants to change into a dragon first?"

Elliott's head snapped up so fast, I wasn't sure how it hadn't fallen off. "Uh...*me.*" He pounded the table. "I said yes the moment it was offered, so you'd better change me before *her.*" He gestured to his sister.

We'd better do this before Peter gets back. If what I'd seen outside was any indication, he'd be plodding in here shortly now that everyone knew Thorn and I were up. I almost asked if Peter was aware of their decision, but I stopped myself. It didn't matter. They were legal adults, and with the danger we were in, it was smart to change them so they could better protect themselves.

Elliott rushed through the kitchen to the front of the house. "Let's go out this way so Dad won't know what's going on. Better to ask for forgiveness than permission."

Unfortunately, that was my answer.

We hurried outside, and Thorn had no problem changing either of my siblings. It was strange because his hands glowed, and the friction still wafted through our bond, but not like before. I sensed he was no longer afraid to use his magic.

"Okay, both of you are done." Thorn dropped his hands from Eva's shoulders.

I wouldn't have known they were changed if he hadn't announced it. But then Elliott clutched his head and groaned, "It's like something's inside me, trying to control me."

"It's your dragon." I remembered how unsettling it had been to feel a new being inside my body, like the dragon and I had two different sets of thoughts. "You can spend time acclimating to it later. We need to see if Mindy and Sol are your fated mates. If they are, they can help you shift more easily."

Thorn ran a hand down his face. "I need to fly, too. My dragon is getting restless, but we'll have to keep a close watch so any nearby warriors don't see us."

The sound of footsteps approached from behind me.

Vlad's group was heading back, likely for lunch, though Thorn and I had just eaten breakfast.

Sol and Mindy glanced our way and stopped in their tracks. Behind me, Elliott and Eva gasped, and hope flared in my chest.

Were both sets of them soulmates?

When they rushed past Thorn and me with a desperate look in their eyes, I knew without question: my siblings had fated mates.

Thorn took my hand and led me to the house. I almost wanted to stay and watch, but I relented. They deserved time alone with each other. Who knew what would happen when we met Uther?

On that note, Thorn and I headed inside to learn what would happen next.

THE NEXT DAY, our group drove four hours south of Nashville, Indiana, to Nashville, Tennessee, where Vlad and Errol had decided to meet Uther. It was a large city and a public place where we could monitor our surroundings and ensure no dragon would be flying overhead, watching us or setting a trap. Once we met Uther, we'd tell him to follow us west to Kingston Springs, Tennessee, where Theron, Sol, Mindy, Hydra, Eva, Elliott, Saphira, Brenton, and Tyson were guarding the backup meeting spot.

I'd thought that Eva and Elliott might argue to stay with me, but they were too excited about flying. Elliott was determined to fly so fast that he could go back in time to harass his past self. They also wanted to stay with their mates, even though neither had completed their bond...yet.

Peter was staying at the house with Tia, Belinda, Merlin, and Ryu. We didn't want him learning who our allies might be and figuring out another way to cause problems, especially since his, my, Eva's, and Elliott's faces were splashed on the news everywhere. The new additions to the group had offered to watch him. Tia liked to remind Peter that both his kids were now dragons. She enjoyed his extreme displeasure.

That left Vlad, Cassidy, Errol, Thorn, and me. We'd split up into the two Suburbans. I'd wanted to be part of the meet and greet, but we couldn't risk someone recognizing me from the news. So Thorn, Cassidy, and I were in a separate Suburban parked beside a Target, where we could watch the whole thing.

Errol and Vlad stood by one of the large red concrete balls outside the store, waiting for Uther. The idea was to get him out of his car, drive by like we were pulling out of the lot, and make sure no one was in his vehicle while he was distracted.

Cassidy was in the driver's seat with Thorn and me in the middle row. Of the three of us, Uther would be least likely to notice her.

I glanced at the time. It was approaching eight o'clock, and the sun was setting. He should be here any second. I fidgeted in my seat, and Thorn placed a hand on my arm.

"Everything will be fine," he assured me.

Vlad had parked their rented white Honda Civic nearby. We'd leased it under another name, so if this was a trap, our Suburbans would be safe. If something went sideways, the plan was simple: we'd meet a few miles south, the two of them would jump into a Suburban, and we'd head out. Cassidy and Vlad would use their fated-mate connection to communicate where to go.

A black four-door sedan pulled into the lot a little too

quickly. My eyes narrowed in on the driver, and my breath caught. It was Uther, and there was a black Tahoe right behind him.

My heart dropped. I'd hoped this wasn't a trap. We needed his help. But the presence of a second vehicle couldn't be a coincidence.

CHAPTER FOURTEEN

A KNOT FORMED in my stomach as my lungs struggled to work. "He's here, but another car is tailing him."

I'd hoped I wasn't wrong about Uther. I'd seen the side of him that didn't like what Drake was doing, but I also understood that people would do anything to protect their own flesh and blood. I would've bet that he would try to warn us. Maybe he had and we'd missed it.

"I'm letting Vlad know." Cassidy hung her head. "I'd wished this would work out, and now we have to get away."

"No." Thorn shook his head. "We keep the plan the same. If they follow us, that'll give us more people to question—as long as more don't follow them. Be on the lookout. I'll call Theron to give them a heads up when we're heading that way."

My belly gurgled uncomfortably. "That's risky." Everyone I loved was part of our group, and some of us, if not all, could get hurt.

Thorn looked at me and chuckled dryly. "The tables have turned."

My brows furrowed. "What?" As far as I knew, we were in the same situation, one we'd attempted to prepare for.

"Normally, it's you trying to convince me to take a risk." He turned back to keep watch over the situation. "That's all."

I crossed my arms, too scared to take my attention away from Uther and the trailing vehicle. I doubted they would take a stand here, but the warriors could have guns. I forced myself to breathe. "Do you care to elaborate?"

"I was just getting ready to." He chuckled again, but the sound was tense. "We have no leads on Drake. No idea what his next move will be. All we have are vague ideas. That's why we risked coming here, and that shouldn't change now. They don't know our numbers, and this is the smallest group they'll send to remain incognito so we don't see the trap coming."

That was a good point, but there could be more vehicles nearby. If Uther left for our secondary location, we'd get a good idea of numbers by following him to see if anyone pulled in behind him. Worst case, we could abort the plan and find an opportunity for Vlad and Errol to get away.

"They could call in where they're heading, or they could have trackers." Cassidy's hand remained on the wheel.

With that many eyes on us, we couldn't risk driving by. Their windows were tinted as well, so it wasn't like we could get an accurate head count. My gaze remained glued on the parking lot entrance, looking for other vehicles that could be holding warriors.

"I know. That's why we have to move fast when we reach the others. Even if we just grab one of them and take off." Thorn tensed. "This isn't ideal, but it's the best chance we have to fight Drake. We won't win unless we get on level footing with him, and even then, it might not work. He has limitless resources and a way to control the message that gets out to the thunders. *All* the power is in his hands, and we need to take some from him or skew it our way."

His words were like a blast of cold water. I'd known we were at a disadvantage, but he'd spelled it out so blatantly that there was no way we were going to win unless we took risks. Worse, if we lost, we'd run out of places to hide. This was potentially our one shot. "He's right." Denying it would be like blow-drying an oil painting—futile and messy.

I could see his smirk out of the corner of my eye. He was eating this up.

Bite me, I connected, pushing my humor and annoyance toward him.

Gladly, but when we get home. I don't mind showing affection in front of Mom, but we have warriors in our midst. Even I have boundaries. He glanced back out the window.

Two could play this game. Though I knew nothing would happen, I couldn't let him say something like that and drop it.

Uther was strolling up to Errol and Vlad, and we were safe—for now—so I leaned over, keeping my gaze on the entrance behind us, and brushed his crotch ever so subtly.

He growled faintly. *Then again, maybe I don't.*

I snickered, surprised I could be somewhat happy in this moment, but I shouldn't have been. Thorn made everything better. I moved my hand, knowing we didn't need more distractions.

You were gloating, so I had to give you hell. Some of the tension uncurled in my stomach. So far, no other suspicious vehicles had entered the lot. That didn't mean we were safe, but at least they hadn't come barreling in, trying to force Errol and Vlad into a car.

The humor between us ebbed as he connected, *Sorry if it came off that way. It just felt nice, needing to convince you of something for a change. I love you even more for being able to admit I was right.*

My heart ached. He'd been dealing with emotions that I'd never fully understand, and he was working through them and seeing things I couldn't. *And I love you for wanting to protect us and your people.*

It just took me time to come around and understand you were right. Thorn leaned forward, toward the passenger front seat. *With Drake in charge, we'll never be safe.* Unease filtered through the bond, and I turned forward to see that Uther had his arms crossed and was frowning.

"What's going on?" Thorn asked.

Cassidy glanced over her shoulder. "Uther isn't thrilled about following us to another location. Apparently, he had a plan of his own, but he conceded."

I grimaced. "Did he say anything about the other vehicle?"

"No." Cassidy tapped her fingers on the steering wheel. "We're all hiding stuff."

Neither side trusted the other. I understood that Uther might feel conflicted about meeting with us, but hell, he was the one who'd contacted us.

Errol and Vlad headed to the new rental car, while Uther went back to his sedan. Vlad pulled out of the spot and headed toward the exit.

We had to be on alert to ensure no one else was following us. My gut churned. What if I didn't pick up on someone following us and we got hurt?

What's wrong? Thorn connected, his gorgeous eyes

scanning me, and my heart skipped a beat. *Do you see something?* His concern added to mine, and my chest constricted.

I had to get a hold of myself, or I'd have a panic attack. The last time I was close to feeling like this was when I'd been struggling with Mom's death. Knowing that if this meeting went wrong, everyone I loved would be at risk had the helpless feeling swirling inside me all over again. *Just worried I might miss something.*

This is a group effort, he replied, taking my hand in his. *If something goes wrong, it's all our fault, not just yours.*

That didn't make me feel better, but if I didn't get control of my emotions, I would miss things because they were ruling me and not my logic. I forced the agonizing sensation away. *You're right.*

Vlad, Errol, and Uther drove past us in their respective cars with our group leading the way. Neither Vlad nor Errol glanced at us, and Uther was too focused on staring in his rearview to notice us.

That was good.

A minute later, the Tahoe pulled out of its spot and trailed behind them, keeping fifty yards between themselves and Uther.

Cassidy followed the same protocol and stayed back the same distance, and I could only pray the Tahoe didn't notice us. We didn't have to keep up with them to learn where we were going, but we had to stay kind of close to see if anyone was also following them.

I gripped Thorn's hand more tightly, realizing this was harder for me than anything else before. I felt helpless sitting in the back seat of a vehicle, waiting and watching. In every other tense situation, we'd been moving or fighting. I'd had the illusion of control, or at least my mind had been preoccupied.

Pressing buttons on the dashboard, Cassidy called Theron on the Suburban's Bluetooth. It rang once before Theron answered. She filled him in as Thorn and I watched the cars between us and the Tahoe. If more people joined them, they wouldn't expect us to be behind them, so they would fill in between Uther's vehicle and ours, likely behind the Tahoe.

The two of them hung up with a plan. Hydra would stay near the vehicles with Theron's phone in case someone saw anything or we needed to call with an update while the rest of them shifted and scouted out the area. Either way, Hydra could use her fated-mate connection with Theron to get the messages across.

Twilight was upon us, which meant humans would have a harder time making out the dragons and hopefully think they were a flock of birds.

A maroon Ford Explorer pulled into the lane beside us and slowed, merging as we got onto the interstate heading west. The woman in the vehicle was taller than average and had long, silky blonde hair. Could she be a warrior? Judging by how quickly she'd rushed up, I had to at least consider it.

We turned onto the interstate, and Cassidy sped up. Breaking my gaze from the Explorer, I noted that we'd fallen behind and she was trying to catch up.

The woman beside us did the same and glanced at me. I jerked my head down, trying to hide—not that it would do any good. The windows were tinted. It wasn't like she could make me out, even with dragon eyesight.

What's wrong? Thorn connected. *Do you see something?*

I don't know yet. There's a woman in the car next to us,

but I'm not sure if she's following them. I bit my bottom lip, trying to calm my raging nerves. *Do you?*

He shook his head. *Not yet.*

At least that was something.

The Explorer dropped behind us, the woman focusing forward, and we barreled toward a split in the highway.

Which vehicle is it? Thorn leaned over the space between our two captain's chairs to look out my window.

Just as he did, the interstate split, and the woman turned east, opposite where we were headed.

My body sagged as anxiety melted away. Although we weren't out of danger, I was relieved that another warrior wasn't following us. *She went east instead of west. It was a false alarm.*

More restlessness swirled through our connection.

Do you see something? I asked, anxiety clawing in my chest again. Wow, that peace had been short-lived. Thorn didn't freak out unless he thought we were under direct threat.

No, he answered as he released my hand and rubbed his legs. *That's the problem. I'd expected us to spot at least one more car by now.*

I scanned the interstate again. A white truck and a blue SUV caught my attention. They'd been near us for a while and had split west with us, but nothing seemed suspicious about the vehicles.

He clucked his tongue. *Maybe we're being followed, but they have a tracker on Uther's vehicle so they're staying far behind. They might suspect we have our own backup.*

That was something I hadn't considered, and the strategy had *Drake* written all over it. Luckily, we were leading them into a public section of woods. *We need to call Hydra so she knows what we're up against.*

Thorn nodded and filled in Cassidy. Once again, she called Hydra, and Thorn voiced his concerns. When the call ended, we settled into silence.

ALL TOO SOON, we neared the parking lot in the woods where we'd planned to meet. If dragons came, we'd have the forest to cover us since there was no overnight camping in the area.

Hydra had called ten minutes ago to confirm the parking lot was empty, now that darkness was thick around us. Theron and Brenton had taken the Suburban and Mindy's car to a nearby parking area hidden by the numerous red maples and cypress trees that were lush and green in the late spring.

Each moment we'd gotten closer, Thorn had grown twitchier, putting me on edge from our shared bond. I tried to practice my yoga breathing, but it was futile. I was too focused on watching every damn car that passed us. Yoga wasn't just a physical technique. Emotional health was equally important, and I couldn't find my center.

We turned down a road and switched off our headlights as Vlad and Errol's car disappeared into the parking lot with Uther on their tail. The Tahoe slowed to a stop twenty feet away from the turn, allowing the trees to hide us, and turned off its engine, likely so that Vlad and Errol wouldn't hear or see the vehicle.

My stomach bunched until I swore a tourniquet had been tied around it, cutting off the blood flow. They were trying to hide their presence, and what terrified me was that it might have worked if we hadn't followed them.

"Let's sneak up on them." Cassidy turned off our vehicle. "Stay in the woods and hurry. We need to get there before they get out, or they could hear us." She opened the glove box. We'd stashed three guns inside. She pulled out two and passed them back to us.

Hands shaking, I took the weapon. I didn't know how to shoot a gun, but I could point and pull the trigger. I knew that much. When we got home, I'd need Thorn or Vlad to teach me how to shoot for real.

Cassidy and I climbed out, with Thorn following me. He murmured, "Don't shut the door in case they opened theirs at the same time. They can't see the open-door light, but they could hear the door shut."

Good idea. And if we needed to rush back to the Suburban, we could jump right in without pause.

We hit the woods to the left of the Tahoe, stepping in deeply enough that the lush branches would hide us for as long as the occupants stayed in human form.

With each step I took, my heart pounded louder in my ears, and the cold metal of the gun had my skin crawling. I kept expecting them to open their doors and try to sneak behind Errol and Vlad, but no one had made a move...yet.

A few owls hooted in the distance, and a flying squirrel jumped from branch to branch right above us. When we reached the side of the Tahoe, we all took a tentative step forward, but we couldn't make out anything through the tinted windows.

There was no telling how many warriors were in the car.

Thorn's jaw twitched, and his anxiety peaked. My blood whooshed through me.

The driver's door opened.

Thorn whispered so low I almost didn't hear him, "Surprising them is our best option. On the count of three, we run and surround them."

Another door opened, and Thorn lifted a hand, raising one finger...then two...and three.

I took off, my lungs seizing, desperate to get there before I froze.

HAND SHAKING, I kept the gun at my side. Holding it felt so unnatural that lifting it before I had to could be disastrous.

Out of the corner of my eye, I noticed Cassidy run around the back of the Tahoe to the other side. I remained focused on the side closest to me.

Thorn stayed beside me, and I knew why. He could feel my emotions. He knew I didn't feel comfortable doing this...at all.

Wings flapped overhead, and I could make out two distinct sets. I didn't risk looking up to see who the dragons were, but they were currently my favorite people.

When the driver stepped out of the vehicle, Thorn pointed his gun at him.

"Drop your weapons. Now," Thorn growled. "How many of you are there?"

"Shit," the driver rasped. "This isn't how it's supposed to go down."

"Yeah, we know. You wanted to get the jump on us instead." Thorn's jaw clenched, and his eyes flicked to the woman in the front passenger seat. "Answer me. How many people are in this vehicle?"

Saphira's butterscotch dragon landed in front of the Tahoe, and Tyson's maroon dragon landed behind Thorn and me. With the vehicle too close to the trees, there was no room to land on the other side next to Cassidy.

Footsteps from the parking lot ran toward us, and I heard Uther yell, "Wait! Don't hurt them."

He might as well not have said anything. Thorn, Cassidy, Saphira, Tyson, and I were on high alert. If the warriors had been hoping to surprise us, their attempt had been futile, and this was what they'd say.

"How many?" Thorn asked again. "This is the last time I'll ask you."

The back passenger door in front of me swung open, and the driver growled, "Chandra, close the door *now*."

I grabbed the edge of the door, yanked it all the way open, and lifted my gun. My hands shook so hard, I was surprised I didn't drop it.

The woman froze. Her cognac-brown eyes widened.

"Hands up," I said, barely above a whisper. The words rubbed my throat raw. This felt *wrong*.

She immediately lifted her hands. A strand of her auburn hair fell out of her ponytail and into her face, and her bottom lip quivered.

This woman didn't look like a warrior. She was tall, which was the dragon norm, but her face held a softness that most warriors lacked, like she was still innocent. Hell, even my face didn't have that innocence anymore, and I'd been fighting for a month, if that.

"Listen. This is one big misunderstanding," Chandra said.

Then the driver cut in, "We're here because we need your help."

There was no doubt that the driver and front passenger were warriors. The guy had a square-cut jaw and muscular arms, and the way his charcoal eyes scanned the area for more of us screamed experience. His confident stance, despite having a gun pointed at him, sealed the deal.

The female warrior had the same sort of composure. Her long, straight, dark brown hair was pulled into a low ponytail, and her dark chocolate eyes looked flat and emotionless, like she was assessing every possible scenario.

Behind me, Tyson snarled, but I wasn't sure if it was from curiosity or a threat.

Uther rounded the edge of the woods on the road that led into the parking lot. Vlad and Errol were on his tail as they reached us.

Smoke trickling from her nostrils, Saphira prepared for a fight.

"Oh, gods," Chandra groaned, pulling my attention back to her. I caught a flash of long golden hair in the back seat of the car. A child called out, "Are they going to hurt us?"

A lump formed in my throat, and suddenly, I was looking into cobalt irises surrounded by thick black eyelashes. A girl no older than six stared right back at me from behind Chandra. I lowered my weapon. I couldn't put a child through this.

Cassidy gasped. "Why do you have a little girl back there?" She swung her gun toward the warrior woman sitting in the front passenger seat.

"Wait. *Please.*" Uther's face twisted in agony. Errol and Vlad now had his arms restrained.

The little girl's eyes stayed locked on me. She scooted

forward as a middle-aged woman in the middle row on the passenger side grabbed her hand. This woman also had long, straight, dark brown hair and dark brown eyes. She was almost an exact replica of the woman in the front passenger seat, like they were twins, but her features weren't as harsh as those of her clone.

"Are you Everly?" the child asked, and tried to wiggle out of the middle-aged woman's arms to reach me. "You have to help my daddy. Listen to him, *please.*"

I forgot how to breathe. "Are you Uther's daughter?"

She nodded, and when I glanced at Uther, a tear trickled down her face. "Yes, I'm Reece. He said we needed to come here and meet you. That you reminded him of my momma and that you would protect me."

My heart broke, and Thorn's tumult of emotions swirled between us.

"What is she talking about?" Thorn asked while he kept his gun trained on the driver.

Uther dropped to his knees. "We aren't here to attack you. I should have known you guys would be wary, but I wanted to make sure you were willing to listen to me before I brought up the others."

Thorn lowered his gun a few inches but not enough that if they made a move, he couldn't still shoot. "Yeah, you should've. This could be a trap."

"It's not." Uther hung his head. "I wouldn't risk my daughter's life like that."

Saphira turned and hissed in Uther's face.

She didn't trust him, that much was clear. Even Thorn's distrust floated into me, but Uther's words tugged at me, making me hesitate.

I'd heard how much he loved his kid. "You might not

have a choice. This might be the only way you can save her —by turning us in."

"Uther isn't the only one Drake has leverage over. He's threatening all of us with people we love," the woman in the front seat said as she lifted her hands, too.

They were making sure we knew they weren't armed... that they weren't a threat. Something inside me already trusted them, but the others weren't convinced yet.

I took a step toward the vehicle, and Tyson edged a wing in front of me.

"I handled this poorly. I see that now." Uther's remorse sounded sincere. "I should've been forthright when we got to Target, but I didn't see you, Everly. You're the only one I know I can trust, and I didn't want to risk Reece. So...I asked where you were, and when Vlad and Errol insisted I come here, I assumed it was because you and Thorn were waiting to talk with me. I...I knew you would have people watching us, but I thought you'd be part of the party we were meeting with here. Now we look like we can't be trusted, but I did this because our time here is very limited. Our vehicles are being tracked."

I clenched my teeth so hard, my jaw ached. His story made sense, and it wasn't like he could've told me this over the phone since we'd used Errol's contact to send him the location.

"Why should we believe a word you say?" Thorn growled. "Talk to me, not my mate. You're pulling on her heartstrings, and it doesn't take more than a minute in her presence to realize what a kind, sympathetic woman she is."

"Fine." Uther straightened his shoulders as if he weren't being gripped on both sides. "I protected your mate more than you realize when she was captured. Drake put the fear of the gods into us, saying that if we treated Everly with too much kindness—or even *looked* at her kindly—and if any of us showed her any warmth, there would be hell to pay. But even with those threats, I protected her the best I could by deflecting Falkor and Ladon when they wanted to harass her through Eva or enter the room while they were sleeping. I did all I could while keeping my daughter safe, but I want to do more. That's why Jerry, Gemma, and I brought our family here. Drake is trying to use them against us."

Vlad tilted his head. "You want to leave them with us." He wasn't asking a question but stating a fact.

"Yes." Uther nodded toward the Tahoe, and his gaze met Thorn's before he continued, "Jerry and Gemma"—he pointed at the man and woman in the front seats—"brought them here so they can stay with you. We're asking you to protect them and hide them with you. They can't protect themselves—that's why Drake's leverage is so effective."

Saphira shook her head and huffed.

Cassidy crossed her arms. "You can teach them to fight. You don't need us for that. For gods' sake, you three are warriors."

"Training won't help." Gemma closed her eyes. "If Kari could handle it, I would've trained her alongside me."

Then it clicked. "They're injured." My gaze swooped to the back seat, looking for signs. Narrowing my eyes, I saw how Reece had gotten out of Kari's grasp—Kari had a deformed hand. I didn't see anything different about Reece or Chandra, though.

"In the womb, you took most of the nutrients, and that's why Kari has that injury." All my premed classes were churning in my mind, highlighting info about twin pregnancies.

Gemma frowned. "Yes." Then she opened the car door and stood.

"That's not surprising, especially since it's hard for dragons to get pregnant. We definitely aren't built to carry twins." Cassidy lowered her gun. "In fact, I've never heard of twins before."

Neither had I, but that wasn't saying much.

"Chandra—my mate—her tail was injured when she first shifted by one of her thunder members. It was an accident." Jerry glanced over his shoulder adoringly. "She's fine unless she needs to move quickly."

This was heartbreaking. Just because these people were a little different, Drake considered them to be disposable and insignificant.

My attention kept slipping back to the little girl with the kind eyes and gorgeous blond hair that made her irises brighter. "What about Reece?"

Uther sighed. "She has a limp."

She was so young. Now my brain flicked through medical reasons for an uneven gait. Unless someone had done something to hurt her. My blood heated at the thought.

Uther bit his bottom lip. "Her mother, my *wife*, was human. Tashya struggled throughout the pregnancy and died giving birth. We had to cut Reece from her womb."

My mind flashed to Emily and baby Thorn. If my mate hadn't changed Emily and the baby had survived, he might have been in a similar state. "I'm so sorry." Reece had been so right when she'd said that her mom had protected her. Her mom had given up her life for Reece.

"But you aren't from the kingdom's lands." Errol released his hands and paced a few feet away. "How did you get involved with Drake?"

"It happened when he turned eighteen and started visiting the thunders." Uther rolled his shoulders, his attention flicking to his daughter, whom he could see through the front windshield. "He had an ulterior motive —he was trying to get an idea of the region-wide average age of our population to see if there were other weak dragons like"—he lifted his hands to do air quotes—"a 'useless' dragon who lived near the château. Unfortunately, we didn't know that, so when Reece ran out with her limp, we thought nothing of it. But he took notice immediately. When he told a warrior to grab her for questioning, I interceded and took the guard down. That was when he made the deal with me: come work for him, and Reece would be safe."

Tyson snarled, fire trickling from his mouth.

What Uther had said was horrible on so many levels. The "useless" dragon Drake had referred to must have been Tyson. And to consider killing a child? That was even more unforgivable. I hadn't thought I could think worse of Drake, but I'd been proven wrong...again.

"Similar story happened to us." Gemma leaned against the hood of the Tahoe. "Drake zeroed in on Kari's hand like it was a beacon."

That wasn't abnormal. People tended to focus on things that were different.

I believe them, I connected. I needed to know where Thorn was with this decision. His emotions were all over the place. He wasn't as angry anymore, but he hadn't put away his gun, either.

Me, too. Finally, he lowered his arms and scanned the group.

Tyson and Saphira both seemed more relaxed, but they weren't budging, and I was thankful to have them here in dragon form. If something happened, they'd be extremely helpful.

Now we needed to see if Uther would deliver on his promise. "You said you had information for us?" I pressed.

Even though Vlad had let Uther go, he hadn't moved away, and his gaze kept flicking around the group, searching for any signs of dishonesty or threat. I'd learned that about Vlad—he was always on guard. I suspected Cassidy getting kidnapped had stripped him of any sense of comfort he developed over the years.

"I do...*we* do." Uther gestured at himself and the others. "But we need you to promise you'll protect our loved ones first. That they can go with you."

Our group glanced at one another. This was less than ideal, seeing as we couldn't talk about it before committing. This was a big ask. We'd be taking in three more people, and we were already struggling to stay hidden.

Vlad cleared his throat. "Isn't Drake watching your loved ones? He'll notice they're missing."

"If we work together, he won't know they're gone before we execute our plan." Uther's neck corded. "Reece lives at our old thunder home, and everyone wants her safe. These two live on the château grounds, but they're reclusive and stay in their house because Drake has made it clear he doesn't want them near him. As long as we don't give him a reason to suspect us, he shouldn't find out. But if he does... well, that's why we need them to stay with you—for protection."

What do you think? I needed to hear Thorn's thoughts before I shared mine.

We have no choice, Thorn answered and turned his head toward me. His irises lightened with all his emotions. *We have to take them in. We need Uther's help, and these three deserve a safe home where they'll be welcome.*

Vision blurring, I nodded. *I agree. They wouldn't hand*

them over willingly if Drake was involved. If Drake attacked, they'd be stuck in the crosshairs.

Thorn glanced at his mom, who nodded and turned to Errol and Vlad. When they didn't counter, Thorn straightened his shoulders. "Fine. We'll keep them with us as long as we can check them and anything they brought for trackers."

Jerry exhaled, the lines on his face smoothing out. "Thank gods. I can't keep living with the worry that today will be the day when Drake snaps and kills her."

That was what I needed to hear. The genuine relief was justified and not something Drake would have wanted them to say. He didn't like people speaking ill of him.

"Let them out. Errol, Cassidy, and I will check them and their bags before taking them to our vehicle." Vlad marched to the back door of the Tahoe.

That meant Thorn and I would be staying behind to chat with the warriors. Gemma, Jerry, Uther, Thorn, and I moved to the front of the Tahoe so we wouldn't be in the way.

Uther removed a cell phone from his back pocket and handed it to Thorn. "I was told to give this to you. It's a burner phone that can't be traced. The numbers you need are already programmed into it. And Drake's coronation is in two weeks. If it happens, he'll have all the power he wants. For now, he has to work through red tape to get thunders to support his claim to the throne. Two weeks is all we have to make a plan and execute it. We don't have time for mistakes."

Two weeks.

That wasn't enough time.

"We've already stayed in this location too long." Jerry

fidgeted. "If someone is watching us, they'll have questions. We need to go."

"Let's say a quick goodbye first," Uther replied and locked eyes with me. "Please make sure Reece is all right."

I placed my hand over my heart. "I promise."

"Okay, your first message is already on the phone. Now I'm going to say goodbye to my daughter."

Chandra, Kari, and Reece hurried toward the Suburban while Thorn swiped the phone.

My breath caught when I saw the name of the person who'd messaged. Maybe this was a trap after all.

CHAPTER SIXTEEN

I LOOKED AT THORN, feeling every ounce of his disbelief, anger, and longing. His face was twisted in the most heartbreaking combination of those three emotions, his eyes wide and his jaw clenched. He brushed a finger along the message like it was a life force.

The message was simple.

A Devastated Mother: I'm sorry for everything. Words can't express the depth of my regret and the love I've always had for you, but we don't have time for that. I'd rather say it in person, but what I have to say is that your father and I were so wrong about you. I know Drake killed Arman, and it's time for us to work together to ensure he doesn't lead our people. That right belongs to you. Let me know when you get this.

He must have longed for a message like this as a boy, and it was almost a slap in the face for him to receive it now.

I placed one hand on his arm, wanting him to know I

was here for him in all ways...the ways that mattered. "Babe, we've got to move. If someone has pinged the spot, there's no telling where the warriors are. Some could be close. We can't risk staying any longer."

My heart squeezed uncomfortably. But I'd felt worse, and so had Thorn, and unfortunately, that had been because of *my* bad decision. The one where I'd sneaked away from him after completing our fated-mate bond to turn myself over to his brother.

That thought crushed my heart further. If not for the sound of my heartbeat, I'd have believed it had stopped.

Every bad thing that had happened since Thorn's parents abandoned him was because of Drake. Their parents had been content to let Thorn live in hiding, despite knowing where he was...until Drake had learned about him.

He sighed and put the phone in his back jeans pocket. "You're right. Let's move. We can figure out what to do about her."

My heart filled again. We were truly one, and we both knew it.

Hand in hand, we rushed toward the Suburban. Halfway to the vehicle, Uther, Jerry, and Gemma stepped into view, heading back to their own vehicles. Uther's eyes were glassy with unshed tears, and that vise tightened once more.

Uther stopped in front of me. He stared into my eyes as a tear trickled down his cheek. "Everly, please take good care of her. She's going to cling to you."

He didn't have to explain; his daughter already had. "I will. I promise." Not only would I protect her but every person Drake threatened.

"And that's the only reason I can walk away from her again." He wiped the tear as Jerry and Gemma continued to their Tahoe. "This has to end. I need to be with my daughter...to watch her grow up without worrying *he* might kill her. I need to be her father. She's already lost too much."

Thorn placed a hand on Uther's shoulder. "Everly and I will ensure she's always watched over. You have my word. You protected my mate, and I'll protect your daughter."

Taking a shaky breath, Uther turned to Thorn. He squinted as if Thorn were a puzzle, but then he nodded. "Tashya made me a better man, despite her not being a dragon. The two of us revolved around each other as if we *were* fated to be one. If she could do that to me, I can only imagine how a fated mate could influence someone else. I know the emotions and feelings are supposed to be stronger, though I don't know how that could be possible. But it has to be because the man standing before me isn't the same one who saved Everly from the château. It's a man I wouldn't mind following after all."

"That's the thing, though—I don't want to be *followed*. I just don't want Drake to destroy our kind...like my grandfather did." Thorn dropped his hand and scowled.

"Fair enough." Uther huffed and glanced back at the Suburban hidden by some trees. "Sometimes, it's the one who doesn't want to lead who makes the best leader. I'll call you later after we visit a thunder near here to see if they know anything about you. At least with the location you chose, there's one close enough to justify an excursion out here."

"Be safe." I'd always been fond of him, but now he was truly putting his neck on the line. I wasn't foolish to think it was for me; it was for his daughter and the future he wanted her to have, but he was still risking everything to better the lives of all the shifters. "If something goes sideways, let us know. We'll try to help you."

"I'm assuming the queen gave you the phone." Thorn's hope and trepidation swirled through our connection. "Do you believe we can trust her? Or is Drake putting her up to this? From the Dragonnet, it seems she's backing him."

"That's something you'll have to ask her." Uther lifted his hands. "Drake hasn't been hiding his nastiness since King Arman died, and everyone is at his mercy, trying to survive."

That made the situation worse. I didn't know why, but I'd foolishly hoped that wasn't the case. I'd hoped he would be kinder to those in his employ, given they were potentially loyal to him, but maybe his meanness was just the way he was. He felt entitled to everyone's loyalty, regardless of how he treated them, and he took what he wanted by force—boy, had I learned that the hard way.

"Be safe, Uther. And feel free to call us on a burner phone to check in with Reece. I'm sure she would love to talk to you," I said as I tugged Thorn toward the Suburban.

"You be careful, too, and I do have a burner phone. I saved the number on yours," Uther replied as Jerry and Gemma climbed into the Tahoe and shut their doors. The engine started.

That was good to know. We wouldn't be answering any calls we couldn't identify, and maybe not even all of those. We had to be careful about who we trusted. Even taking this burner phone was a huge risk, but if Uther, Jerry, and Gemma trusted the queen enough to bring it here and hand over their loved ones, that was enough for me.

Saphira and Tyson stood near the Suburban. Their bodies weren't as tense, but they were still being watchful.

My human ears picked up a few faint wing flaps, which meant dragons were flying overhead. I looked up and made out their forms high in the sky. If I'd been only human, I wouldn't have heard or seen them.

Cassidy was back behind the wheel with the engine running. Kari, Reece, and Chandra sat in the back row, the little girl sitting in the middle with Chandra on the passenger side and Kari on the driver's side. The trunk was open while Vlad and Errol searched their bags for trackers or whatever else could be used for locating our home base.

Thorn and I strolled to the back, and I said, "I'm assuming the three of them are clear."

"We checked them first." Vlad zipped up the bag and tossed it in the corner. "And the two bags I checked don't have anything they can use to track us."

"This one doesn't, either." Errol closed the dark purple bag and placed it on the other side. "As long as we can trust that they won't track the phone they just gave us, we're good to go."

It all came back to trusting the three warriors. Every time, I came to the same conclusion—we could—but a little fear still sat hard on my stomach, mainly because the queen was involved. But I'd seen how she'd reacted when she'd learned Thorn was alive. She'd been happy, so that was the only reason I was willing to continue with the plan.

Thorn placed an arm around my waist, anchoring me to him, and connected, *If you want us to change our minds about trusting them, we can.*

He was having similar thoughts. *I think they're all being honest...even the queen. I just worry about her loyalties remaining steady if she realizes Uther wants to kill Drake.* I hadn't put that piece together until he'd forced me to discuss it.

I agree, but I believe she doesn't want him as king. I remember the love she and King Arman had for each other.

They were fated, one of the last few pairs to find each other back then...so I believe she's upset with him. Something like hope spread from my mate. *I think we do trust them, but we don't let our guard down completely. We schedule watches among the thunders so that if warriors come at us, we'll have a warning.*

You're right. This is our best chance, but that doesn't mean we can't take precautions. A plan like that did make me feel better.

"We continue on as planned," Thorn instructed. "But we'll make sure that two of us are always on watch, and we'll rotate the schedule."

"Good." Vlad shut the trunk. "I agree, but caution saves lives. Worst case, it gives us time to work on our observation skills, which we'll need when we attack the coronation."

A humorless laugh bubbled out of me unexpectedly. "First a wedding and now a coronation. He'll be more prepared this time around."

"Yes, he'll be paranoid." Errol nodded. "We can strategize back at the house."

House. Not *home.* The word choice didn't go unnoticed, but in fairness, the place didn't feel like home, either, other than when I was in Thorn's arms, especially with Peter always hovering nearby with a scowl on his face like he was trying to overhear everything.

Turning me toward the back door, Thorn said, "Saphira and Tyson, tell the others it's time to leave."

The two dragons nodded and took off just as the Tahoe turned onto the road, passing us. Uther's black sedan was right behind them.

I glanced skyward in time to see the hint of Elliott's hunter green dragon and Eva's olive green dragon high in the sky.

Just like before, Thorn and I sat in the middle row, where we couldn't be easily identified if a dragon happened to look through the windshield.

"Thank goodness we planned on keeping the car overnight." Cassidy glanced into the rearview mirror. "Otherwise, we wouldn't have had room for everyone."

We'd been torn initially, thinking we should drop the rental car off after the meeting so we wouldn't have to pay for another full day, but we'd realized that we wouldn't be able to get it back before the rental office closed. That was a blessing now.

I didn't want to say it was good luck in case jinxing was an actual thing. I hadn't believed in superstitions growing up—I was all about science and logic—but after learning about an entire supernatural world, I now questioned everything.

Cassidy put the car into drive and slowly turned around, heading back toward the interstate.

"Shouldn't we wait on the others?" I rubbed my hands on my shorts, trying to work out my jitters.

Shaking her head, Cassidy kept her focus on the road. "Vlad said to go on so we can get our new charges settled. We'll be rolling in around two in the morning."

We needed to get these women to their temporary home.

I looked into the back seat, and my lungs froze.

Chandra had her arms wrapped around herself with her legs folded up on the seat against her chest. She was staring at the holes in her jeans like she was in another world.

Beside Reece, Kari stared out the window. Her shoulders were hunched as if the weight of the world were pressing down on her, which it probably was. Every single person in our group had a target on their back, and the same man was hunting us all.

Then there was Reece. Her demeanor was slightly different. Instead of retreating into herself, she was staring right at me. Her eyes glistened, making her irises appear more navy, but there was something mixed in with the sadness...something like hope.

I tried to swallow unsuccessfully.

Thorn's forehead creased with concern, and he followed my gaze. "Are you okay?" A soft warmness swirled through our bond as he examined the girl.

"I am now." Reece nodded eagerly. "I mean, I miss Daddy. Every time I see him, we aren't together long, but I know Everly will fix it so we don't have to be apart anymore."

My head tilted back, and my breathing quickened. "I'll try my best. And one of the best ways to protect you and your daddy is to keep his identity a secret. We need to say we found you and that you needed help. If people recognize you and know who you're related to, it could put us all at risk." I wouldn't promise something I couldn't deliver. I'd never been a fan of lying and did it only when I felt the truth would hurt someone over something pointless, or by omitting something when I thought it would save the lives of people I loved.

"Okay, I trust you." The little girl nodded so confidently that her blonde hair bobbed around her. "Because if you remind my daddy of Momma, that means you're a good person, and you'll protect me just like she did."

A sob swelled in my chest, and holding it back was damn near impossible, but I managed. I wanted Drake gone more desperately than before, and it had everything to do with this little girl. I didn't want to disappoint her. Our plan had to succeed, not only for her but for everyone I loved.

I promise we'll figure this out, Thorn connected and took my hand. *We will all be able to live without fear, and you won't disappoint this little girl. Together, we can take on the world.*

As usual, he'd said what I needed to hear, and his emotions backed up the words. He wasn't saying them just to appease me. I squeezed his hand back and turned toward the window, ready to keep an eye on the vehicles around us. As we'd said, we needed to be cautious.

***

THE NEXT MORNING, I woke up late. Tia and Ryu had taken the night watch in their dragon form. They'd stayed far enough away that if they sensed a dragon, they would have time to warn us, but were close enough that someone would have to be looking for us to be there. I'd learned that thunders tended to stay away from other thunders, so the likelihood of a random dragon flying by was low.

The three new additions had claimed the couch as their bed. Unfortunately, all the other rooms were taken, but the couch was comfortable and large enough to fit all three of them.

A strong arm circled my waist and pulled me against a thick, strong chest. Thorn's breath hit my ear, and my body warmed. We hadn't had sex last night, and I was more than eager to make up for lost time.

I turned to him and smiled as I took in his soft expression. His love and arousal swirled between us.

Then there was a loud knock on the door, and Theron called out, "You two need to come out here and see this."

The urgency had us jumping from the bed and rushing to the door.

That was when I heard the queen's voice. I paused and turned around the bedroom, seeking the source. The burner phone lay on the end table next to Thorn's side of the bed. Her voice wasn't coming from there. So where was she?

Thorn and I raced into the living room, where Elliott had his laptop hooked up to the television so everyone could see what was going on.

The queen stood next to Drake, looking seriously into the camera. Her expression was full of sorrow, but she patted Drake's arm lovingly as she said, "I know some are concerned about Drake taking over too quickly, but the circumstances are unprecedented. The king died before the prince was officially crowned as his heir. But please know we're doing exactly what King Arman wanted, and we must make sure that things continue to go as King Arman planned by crowning my son to fulfill his legacy."

"That *bitch!*" Elliott yelled, as Thorn's feeling of betrayal prickled in my veins.

I blinked, hoping this was another nightmare. If it wasn't, we could be attacked at any second.

CHAPTER SEVENTEEN

EVERYONE WAS HERE except for Peter, who must have been pouting upstairs in his room. The living room was silent as each person took in the severity of the situation. The queen had given a burner phone to Thorn via Uther. Either Uther had been in on it—which I doubted with his daughter here—or she'd screwed him over as well.

My stomach roiled. The queen was helping Drake weed out all the traitors, and we were *all* in danger.

Betrayal, hurt, and anger—the conflicting emotions that swirled through Thorn whenever it came to his biological parents—overwhelmed our bond. All I could do was push my love toward him and take his hand, reminding him I was there.

The queen dropped her arm from Drake and stepped forward, staring straight into the camera. "I ask for you all to trust the process because my mate—your king—and I always strove to do the most important thing in our lives: protect our people." A sad smile took over her face. "Please, be patient as we make the necessary changes to secure a better future for us all."

Drake beamed in the background, the charismatic persona he somehow managed to achieve emanating from the screen. I hated this confident look more than his smug real one. Many people out there would fall for this persona and willingly trust him. Sometimes, a confident face or essence was all people needed to get behind someone without bothering to look under the surface.

"Thank you for listening." The queen stepped back, returning to her place beside Drake.

"The queen looks nice," Reece sighed from her spot on the couch. She was sitting with her rainbow-colored blanket over her legs. "It would be amazing to meet her one day. Maybe I could dress up like a *princess*."

I pressed my lips together, trying to keep the scowl from my face. Obviously, Uther and his thunder hadn't told her everything. She was so young, but it also scared me. She was unaware of the threat the queen posed, and it broke my heart. It wasn't my place to tell Uther how to handle his child, but that didn't mean I wouldn't discuss it with him when he called...if he were ever able to again.

Drake glided to the forefront of the screen. His face contorted with what viewers would assume was worry and despair, and he placed a hand over his heart. "You heard my mother, the queen. These are unprecedented times, and we need to move quickly, especially with my brother at large. I must secure the throne before he attacks again and strips more people of their dragons." He straightened his shoulders, looking straight into the camera like the queen had done. "I vow that I will hunt him down and take care of him and anyone who aids him. I miss my dear, sweet fiancée terribly and hope she'll be returned home safely. Until then, I'll remember every kiss we shared and believe there will be many more in our future."

The memory of the one time he'd forced me to kiss him in front of the king and queen slammed into my brain, and I fought the urge to gag. I clutched my stomach, hoping the bile wouldn't burn my throat. I'd tried to erase that horrible memory for so many reasons.

Thorn shivered with rage. His jaw clenched, and he rasped, "That prick is going to die."

Reece's eyes bulged, and she wrapped her arms around her stomach and shrank back on the couch. Kari and Chandra were beside her, and they scooted closer to her.

We weren't used to having a small child here. *Babe, you're scaring Reece.*

He flinched and pulled his attention away from the television and toward the little girl. He connected, *It's so damn hard to keep my head on straight when he talks about you like that.* His neck corded. *I want to jump through the television and kill him.*

I leaned my head on his arm. *That's what he wants and why I need you to stay focused.*

Does he think I don't know about that kiss? And he's still calling you his fucking fiancée? Thorn snarled, and Reece glanced fearfully in our direction again.

"Reece, that's the man your daddy has to work for to protect you." Kari bent so she was at eye level with the little girl. She continued to talk, but I had to calm Thorn down. Drake had pushed his buttons, which he'd likely intended in case we were watching.

I tugged my mate toward the front door. Saphira hurriedly opened it, guessing my intent. Thorn had a level head on his shoulders when it came to everything but me.

"We'll be right back," I informed everyone.

The late morning sun hovered about three-quarters of the way up in the sky. I faced my mate, cupping his cheek with my hand. "I want to forget that it happened, but Thorn, it did, and he will do anything he can to get a reaction from you. He wants you to act irrationally."

His nostrils flared, but his breathing slowed at my touch. His face contorted with heartbreak. "I know, but that's the thing. It works. How would you feel if another woman was acting that way about me? Claiming me in front of the world and making it clear I'd soon be hers?"

My stomach clenched, and my blood boiled. That would be worse than a nightmare. He wasn't trying to be a possessive, jealous asshole, but we were mates, two parts of one soul, and hearing someone act like one half of us belonged to someone else was maddening. "Babe, I know. I'm not saying this is easy, and I hope you'd be having the same conversation with me if the roles were reversed." I wasn't judging him, but we didn't have the luxury of reacting to emotion if we wanted to win.

Some of the tension released from his shoulders, and he pressed his forehead to mine. He chuckled humorlessly. "I would be."

"Exactly." I smiled softly. "Anytime he talks like that, ignore him. Otherwise, we're giving him what he wants. Do you want to make Drake happy?"

"Fuck, no," he growled as he wrapped his arms around my waist, pulling me against his body. "I want him to be the angry one when he realizes we've won."

I tapped his forehead with my fingers. "You do realize that winning means you might be the one taking over the throne, and the queen might be working with Drake. We could be in a whole lot of trouble right now." The only reason I wasn't completely freaking out was because Belinda and Merlin were out there keeping watch.

He exhaled, the anger ebbing, replaced by uncertainty.

"I've been thinking about that, and I don't want to rule. I've made that clear, but if Drake isn't an option, what if I'm the only choice?"

"We'll cross that bridge when we get there." I didn't want him to feel pressured into making a decision that didn't need to be made now, but I did agree with him. He might not have much of a choice, and I also believed he was the most fit to lead. He'd be the type of leader people would be willing to die for. "But when the bridge comes and you're torn about whether to cross it, don't take my needs into account." Because he would. He would prioritize my wants and needs over his people. I was his weakness and, in some ways, his fatal flaw.

"Of course I will. That's just as important as any other piece," he whispered vehemently as he placed a finger under my chin and tilted my head up so I was staring into his eyes. He pressed, "Your happiness is the most important thing to me. Damn the consequences."

His emotions soared between us, reinforcing every word. Even without a fated-mate connection, I'd have believed him. He didn't lie or sugarcoat truths to make others happy.

"I wanted to be a doctor to help people. To heal the sick or, in some cases, help them toward their end with peace and as much grace and dignity as they can keep." I'd seen what had happened to my mom during her cancer treatment. The denial, the depression, and her body breaking down on her. Through it all, she hadn't found peace until I'd told her she could leave. That I'd be fine on my own. That she could stop fighting for me. Within minutes, she'd faded away.

He nodded, his sky blue eyes darkening a shade, and the diamond flecks in his irises stole my breath. He connected, *I know. That's why you becoming a doctor is a priority.*

"Let me finish." I took his hands and squeezed. "What I'm trying to say is, if *you* want to become king, I'll still be fulfilling my dream."

Tilting his head, he furrowed his brows. "I'm not following."

"Maybe it's not the dream I envisioned six years ago, but I'll still be helping others." I clasped my hands. "We'd be making sure that dragons who are different or elderly aren't persecuted. Think about Reece's situation, all because a dragon shifter fell for a human and no one could help them. If you're king, we can help people the way we helped Emily and baby Thorn." My heart raced thinking about all the good we could do. "We could help those down on their luck in a way that wouldn't be insulting because we can relate to them better than royals who were raised privileged. We could—"

He laughed, the sound refreshing, deep, and sexy. "I get it." His irises twinkled. "You still get to fulfill your dream if I choose to take on the responsibility of leading our people."

"Yeah." I smiled, surprising myself. That really was the case. I hadn't realized it until now, but Thorn ruling the dragons would protect a lot more people, along with our actual future.

"I don't know how I got so damn lucky to have you be mine, but I will cherish you always," he vowed and kissed me. My stomach knotted with the familiar urgent need, but now was not the time or place.

Two seconds was all I gave myself to enjoy the kiss before pulling away. I licked my lips, relishing his minty taste. "We need to go back in and determine our next steps if the queen is working with Drake." All my hope from the night before had left me raw.

Thorn flinched and tightened his hold on me. "I know it was foolish, but I was kind of hoping she meant what she said, which shows that hope doesn't change anything."

"Hope is one of the most powerful motivators. Hope for a better future keeps underdogs fighting." He couldn't give up or become defeated. That was exactly what Drake wanted. "It's what motivates our group to take Drake down, and when nurtured correctly, that hope can turn into a flame of passion. That's what we're going to do." I pointed at the door. "Head in there and spread those flames."

"Okay." He smiled adoringly at me. "Let's go inside and do that. And I have a little girl I need to make up with."

When we entered the house again, not much had changed. Reece, Chandra, and Kari sat in the center section of the couch, with Elliott and Mindy on the ottoman. Sol, Eva, and Hydra were on the left side of the couch, and Tia, Ryu, and Tyson were on the other. Theron, Brenton, Vlad, and Errol paced behind the couch. The sound of pots and pans clanging informed me that Cassidy was in the kitchen, odd for this hour.

One person was missing. "Is Peter still upstairs?"

"Yeah, he went up after dinner." Elliott rolled his eyes. "He said he needed space where there wasn't as much drama."

That sounded like Peter. He wanted Drake to win—I could feel it. "He can't know that people are helping us from the inside."

"Reece, I could use your help," Cassidy sing-songed from the kitchen.

Ah, that must be why she was making something at

such an odd hour. She was using it as a way to distract the little girl while we discussed strategy.

When Reece's feet hit the floor, Thorn strolled over and squatted in front of her. He hung his head and murmured, "I'm sorry if I upset you earlier. The prince was saying a lot of stuff about my Everly, and I didn't like it. However, I shouldn't have spouted off like that. It was wrong."

Reece's smile was blinding. "It's okay. Daddy gets upset, too, when he thinks about how he and I can't be together." She threw her arms around Thorn's neck, pulling him in for a tight hug.

This time, when my eyes burned, it was from happy tears. She was a bright light that we needed so desperately in our world right now.

Standing, Chandra pushed a piece of hair behind her ear. "We should go help."

"Yeah." Kari climbed to her feet. "Let us know if you need us for anything."

My heart ached as the two grown women also hurried away. They were more than welcome to talk strategy with us, but it was clear they either didn't feel comfortable or wanted to stay with Reece. Either way, I wouldn't push them.

Vlad rubbed the back of his neck. "If the queen is working with Drake, they could already have our location."

"I don't know." Errol strolled around the couch and leaned against the edge of the fireplace. He pursed his lips. "If I hadn't seen the broadcast, I never would have believed it. Though giving up Thorn caused problems in their relationship, King Arman and Queen Mira loved each other very much. They were truly fated. I don't see her supporting Drake, knowing he killed his father, her mate. I don't care if he is her son...so maybe she doesn't know or doesn't believe it."

Saphira and Brenton took the spots on the couch our newcomers had vacated. Saphira crossed her legs and leaned forward, placing an elbow on her knee. "Maybe she doesn't think the dragons will support Thorn as king."

"I swear." Tia rolled her eyes and crossed her arms. "The king and queen didn't know what their people would do. Let's be real—most of the time, they stayed holed up in their big, fancy mansion and did shit like this to inform us heathens of their decrees. It's insulting. Even if Thorn didn't have a lick of power, I, for one, would want someone like *him* ruling. He understands not having money and the struggles that we-the-people actually go through. I don't need that scoundrel prick or the spoiled queen making decisions for me."

"Dear." Merlin placed an arm over his mate's shoulders and pulled her close. "Sometimes, it's best if you don't say *everything* that's on your mind."

Elliott shook his head. "Don't listen to him. Say it. I love hearing it." He glanced at Mindy and shook his head. "Babe, it's a good thing she's taken, or you'd have some serious competition."

Giggling, Tia blushed. "Oh, that boy makes me feel young."

Instead of getting growly, Merlin chuckled. "It's a damn good thing I know you would never stray, or I'd be teaching this young man here a lesson or two."

"Oh, I'd be helping you." Mindy placed her hands on her hips and narrowed her eyes at Elliott. Unlike the older man, she wasn't teasing. They weren't fully mated yet, so there was no doubt super-heightened emotions were swirling through her.

Tyson snorted. "Dude, you're in trouble."

Luckily, that wised Elliott up. He lifted his hands. "Babe, I was kidding. You know I love you." Then his face blanched, and his mouth dropped open.

I don't think your brother has said the L-word to her before, Thorn connected, mashing his lips together.

Mindy's breath caught. She blinked several times. When she opened her mouth, a phone rang.

The ring had come from Thorn's and my bedroom.

That broke the moment, and utter silence fell, even in the kitchen. It was the burner phone that Uther had given Thorn.

When it rang a second time, Thorn sprang into action and raced to the bedroom. Vlad and I were hot on his heels, with Theron and Saphira right behind us.

He snatched the phone from the end table, swiped it, and put it on speaker. He snarled, "Are you calling to gloat and inform us that warriors are on their way?"

It was the queen. I shouldn't have been surprised, but the pain etched into Thorn's face tore me in two.

No matter what, I'd make sure this woman never made him feel like this again.

THORN'S ADRENALINE spiked as my throat constricted. I hadn't realized I'd put so much hope in all of this panning out so we'd have a chance to beat Drake at his own game. My heart felt obliterated.

Finally, the queen sighed on the other end of the line. "I shouldn't expect your trust. I haven't earned it."

Thorn laughed cruelly. "Well, we did just watch you say that you're backing Drake as the king, so forgive my problematic attitude."

"You heard me say I would back my son—the one I know will continue on his father's course. I won't lie. Part of me wishes it were Drake. It would make things easier. But there was a reason I didn't use his name."

Thorn's hurt sliced through our bond, stealing my breath with his agony.

I placed a hand on his shoulder. "Stop the games. You can't keep playing both sides."

"Everly, I'm assuming that's you." The queen wasn't asking. She knew.

I didn't humor her with a confirmation.

After a pause, she huffed. "You saw my shock the day I learned Thorn was alive. I couldn't fake that. Then I saw him at the wed—"

Thorn snarled so loudly the sound hurt my ears.

"Do *not* finish that word," he seethed. "You were going to let that arrogant *douche* marry my fated mate."

"I didn't *know*." The pain in her voice was evident. "I didn't have a clue."

I was tired of everyone's bullshit. "When Drake forced me to meet you two at breakfast, you thought you caught a whiff of Thorn's scent as I sat down. You reacted so strongly that the table almost toppled over."

Errol and Vlad moved closer, coming to stand on our other side so we could all see one another. I could smell Saphira and Tyson and hear them breathing at the threshold of the door.

"If that was the case, Mira," Errol said, frowning, "you would've known she was mated to Thorn."

"I couldn't believe it." Her voice sounded so sad...so weak. "First, I learned that the son I thought was dead had been alive all this time, and then the son I did know brought home a fiancée who reminded me of the son I thought was dead, and things just spiraled out of control. I didn't want to face what any of it could mean."

She'd been in denial. Gods, I understood that. I'd seen what Mom went through when her entire life changed. Though this situation wasn't a terminal illness, it was still life-altering. Sometimes it was easier to turn a blind eye to something that could change things fundamentally than it was to deal with it...until you had to.

Some of my anger fizzled, but Thorn's didn't. He hadn't gone through anything like this before, not really.

"That's why you kept the announcement generic." Vlad

rubbed the scruff on his face. "You didn't mean Drake when you were saying that. You meant Thorn the entire time."

"Yes. I will *not* betray Thorn...not again." Her voice shook as if she were suppressing a sob. "Drake went too far in killing Arman, but he threatened to injure more people I care about if I didn't partake in the video and make it look like I supported him. I...I can't...handle causing more pain through my decisions and indiscretions."

Errol clenched his jaw. "He's threatening you?"

"No, but he will if I don't play the doting mother. He isn't aware that I know he killed Arman. He told me it was Thorn, and that opened my eyes to what's been happening all along. Thinking back, Arman and I ignored so many signs. We focused everything on him because of our guilt and grief over what we'd done to Thorn."

That all-too-familiar stream of emotions swirled between my mate and me. Again, Thorn felt hurt, sad, and betrayed, but with hope also blending in. The sensation was so intense that my body weakened. Even the buzz of our connection didn't ease what he was going through, and I wished I could do something beyond just standing next to him. I wanted to fix the problem...but it was something only time could heal.

"How did you find out?" he asked roughly.

There was a pause. "I can't tell you. I promised them."

It sounded like someone the queen trusted had told her everything. *Do you trust her?* I connected with Thorn, needing to hear his unbiased opinion before the inevitable group conversation.

He glanced at me and took my hand. *I do, which makes this harder.*

Just like the king's death had taken a bigger toll on him than he wanted to address, I could sense his sadness. It was easier to think of his biological parents as bad people than as flawed beings who had made a terrible mistake. *Me, too.*

He nodded.

"What's your plan, Mira?" Errol covered his mouth with his hands.

She sighed in relief. "Someone in Drake's inner circle is feeding me information. I can tell you where Drake's going and what his plans are so you can save the people he's trying to..."

The silence was thick, and the four of us glanced at one another. None of us spoke up to finish her sentence. If she was saying what I thought she was, then I needed to hear *her* acknowledge it, and we needed to find out how much she knew.

"That he's trying to k-kill." Her voice broke on the last word, but she'd said it solidly enough for us to understand.

She knew everything.

"I can't get over that. The way he's been manipulating us while hurting our people." She sniffed. "And my poor, sweet Arman paid the cost for our obliviousness. But no more. This has to end."

"That information will help us save our people, but to stop the coronation, we need to know more than the locations Drake plans to attack or search," Thorn said, tugging me to his side so our bodies pressed together.

The sizzle of our connection exploded, but I couldn't enjoy it in the current situation.

Queen Mira exhaled. "I'm figuring that part out, but we need allies. I need you to help thunders and find the guards who fought for you. That's your first assignment. A dragon shifter flying near Pilot Mountain in North Carolina noticed a group of ten warriors in the woods. They think the guards are loyal to *you*, Thorn. Drake is preparing to send fifty warriors there tonight to kill them. You need to get to them first."

Our group became silent. This was a huge risk, one that would surely send us into a trap if she was working with Drake. But if she was telling the truth, we would have ten trained men fighting alongside us. That would be a huge increase to our extremely low numbers.

"Okay." Vlad nodded. "That's close to Mount Airy, so it makes sense they'd be near Theron's thunder because they couldn't risk flying for too long. They didn't venture too far, which the warriors wouldn't expect, but moved farther from the king's lands in case they had to run away. Also, it's near the mountain from which the town got its name, and the location is a draw for human hikers, so Drake's warriors can't search the area easily in dragon form."

A knock came from the other end of the phone, followed by a woman's voice calling out, "Queen Mira, Prince Drake has requested you come to the office. He wants to chat with you."

"Of course," Queen Mira responded with a strong voice that sounded significantly different from the one she was using with us. "Tell him I'm changing and will be down in a few minutes."

"Yes, ma'am." Then the sound of the maid's footsteps receded.

There was a shuffling noise, and the queen's more urgent voice came over the phone. "I've got to go. Text me when you have the warriors, and hurry. Drake won't sit on this knowledge for long. He'll want to attack when it's dark to hide from the humans. I won't have my cell phone on me. I can't chance Drake finding it, or all of this will be ruined, but I'll check it periodically, especially at night when I retire."

At least, Drake was determined to keep dragons a secret from humans...for now. There was no telling what Drake might be planning for the future. Knowing him, ruling the dragons wouldn't be enough. He craved power, and the only way to satisfy that craving was to conquer more.

"You all be safe, and Thorn...I love you," she breathed. "I'm sorry it's taken me so long to see the truth."

A burning sensation slammed into me, and it felt as if I'd been stabbed in my chest near the core of our connection. If I hadn't known better, I would've thought I'd been stabbed in the heart just like King Arman, but this was emotional suffering, not physical.

"You stay safe, too." His voice was a deep rumble. "Bye." He hung up the phone, not waiting for her to hang up first.

The silence was heavy for a few beats.

I moved where I could see Saphira and Tyson. We all wore varying expressions of dread. Whatever choice we made would be risky. This could be a trap, though I doubted it, and if it wasn't, where the hell were we going to put ten more people? We were already out of rooms, and the couch was taken.

"It's about damn time people realize who Drake truly is." Tyson sneered. "Seriously, if they hadn't overlooked his shit, maybe the king would still be alive."

Thorn grunted so lightly *I* almost didn't hear him, but the sadness and regret emanating from him whenever he thought of or talked about his biological father pierced between us. Errol's mouth tugged into a frown.

Taking a ragged breath, I gritted out, "That may be true, but people here have ties to the king, and those words were hurtful. Though Arman acted like a coward by ignoring signs of the person Drake was becoming, he didn't do those things, and he died trying to do the right thing. At least

Queen Mira is still trying to fix the problem. Don't waste your energy being mad at the wrong people."

Flinching, Tyson stepped back. "You seem so nice most of the time, then *bam*. You're the scariest one of us all."

"Dude, try being her brother," Elliott called from his spot in the den.

All of them, especially Elliott, had been listening to the entire conversation.

"One day, when I was ten, I hit a beehive with a stick to see how much it would take for the hornets to spew out and attack me," Elliott continued, confident we all wanted to hear how his story tragically ended. "Let me tell you, it didn't take much. As I was running in the front yard for my *life*, I saw Everly standing on the front porch, just watching me. *Watching me.* She yelled at me to run faster and opened the door for me to run inside. I got stung five times, and she rolled her eyes as she took care of me. She told me if that didn't fix my curiosity, nothing would. She gave me no sympathy and definitely didn't kiss my boo-boos."

Out of all the things he could have brought up, that was the story he'd chosen to tell? I rolled my eyes. "A *swarm* of hornets was chasing you. What did you expect me to do? We would've both wound up stung. And I'd told you the day before not to bother the hive! You had it coming."

"Exactly! Siblings are supposed to stick together, but no, you stayed safe and sting-free on the porch, watching me."

I pressed my head into Thorn's shoulder. "You'd *just* started running. You make it sound like I was watching you run in circles, laughing maniacally in the background. I was about to yell at you to come in when you saw me." Some-times, it was exhausting to be around him. I'd forgotten that over the past six years since the twins had retreated into themselves.

"That's the version in *my* head," he countered.

"This is why the invention of video games was so horrible." Tia sounded disgusted. "These young'uns don't know reality from fiction."

"I thought I did," Elliott retorted. "Then I learned that dragons, wolves, and who knows what else are real! It's all fair game now."

"Despite the usefulness of this conversation, we should focus on the ten warriors we need to rescue." Vlad smirked slightly and leaned against the wall between the end table and the bathroom door. "It's a five-hour drive. We need as much time as possible between when we get there and when Drake's team arrives so our scents won't be in the air. They won't be able to piece together that the men are with us."

The lightness Elliott and Tia had provided was gone. Vlad had a good point. "What are we thinking? Do we know for sure it's not a trap?"

"I don't think it is." Errol paced in the open area of the bedroom. "But I'd hate to not be wary. For all we know, Drake bugged the queen's room and can hear everything she plans."

"Which means we need to be careful. Luckily we have the rentals cars under various aliases of Vlad and Cassidy." Thorn tossed the burner phone on the bed. "We'll need both Suburbans to bring the ten new additions back with us. So, two of us in each vehicle—the driver and a passenger in front."

"Fated mates will make the best teams so everyone can communicate quickly without worrying about dead spots." Vlad pursed his lips. "Cassidy can stay back with the group here so we can keep each other updated, and Everly can ride with me in one of the Suburbans."

My stomach knotted. Vlad had been nothing but great to me, but we hadn't spent a ton of time alone. Sitting in the car with him for five hours might be uncomfortable, but his plan had merit.

"Theron can ride with me, and Hydra, Errol, and two others can ride in the rental car." Thorn licked his bottom lip.

"I'm going." Saphira wagged a finger. "I may not have a fated-mate connection, but I want to be involved. These people know me, and more familiar faces will be helpful."

I hadn't thought of that. The guards the king had brought had likely worked with him for years.

"Brenton should go as well. He'll know some of them, too." Errol strolled to the door to leave the bedroom.

Tyson blocked it. "Why shouldn't I go? Is it because I used to be injured?"

"What?" Errol shook his head hard. "That's not it at all. It's because you were more of a recluse, and Brenton was an advisor to the king for almost as long as I was. People will recognize him, especially since he's older."

Tyson's head hung, and his cheeks burned. "Oh, yeah. That makes sense."

My chest hurt. Even though he was healed, the way he'd been treated still affected him. I hated that Drake had made him feel like less of a person when he was just as whole as any of us.

"We've got a plan." Vlad clapped his hands. "Now it's time to execute it. Everly had a good point earlier—do *not* mention anything to Peter about who our source is. If asked, we saw someone mention this on the Dragonnet. Don't trust him."

Our group dispersed to get ready to head out for another long day.

THE CAR RIDE with Vlad wasn't as awkward as I'd feared.

I wore one of Thorn's baseball caps, keeping it pulled low over my face in case we passed anyone we knew. Thorn had done the same, and I learned he kept caps around for when he wanted to hide half his face.

Cassidy had packed us some lunch and snacks so we wouldn't have to stop often on the way there or back. We also brought large coolers filled with sandwiches. There was no telling when these ten guards had last eaten. For all we knew, they were living off the land.

I learned that Vlad had similar tastes in music to Thorn, and I realized Vlad had probably influenced Thorn's taste growing up. We talked about our hobbies and interests, and when he learned that I loved to paint, his eyes glowed. Though Vlad wasn't a painter, he'd loved collecting paintings...until his life had changed twenty-one years ago.

As we pulled into our destination parking lot, I stared at a mountain of rocks surrounded by trees. We jumped from our vehicles, ready to search the area for any signs that Drake's warriors were already here, but as the queen had promised, they weren't here since darkness hadn't fallen.

We trooped into the thick black gum, eastern red cedar, and tulip trees. The air was warm, around eighty, and a herd of elk roamed nearby.

Thorn came to my side as we walked deeper into the woods. None of us spoke, afraid we might scare the warriors or miss the sound of a threat. We tried to keep our steps light...feeble.

Vlad and Theron led our group, with Thorn and me right behind them. Hydra and Brenton took the rear, with Saphira and Errol between us.

I found myself enjoying the sun on my skin and being part of nature—something I'd despised as a human. My dragon inched forward, the animal side of me reveling in being free and unbound.

We must have been walking for over an hour when something startled us to our right. It was too large to be an elk and too small to be a bear.

Our group turned and tiptoed toward the sound. I stifled a gasp when I saw one of the king's warriors who'd been at Theron's thunder.

One of us kicked a rock. At the rattling sound, the warrior jerked his head around, right toward Hydra.

Someone he didn't recognize. He spun and ran away as quickly as possible, forcing us to chase him.

The man yelled, "They're here! Run! They've found us."

"Wait!" Thorn shouted, but that only made them run faster.

They didn't recognize his voice, which wasn't surprising. They hadn't heard him speak much before. Between seeing Hydra and hearing an unfamiliar voice, their panic took over.

Shit. We had to stop them before they disappeared...or Drake's warriors found us.

CHAPTER NINETEEN

I RAN AS FAST as I could. Our only saving grace was that human hikers could be in the area, and this site could easily be seen, so the men weren't likely to shift into dragon form unless they were super desperate and afraid. But these were the king's warriors, and they were loyal—keeping the secret of the existence of dragons even while in danger would be important to them out of respect for their former leader.

We could hear more hurried footsteps now. The other warriors were running, too, but that was a blessing. At least they'd stayed close together.

We all must have tapped into our dragons, because our group picked up its pace, and so did the man running ahead of us.

Thorn, don't hold back. They need to see you before they scatter, I connected. Though he hadn't been feeling anything other than determination, I also knew he didn't want to leave me behind, which would slow him down. *If I get into trouble, I'll let you know.*

He tensed as he ran past the other side of a red cedar and then past me. Finally, he replied, *Are you sure?*

Yes. Now go. That was the whole point of coming here, but I knew he needed to hear me say so.

He picked up his pace and flew by everyone, confirming what I already knew. He was the strongest of us all...hell, probably out of all the dragons. No one had told me this outright, but there was a reason the royal line ruled—they emanated power. Thorn had the same raw power as his father. He was strong, and with his mark, he could be unstoppable, which was how his grandfather had terrorized their world. To me, Thorn's situation was different because he was my mate. Even though I knew he was powerful, that power didn't affect me. Not in the same way I saw it affect others until they got to know him and saw the man he was.

Theron and Vlad surged forward, leaving Brenton, Errol, Saphira, Hydra, and me behind. They weren't as fast as Thorn, but they were stronger than the rest of us.

The warrior was pulling away, but I could still see the back of his head. I had to split my attention between him and dodging the trees in front of me. He was smaller than the other warriors I'd met, but with each pump of his arms, his triceps bulged. I was certain that even though I'd become a dragon, the loose skin of my underarms still wobbled every time I moved my arms—though with all the training we'd done, I hoped I was getting more toned.

Thorn was gaining speed, and his frustration swirled through me.

I noticed the other footsteps had gone silent...like they'd stopped running. *Thorn, something's up.*

Before I could say more, a clearing came into view. The other nine warriors stood waiting, rifles pointed right at us.

Bile burned in my throat. Out of all the possible scenarios, I hadn't considered *this*. Maybe the warriors regretted their decision and had turned on us. That would be the best way to gain Drake's forgiveness if they wanted to rejoin what could be the winning side, especially with our limited resources.

The man who was running blew past the two tallest men in the center of the group. A gigantic, ripped, deep-bronze complected man whose braids of ebony hair were pulled into a bun on top of his head had locked his graphite eyes on Vlad, while a fair-skinned male with dark blond hair styled upward, who was only a few inches shorter and not quite as buff but could still take on an ox, had his sapphire eyes on Theron.

"Stop where you are and raise your hands," the bigger man snarled, his voice as deep and menacing as his muscles.

We all slowed, even Thorn, and his fear peaked within our bond. I knew exactly why. He wasn't afraid for himself —he was freaking out because he was fifteen feet away from me and not able to protect me.

We weren't as prepared as we'd thought, and I feared we'd walked into a horrible trap.

The guards at either end of their line, both women, were focused on my mate, while the remaining five focused on the rest of us. I recognized them vaguely from our brief time together in chaos.

"Wait." The tan-complected woman on our left with dark brown hair lowered her rifle a few inches. The skin around her midnight-black eyes tightened as she let out a deep breath. She lifted a hand and tilted her head. "Who are you?"

Thorn straightened his shoulders and lifted his chin. "Thorn Wight."

"No way." The female warrior on the other end snarled. She still had her rifle trained on my mate, her cinnamon irises glowing with anger. "This is a trick. Maybe witch magic?

Thorn wouldn't be able to find us. He's in hiding and doesn't have the resources." She jerked her head back, the ends of her golden brown ponytail swishing over her shoulder.

"It *is* him." Errol pivoted around me and came into view. "Drake has learned where you are. A dragon shifter saw you and reported it. His warriors will be here tonight to eliminate you."

The guy who'd been running from us gaped. "Errol? Is that really you? Prove it."

"First off, witches don't interact with dragons, and second, I was there when the king asked you to become part of his inner circle. He told you that he'd noticed your passion for doing the right thing, and he needed you at his side."

He sucked in a breath and nodded. "It is you."

"And this *is* Thorn. There's no deception involved." Errol gestured to my mate.

Tragedy had a way of messing with details, and when they'd last seen us, we'd been naked. My dragon snarled at the thought of the others—especially the women—seeing my mate unclothed. It was a good thing they weren't certain they recognized him, or I might have had to kill them for that reason alone.

"This isn't a trick," Errol finished. "We have a source inside the château who notified us that you were hiding in this area."

I appreciated that he didn't divulge who the informant was, but it wasn't surprising. He was the king's advisor, after all. Though these warriors were loyal to the late king, that didn't mean we could trust them yet.

The ten scanned each other, and Runner Guy nodded. "Lower your weapons."

I was surprised Runner was the leader of the group. He was the scrawniest man in the mix, but if the two who flanked him hadn't been so huge, he probably would've appeared much stronger. He did appear older, so maybe that had something to do with it.

Everyone listened without hesitation. It was clear this group trusted Runner, which was good for us.

Doubt crept through our bond from Thorn. He wasn't sure how to handle this situation.

"I'm sorry we startled you." I walked over to Thorn, the warriors watching me the entire way, and took my mate's hand. "That wasn't our intention."

"Wait," the third and final female guard said from the other side of the dark bronze, muscled man. She lifted a hand. "You're the one Drake is determined to marry."

Thorn snarled, his pupils slitting. "She is *my mate* and *wife*." Tension filled the air as the warriors' expressions turned to various levels of wariness. They didn't trust Thorn yet, despite the king's dying wishes. Unfortunately, they'd hit the sorest subject possible when it came to him.

Squeezing his hand comfortingly, I rolled my eyes and pushed my calm toward him, trying to keep the situation from escalating again. Though they'd promised their allegiance to Thorn, it had been on King Arman's say-so. We didn't need to scare them away. We needed their help.

"Drake proclaimed he'd make me his wife when he realized Thorn and I had completed our fated-mate bond." I smiled sadly.

"And he goes cuckoo where she's concerned because of that." Saphira snorted as she sidled over beside me. "Hell, even when she was human, those two circled each other like they might combust."

The jaw of the fiery pale girl on the end dropped. "You were *human?*"

You need to step in, I connected. He had to be seen as our leader. We needed them to be confident about King Arman's decision. *These people will follow you. Just focus on our goal—where Drake isn't around to terrorize us anymore.*

Inhaling, Thorn stepped closer to me and said, "Yes, she was. She got hurt, and I had to change her, or she would've died. I had no idea I was changing the woman who would become my fated mate."

The fiery girl smiled dreamily. "That's romantic."

I hadn't thought about our situation like that, but she was right. No one else had a story like it.

"I'm not trying to be rude, but what Errol said is true. We came to bring you back with us." Thorn flinched, then added quickly, "*If* you're willing."

That addition wasn't needed, but that made me fall for him more. It was another reminder of the type of man he was—kind, considerate, caring, and the ultimate leader who would let someone choose what was best for them as long as it didn't hurt others. And he was all mine.

The ten warriors glanced at one another again, like they were talking telepathically, though it wasn't possible.

"Actually, we would *really* appreciate that." Runner stepped forward, all sense of wariness removed, as if they'd decided something. "We're starving, and we've been too afraid to go inland. We've been staying out here to avoid hikers, though not well enough." He shook his head and pointed at himself. "My name is Arrow." He nodded at the others.

"I'm Echo," the gorgeous dark-bronze freight truck added.

The woman beside him lifted her hand, her warm smile reflecting in her amber eyes. She was about a foot shorter than Echo, and her dark brown hair was pulled into a tight ponytail as well. There was dirt smeared on her cheek, contrasting with her deep tan complexion. "I'm Opal."

"And I'm Fury," the fiery girl at the end added bluntly.

The other huge guy flanking Echo introduced himself. "Smokey."

Putting his rifle through the loop and on his shoulder, the man next to Smokey lifted his chin, his dark brown eyes hesitant. Somehow, his black hair was still spiked, even though he'd been out here for weeks, and his ebony scruff was thick. He was almost as short as Arrow but stouter, and his medium-brown complexion glowed. "Blaze here."

Beside him was a man with gorgeous tan skin. He had dark, unruly, curly hair and mesmerizing carob-brown eyes. He was only an inch taller than Blaze, but there was something happy about his presence. "Most people call me Amazing, but I also go by Owen."

"That's the Prince Heir, and you're pulling that shit?" The next warrior rolled his pine green eyes. Though he wasn't as ripped as Echo and Smokey, he was pretty damn close. Light auburn hair hung in his face, and he had black smudges, like war paint, across his cheeks, making his lighter complexion look ghostly compared to everyone else's.

"He's Rex," the woman on the other end added while glaring at the guys. "And I'm Sydney."

I was hoping I could remember each name.

Thorn stepped in and introduced our group one by one. Once introductions were done, the mood changed. The warriors began to fidget, eager to get away. I didn't blame them. Though I didn't mind nature anymore, if I'd stayed out here for as long as they had, my human side would've been ready for a shower and clean clothes immediately. They were still wearing their black warrior outfits, and while that had likely helped them blend in, especially at night, it was long past time to do some laundry.

"Follow us," Theron said, and he started back toward the vehicles, Hydra walking next to him.

Saphira and Brenton followed, with Errol and Vlad next. Thorn and I fell in behind them, and Opal and Arrow followed us. The rest of the warriors broke into pairs, but I didn't glance back. I wanted to get the hell away from here before Drake and his warriors arrived. They could fly, which meant their travel time would be significantly less than ours, but they would have to wait until it was dark to land. It was getting close to five, so we might hit traffic on the way back to the house. That was fine. I just wanted time for our scents to dissipate.

Our trek was quiet, and though the warriors' footsteps were steady, something uncomfortable nudged at me. I couldn't place what it was, but the hairs on my neck rose.

With each step, the sensation of being watched intensified, and a cold warning coursed down my spine. Thorn didn't appear to be affected, and no one else did, either. Maybe my anxiety was getting the best of me.

What's wrong? Thorn connected, sensing my unease through our mate bond. He stiffened beside me, tugging me closer to him.

I know this sounds weird, but I feel like we're being watched. A shiver ran down my spine. I couldn't kick the sinking suspicion.

Thorn scanned the area, and his breath caught. *Something is following us on your side and slightly behind us. I hadn't noticed it.*

I glanced over my shoulder, frowning.

The warriors had stern expressions like there was a threat nearby. They sensed whatever it was, too.

"The wolves," Arrow said tensely. "They came across us the first day we settled here and talked with us. We're technically in wolf territory. When they heard what happened, they were fine with us hiding here. Other shifters told them about what Drake's been up to. They think he'll come after the wolves once he conquers the dragons, and they don't want him in charge."

The wolves surrounded us, and my heart thundered. They were tense, as if they might attack. When the group in front of us stopped, Thorn hissed beside me.

Since I was shorter, I couldn't see what was happening, but then a deep voice sounded from in front of us. "What's going on here?"

When Thorn wedged us between Vlad and Errol and released my hand, my heart ached. This was the first time he'd ever left me behind without me urging him to.

"We came to take Arrow and the others to safety." Thorn continued to push forward, and when Theron and Hydra parted, I caught a glimpse of the action.

A naked older man blocked our path. He had short gray hair and a matching goatee. His arms were bulging without him flexing. At one time, he would've been the buffest man I'd ever seen...but now I'd met dragons. Despite being older, nothing on him was sagging, and unfortunately, that was yet again something I couldn't unsee.

"I didn't realize we were on wolf territory, and I'm sorry we didn't alert you to our presence." Thorn looked over his shoulder and scowled when he saw I had a clear view of the naked man. He moved to block the older man from my view.

Thank you for that, I connected. I had no desire to see anyone naked but him, and it unsettled me that this man had no problem standing in front of us completely nude.

"Why didn't you know this is wolf land?" the older man pressed, his voice turning gritty.

"Because I haven't been involved in the supernatural world for over twenty-one years. I've only recently acclimated again." Thorn lowered his head, but not in submission—in respect.

It was strange how I picked up on things like that now.

"You're the prince the warriors here are so desperate to protect." The older man's voice softened. "You're the true heir to the dragon throne?"

I couldn't breathe. Whatever Thorn said now would set the course for our future, and I was grateful we'd talked about it earlier.

"Yes, I am." Thorn nodded, and something shifted in our bond...acceptance.

"Good." His answer was so simple. "My name is Lowell."

"I'm Thorn."

A wolf howled in the distance, and the sound was chilling.

"Nice to meet you, Thorn," the wolf shifter replied. "Are you expecting more of your people?"

I sensed the warriors behind me tensing, and Vlad's neck corded.

Thorn shook his head. "No. Why?"

"Because twenty more dragon shifters are entering the woods two miles west of here."

CHAPTER TWENTY

MY LEGS ALMOST GAVE OUT. We'd expected Drake to send people here after sunset, but they were already here, and we were outnumbered. I feared we were about to find out how badly our warriors were suffering from malnutrition.

Considering how well things had been going today, we should've been prepared for this. Our luck always ran out, a fact I tried not to focus on too often. So far, we'd scraped by, but that particular silver lining could vanish at any time. It was too scary to consider because I could lose Thorn...forever.

Overwhelming sensations surged through our connection. Thorn felt the same way that I did...and adding that to the emotions rolling off the dragon shifters surrounding me only made things worse. Like I was drowning on land.

When Thorn stopped blocking my view of Lowell, allowing me to see the older man's naked form again, that was the icing on the proverbial cake. He was so worried that he didn't care about my view of the naked older man anymore.

"Those are *not* our people. They're loyal to Drake." Thorn tensed. "But thanks for the warning. We need to move before they find us."

"It won't be long." The older man stepped aside into the thick brush. "But I can buy you some time."

"Don't." Thorn jerked his head toward the vehicles, indicating he wanted us to move. "I'd hate to drag the wolves into this mess. It's bad enough with dragons suffering. We don't need more of our brethren species getting involved."

Lifting a brow, Lowell scanned my mate again, seeing him in a new light.

Saphira and Brenton took off toward our vehicles with renewed vigor.

Thorn gestured for Theron and Hydra to move next, but no one budged, and even Saphira and Brenton paused when they realized no one was coming behind them. I went to my mate, refusing to leave him. The warriors followed suit, remaining right behind me.

"I'll take up the back." Thorn gestured more urgently while leveling a heavy gaze on me. "And make sure I don't see anything."

I'll be in the back with you. I pushed my determination toward him and planted my feet on the earth. He needed to know I was unyielding on this.

"No, Your Highness." Arrow shook his head and crossed his arms. "We are here to protect you, not the other way around. And I'm certain I'm talking for everyone here and not just us warriors."

Nodding curtly as if he'd come to a decision, Lowell clapped my mate on his arm and said, "If you hurry, you'll make it out of here. I can buy you time with little risk since they're on wolf lands. Drake might not like it, but it won't seem like we're aiding you. So go. Now. For the sake of all supernaturals, we need you to take the throne."

I smiled and took Thorn's hand in mine. I was certain that Lowell was the alpha of this pack and had made a decision about Thorn. Best of all, he approved of my mate. We needed any help we could muster.

Surprise filtered through our bond, and Thorn's heartbeat quickened slightly, but my mate's face remained a mask of indifference. "Thank you. But please don't cause problems for yourself and your pack."

"We appreciate your concern." Lowell stepped into the trees, his hunter green eyes glowing. His voice changed into one that sounded half human, half animal. "Now go."

Bones cracked, and fur matching his hair color sprouted over his arms. I'd never seen a wolf shifter before, let alone one shifting, and I was intrigued, but we didn't have time to loiter.

Everyone watched Thorn and me, waiting for us to make the first move, as if they were afraid to run in case we lagged behind.

Instead of arguing, Thorn took my hand, and we moved in unison. Appeased, Brenton and Saphira spun on their heels and took off again, this time with Theron and Hydra. Vlad and Errol paused and settled in behind us and in front of the warriors, likely so Vlad could keep an eye on Thorn and make sure he didn't do something noble to save us. There was no guarantee that Lowell's plan would work.

As we picked up our pace, I heard the wolves running away on our left. At least Drake's warriors hadn't parked in the same lot we had. There must be one on the other side of the mountain.

Each breath I took was harder than the last, mainly because I was listening for any signs of someone approaching. With the adrenaline coursing through my veins and fear's cold claws digging into my chest, my hearing seemed better than usual, even being tapped into my dragon. But all I could hear were the wolves running away and the sound of our footsteps, along with some squirrels scurrying through the trees. Between that and the scents of dragon shifters, trees, and sunshine, I wasn't losing my mind.

Well, maybe I was. I *smelled* sunshine, which I'd never noticed before, but with the warmth on my skin and the fresh smell surrounding it, there was no denying it.

The tree line came into view, the parking lot peeking between outstretched branches. We were close, but I didn't want to get my hopes up, not with the warriors laboring to breathe behind us.

Hints of their hunger bled through, weakening their magic and their endurance. It wasn't drastic, and they were keeping up, but if we had to engage in a fight, there was no telling how long they could hold up against other well-trained warriors who hadn't been suffering like they had.

Noises came from the left, and my heart stuttered. *Do you hear that?* The source wasn't small like a wolf; it was more human-sized but moving too quickly.

Yes, I do. Thorn kept his attention focused forward. *Keep running. If we start scanning the area, it'll slow us down. They're far enough away that we should be able to get to the car without trouble.*

The warriors behind us stiffened, their movements not quite as quiet, confirming they were also straining and on high alert. Everyone's footsteps remained strong and steady.

When Saphira and Brenton broke through the trees, part of me felt relieved, but I locked that down. We weren't out of the woods yet, and I didn't mean literally. Until we were in the vehicles, driving away with no one following us, we could still be attacked.

My dragon roared, inching forward and ready to be released for battle. I could see a few cars with humans hanging around them close to our vehicles. Shifting would not be possible, but at least Drake's warriors would have to be careful around the prying eyes.

A few seconds later, Thorn and I were on the dirt path to the parking lot.

I could hear feet pounding from about a mile away.

We'd get out of here, but not without Drake learning we had the ten warriors and that Theron and Hydra were part of our crew. I only hoped that didn't mean something worse for their thunder, but we'd discuss that once we were on our way out.

Brenton jumped into the driver's seat of the rental car, while Saphira took the front passenger side. The rest of us split up, heading to the vehicles we'd ridden in to get here.

Over his shoulder, Thorn told the warriors, "Five in each Suburban."

As we jogged past two families getting hiking gear together to head into the woods, they all stared at us. We were running, maybe in an obvious hurry, but not so fast that we screamed supernatural...at least, I didn't think we did.

I realized that wasn't what had caught their attention. It was the ten warriors with rifles on their backs.

"Honey," a middle-aged mother said as she scurried to her two preteen kids. "We need to go."

The father nodded abruptly and ran to the driver's side door to unlock their vehicle.

I hated that we'd scared them, but there wasn't much we could do. I ran to the Suburban parked closest to the road and jumped into the front passenger seat. I wanted to ride with Thorn, but using our fated-mate connection could be beneficial. Caution would help us in this situation.

Echo, Blaze, Fury, Owen, and Opal climbed in the back of my vehicle, and as soon as the door shut, Vlad put the car in reverse and peeled out of the lot.

I turned around in my seat, searching for the enemy dragon shifters. One of the human families that had been squatting when we'd run by had stayed, while the other family had piled into their car. The warriors chasing us must have split off, casing the area outside of the woods. They couldn't move too quickly and were still three-quarters of a mile away. Luckily, the other cars in the lot blocked our tags, so all they'd see were the types of vehicles we were driving.

Thorn and Brenton backed their vehicles out, and the three cars raced to the road. I could hear seatbelts buckling in the back as the warriors settled in. Fury sat in the middle of the far back row, with Opal and Echo flanking her. I was surprised that of the three men in the car, the largest one had gotten shoved into the far back until Echo placed an arm around Fury's shoulders. They must be together, but they had distinct scents, meaning they weren't bonded yet.

"I need you to keep an eye out and make sure no one is following us," Vlad said as he stepped on the gas, going fifteen miles over the speed limit.

I wanted to tell him to go faster, but that would be reckless. We could get pulled over, and that would only cause more problems.

"We're on it," Blaze said from his spot behind me.

My head rolled back as the world spun. I forced out a breath I hadn't realized I was holding, then filled my lungs to capacity.

All the vehicles were moving, and we were making headway back to the safe house. Even better, trained warriors were keeping an eye out in case someone was following us. That hadn't gone over so well with me last time, so I focused on calming down.

I'd give anything to be in that vehicle with you, Thorn connected in my head, his nerves still frazzled.

Unlike me, he didn't show them, and since we were going to rule over the dragons once we took Drake down, I'd better develop a poker face of my own. With Peter, I'd managed to hide my emotions because he'd always been indifferent and mean to me. That was easier to take than people I loved being in danger. I was damn sure they could see every emotion rolling across my face.

Me, too. I turned to stare into the side mirror. I wanted to do my part, even with warriors in the vehicle, but I did feel better that I wasn't the only one watching for tails, or I'd think *every* car was following us.

After twenty minutes of no one saying anything, some of the tension eased. I told the warriors there was a cooler in the back with sandwiches, and Fury immediately leaned over the back seat and dug in.

When they passed me a sandwich, I settled back and continued to keep watch...just to make sure. I suspected it would feel like a much longer ride back.

THE NEXT MORNING, Arrow, Echo, Errol, Vlad, Theron, Cassidy, Thorn, and I were in the kitchen after breakfast. Despite Peter's protests, Elliott and Eva had dragged him outside to train with the others, saying that even though he was the only human, he had to learn to defend himself.

We'd gotten back late and hadn't discussed our situation because the warriors had been exhausted. We'd found extra sheets and pillows, and they'd camped on the floor of the den, promising it was the most comfortable they'd been in weeks.

The table had been cleared of dishes, and everyone but Errol was sitting around it with cups of coffee, the scent of bacon still lingering.

Cassidy placed her teal coffee mug on the table. "So, they know these warriors are with us. We wanted to have that be a secret advantage."

"There was nothing we could do." Thorn leaned back in his seat across from her. "They arrived. If those wolves hadn't warned us, they might have chased after us and caught us." He leaned over and took my hand resting on top of the table.

Vlad ran a hand through his thickening scruff and placed his elbows on the table. He didn't say anything, but his forehead was lined with worry.

"We need more allies," Errol stated as he paced behind us. "But how can we achieve that while we hide?"

Arrow rubbed a finger against his bottom lip. He was sitting at the end of the table between Thorn and Cassidy. "One thing we can do is train *everybody* like the warriors. We'll teach them the way we...er, the enemy thinks. They'll surprise Drake's people and have a better chance of escaping them."

Excellent. This reminded me of something from a few days ago. "We should train them with weapons. I had to hold a gun the other night, and I was uncomfortable. I need to learn to shoot."

"Why did you need a gun here?" Echo scowled and examined the room like it held answers.

"It wasn't here," Theron said from his spot near the back door, a few feet away from Arrow and Cassidy. He'd been watching the others train outside. "It was when we met with Uther, Gemma, and Jerry, and they gave us a burner phone and asked us to take in their family members, who Drake was using as leverage to force their loyalty."

We filled the warriors in on everything that had happened to date.

"Those three are good people." Arrow took a sip of his drink. "I can think of several others who would ally with us, but it's too risky to reach out to them."

"There might be another way for us to gain more allies." Thorn cleared his throat as something brimmed through our bond: anticipation.

Hope sparked inside me. He had a plan. "What?"

"Theron, you still have access to the injured dragons' network, don't you?" Thorn winked as a warm feeling spread between us.

I tilted my head. I had no idea where he was heading with this. "Do you want us to move again?" I asked. The bouncing around was hard, but if they thought we might be at risk, I was willing to do whatever was necessary.

"That's not what I'm getting at. What if we coordinate meetings so I can heal more injured dragons?" He gestured at me. "And Everly could help with those who were injured in human form and give them some relief."

My heart leapt. "That won't guarantee us allies."

He shrugged. "Doesn't matter. It's the right thing to do —as long as we know our meeting location will be secure."

"I'm telling you, the people in this network—they aren't like that." Theron turned to the table, his eyes lighter than I'd seen in days. "Just the fact that you're willing to help would make a world of difference to so many."

"And word will spread, and other thunders won't be afraid of you." Errol grinned. "Some will want to ally with you just because of the good you're doing for the community, and that will make it easier for others to follow you two."

Us two? "You mean him," I said.

"The king is only as strong as the queen beside him." Errol smiled kindly. "Mira is capable of so much, but none of you had the opportunity to see it because all the light was on King Arman."

Echo chuckled. "That lady is as strong as they come. I've seen it with my own two eyes—when she walked into a room and spoke, King Arman listened. Their love was inspiring."

His words dampened my mate's spirit, and I understood why. He hadn't gotten the chance to notice it...not as a man. He could remember it only through a little boy's eyes.

I glanced out the window and saw Peter scowling with his arms crossed on the sidelines. He'd been a constant pain in the butt, and ever since Elliott and Eva had been changed, he'd become sulky and silent, dragging us down.

Reece was outside, despite not training like the rest, and stood next to Peter, trying to talk to him, but he ignored her just as he'd done to me when I was her age...at least, when my mother wasn't around.

Something clicked, and a lightness filled my body. "I know what we can do to completely derail Drake and solve another problem."

CHAPTER TWENTY-ONE

ALL SEVEN PAIRS of eyes pinned me. The idea had rushed at me so quickly. We'd have to work out logistics, but I believed it could *work*.

Thorn quirked an eyebrow. *Are you adding to the suspense?*

Bite me, I replied as I lifted my hands, getting ready to talk.

Gladly. He inched forward. *I didn't get the opportunity this morning, so I have no qualms about doing it right here at the table in front of everyone.*

Heat flooded my body, and my dragon surged forward. Never would I have believed I'd be the type of girl who'd love a man this possessive and unafraid of public affection, but here we were. I hoped it never changed.

"What if we use Peter for something useful?" I rubbed my hands together, focusing back on what I'd been planning.

Thorn thumped a hand on the table like a drum. "Sold. I don't need to know anything more. Let's get rid of the man who keeps glaring hatefully at my mate *before* I lose control and kill him."

I laughed, surprising myself. Thorn had a way of making me smile, no matter the circumstance.

"Though I want to agree with Thorn, Peter knows too much about us." Vlad's shoulders sagged. "And I'm not sure how he can be useful."

"Hear me out." I lifted a hand. "Obviously, we'd have to get Edna and the thunder on board, but what if we can find a place where we can all work together to tend to the injured, but we paint a different story for Peter and let him sneak away?"

Errol paused mid-step but said nothing.

"What do you mean by 'paint a different story'?" Theron squinted as if he were trying to see the bigger picture.

"We tell him Edna freaked out and said we needed to find another place on our own to hide." I started tossing out ideas without thinking any of them through. "And then make it sound like the warriors abandoned us so Drake thinks we're on our own again, with no place to go."

"I mean, they're training the others outside." Arrow gestured to the door. "Why would we be training you if we planned on leaving?"

Cassidy chewed on her fingernail. "No, wait. This could work. You all hid, and when they came to bring you back with us, you realized your location had been compromised."

"We can say we were tired and hungry, man." Echo smirked. "We took a chance to get out of there and get some food. Then we'll let slip that when Edna kicks Thorn and the others out and they have no place to go, their usefulness is over. After all, King Arman is dead, and there's no way Thorn and Everly can win."

I hated how that sounded and almost regretted bringing up the idea. Maybe the warriors would realize they were invested in a sinking ship.

"So we cut our losses." Arrow winced. "That sounds awful, but it would make sense. If they had nowhere to go, we would separate so we only had to worry about ourselves...the ones best trained for the situation. Some might not buy it, but hell, we just need Drake to."

"And he would." Vlad snorted humorlessly. "He only looks out for himself. His focus will be on finding Thorn before the coronation to ensure nothing goes wrong, and he'll believe that you warriors would know that and try to save yourselves."

He was right. Though none of us were like that, Drake was. That sort of rationale would make sense to him because that was what he'd do—cut his losses and save his own ass.

"Edna would have to be willing to leave with her thunder," Thorn said as he placed a hand on my thigh. "Even if we have her pretend to send us away, Drake wouldn't let her go unpunished."

"We would have to take her with us." Theron nodded. "And it wouldn't be ideal. I'm not even sure where we *could* go. They have a thunder of over one hundred people. We can't all cram into one house."

Unfortunately, that was a good point. "We'll have to split up, if you think we can find enough safe locations."

"If we first help the injured dragons to those who hide us, I think we can find a handful of people who can take us all in." Theron removed his phone from his back pocket.

"That would also allow us to spread apart and be harder to locate."

"We have Uther and Queen Mira to warn us if Drake and his warriors are coming to our location." Thorn shrugged. "Uther calls us every night to talk to Reece, anyway, but we aren't making that public knowledge because of the human hanging around. He'd rat us out in a heartbeat."

That was true. Uther called often, and the queen had helped us yesterday. They were coordinating who could get a hold of us best.

"It all comes down to whether Edna will agree." Cassidy ran a finger along the edge of her coffee cup. "Do we think she will?" She glanced at Theron.

"There's only one way to find out." Theron swiped on his phone. "But I suspect she will. Why don't you all head out there and train while I talk to her?"

Thorn's hand tensed on my leg, and he connected, *Don't get me wrong. I like you being able to defend yourself and find you training sexy as hell, but I hate it when you get hurt. It's worse than when I do.*

To his credit, he rarely got hurt, even when he trained with Vlad. Thorn was the strongest out there by far, and when he, Vlad, and Cassidy had been living in hiding, he'd worked construction jobs so he could get paid under the table. He was fit, tough, and all dragon—then add in his strong alpha royal genes, and he was a beast. With the warriors we had in tow now, he might struggle a little, but not like the rest of us.

I know, but it's good for me. I turned and brushed my hand over his cheek. Just like Vlad, he had a little scruff on his face, and it scratched my fingertips. *And I don't get hurt as often anymore.* I was about on par with the others now.

Though I was smaller and not built as sturdily since I wasn't born a dragon, I could get out of tight spots more easily due to my size. It helped me as often as it hurt me. That was one thing Vlad and Theron were trying to focus on with me: using my differences to my advantage.

After a quick kiss, I stood and flicked my gaze between Echo and Arrow. "Will one of you teach me to shoot a gun? I'd like to be more confident if I ever need to use one again."

"You have a very smart wife and mate, Your Highness," Arrow said as he smiled at me.

"Thorn." Thorn cleared his throat uncomfortably. "Just Thorn, and I know. I'm one lucky man."

Vlad climbed to his feet. "I'll run out to get some weapons and meet you in the back."

Our group dispersed, and even Cassidy joined us outside. Though she was trained, we all had to be in top shape for what came next. And that was exactly what we were going to do.

THAT NIGHT, our plan was in place. Edna had agreed. She'd said she would feel better at another location, anyway, in case the warriors learned that Emily had been changed or caught hints of Tia, Ryu, Merlin, and Belinda and their age. After all, the two empty houses had clearly been occupied. It would lead to questions. Apparently, she hadn't been sleeping well, worried about the situation as it was.

After Edna talked to the thunder and they all agreed, she and Theron reached out to other thunders in their network. Though it was less than ideal, we were looking for places farther from Asheville so we'd be centrally located for the thunders that wanted to bring their injured there for Thorn to heal.

The plan was in place—we were doing this tonight. The sooner, the better, so it would be more believable that Edna was kicking us out for bringing the warriors here. Arrow had discussed the plan with the nine warriors so they'd all play along, but we didn't inform anyone else since we needed the others to react accordingly.

We were all eating dinner—a quick, simple meal of hamburgers, steaks, and veggies that was easy to pick up, but nothing out of the ordinary for us—when there was a pounding on the front door. Mindy, Elliott, Cassidy, Vlad, Eva, Sol, Reece, Chandra, and Kari were crammed around the table with the extra chairs we'd added.

Five of the new warriors, plus Errol, Theron, Hydra, Belinda, Tia, Merlin, and Ryu, had gone outside to eat on the front porch, and Arrow, Echo, Sydney, Fury, Rex, Saphira, Tyson, Brenton, and Peter were sitting on the couch. Thorn and I sat on the ottoman facing the door, trying to appear relaxed, but it was so damn hard. We had a plan, but I worried something would go wrong. Something *always* went wrong.

Another knock sounded, and Peter's eyes widened, either from fear or hope. I doubted he'd be upset if Drake found us and came swooping in. That was why he needed to go.

"Edna, what did you expect us to do?" Theron asked more loudly than necessary so Peter could hear everything, too. Thorn set his plate of food down just as the door opened.

Edna's face was pink, her hands clenched at her sides. "It was *one* thing when it was just you all. I still wasn't thrilled with that, remember? You had your bags packed to leave. But now you've brought Drake's warriors here as well? There's only so much risk I'm willing to take!"

I placed my empty plate on the floor, and Thorn and I stood, needing to appear concerned and on edge.

Following our lead, Arrow placed his plate on the couch where he'd been sitting. He'd picked the side of the couch closest to the door and quickly pivoted around it to stand before Edna. He lifted his hands in surrender. "We aren't Drake's warriors. We turned against him when he killed the king—after the king decreed he wasn't the true heir to the throne."

"You're smart, but that doesn't change things." Edna karate-chopped the air. "The more of you here, the more mouths I have to feed and the greater the worry that you'll be spotted. I have my own thunder to think of. You all need to leave. I'm sorry, but Tia, Belinda, Merlin, Ryu, and Mindy are the only ones who can stay."

Chairs scraped against the floor in the kitchen. Then footsteps hurried toward us.

Vlad marched in. "Edna, look. We should've talked to you about it. We're sorry. You're right, that was inconsiderate. But there was a tip on Dragonnet about them, and they'd protected us at Theron's thunder when Drake and his warriors had been ready to capture us. We owed it to them to help."

"That's fine." Edna spread out her arms. "I'm all for acts of kindness. That's why I've let you stay here for as long as you have. But even kindness has a limit, and mine has been reached. You need to pack up and leave, *tonight.*"

"Mom, you can't be serious." Mindy pushed past Vlad and hurried into the living room. Her eyes were wide, and her mouth trembled. "You want to split me up from my *fated mate.* This has to be a sick joke. These people are part of our *family* now."

Edna flinched, her face twisting in agony. "I'm sorry, honey. Elliott can stay, too."

My stomach dropped. *We should've told those two.*

Brushing his arm against mine, Thorn responded, *They'll understand later. Their reaction is genuine.*

He was right, but seeing the hurt and anger on my brother's and his fated mate's faces tugged at me. I knew how I'd be feeling if this were happening to Thorn and me.

"Can you give us one more night to get our things together?" Thorn clasped his hands in front of his chest. "I understand you don't want us here, but just give us a night's rest, and we'll leave first thing in the morning."

"That's the right thing to do, Edna." Tia *tsk*ed from the front porch.

I didn't need to see the older lady to know she had a disapproving look on her face. That was one thing I loved about her. She didn't have a problem speaking her mind, similar to Elliott and Saphira. The only difference was she was old enough to use her age as an excuse, though we *all* knew better.

"Fine." Edna's jaw clenched. "But that's it. At dawn, you must go. No do-overs this time. And until then, you need to stay in the house unless it's to load your vehicles. I mean it."

Mindy stomped, then winced like she'd done it too forcefully and hurt her back. Her voice was laced with pain as she rasped, "I'm going with them. I can't ask Elliott to leave his sisters and father behind when people are *hunting* them."

"Babe, it'd be safer if you stayed—" Elliott started.

Mindy spun on her heels, her pupils slitting as she

waved a finger in his face and sneered, "Do *not* finish that sentence. I may have a bad back, but I'll find a way to kick your ass if you do. There is no way we're splitting up. It's you and me together, just like your sister and Thorn. Got it?"

He winked. "I may need you to take me to any room that will give us some privacy so you can show me *exactly* what you'd do to me, but you know, in a more fun way that results in us—"

"*Nope*," Eva said, uncharacteristically forcibly. "I'm stopping you right there. You're my *twin*, and there are some things I *never* want to hear."

"And I'm Mindy's mom." Edna leveled a dark gaze at him. "I know what fated mates do, and we don't need any visuals."

Peter huffed and rolled his eyes, unhappy with this situation. Frankly, I didn't care. I was glad he was the one on the short end of things, for once.

"Dawn. That's it," Edna said and hugged Mindy. "And you do what you have to do. I understand." She headed to her car.

"Well, she woke up on the wrong side of the bed," Tia muttered from outside, loudly enough for Edna to hear. "She usually keeps a level head, but she's gone off the wall."

"Hun," Ryu warned.

Belinda didn't hold back. "She can still hear you. You aren't as quiet as you think you are."

"Damn being old," Tia muttered, and Merlin chuckled.

The people on the front porch entered the house and shut the door behind them while everyone in the kitchen joined us in the living room. It was standing room only, and everyone was on edge.

Good. That was what we needed.

"What are we going to do?" Tyson asked from his spot between Saphira and Opal.

Thorn stood up straight, but the emotion coursing through the bond made my skin itch. Shame. "I know I was thinking we could fight Drake, but if we have nowhere to go, there is only one option—the one I thought was best from the very beginning. We need to leave the country. It'll be harder for him to search for us outside of the States, and yeah, we may have to hide, but it won't be as dangerous as staying here."

Now I had my part to play. "But he won't stop hunting us...ever." This was a conversation we'd had over and over, which was why we'd thought it would be believable if he pitched it.

"And my business is here." A vein in Peter's neck throbbed. "I've already been gone too long. I've got to get back. People count on me."

And we wanted to make Peter desperate.

"You mean *Drake* counts on you. He's your biggest client. Do I have to knock you out again?" Thorn snarled, turning the disgust he had with himself on Peter. "I've been itching to do that again for a while, now."

Vlad ran a hand through his hair. "I hate to say it, but we might need to leave until we can figure out a more permanent solution."

Reece whimpered and buried her face in Chandra's shirt. My heart hurt again for not letting everyone know.

"There's no way in hell I'm leaving the country." Arrow shook his head. "Besides, there aren't enough vehicles, so the warriors and I will go our separate way. It'll be best for all of us."

"What?" Saphira's jaw dropped. "You've got to be

kidding. Splitting up is the worst thing we can do. That's the worst excuse I've ever heard."

"Just say what you mean, man." Echo looked down his nose at us. "Arrow doesn't want to tell you the truth. The truth is, we don't want to be here. We were loyal to the *king*, and there's no way in hell Thorn can take the crown from Drake. He doesn't even have a place to sleep starting tomorrow night. The best thing we can do is cut our losses—and that's all of you."

A few of the other warriors nodded uncomfortably.

"But we saved you from Drake." Errol shook his head. "And now that we don't have shelter for you, you're bailing?"

Sydney shrugged. "We made a mistake, but putting more cards in with your losing hand will only worsen our problems."

"You guys are assholes." Elliott wrinkled his nose and spat on the floor.

Of course he would actually spit on the floor. That was my brother. In fairness, he was mad at the warriors and Edna, and this was *her* house.

"There's no point in fighting." It was still light outside, and Peter needed to feel comfortable enough to run. He was a coward and wouldn't leave in the dark, so we had to speed this along. "We all need to clean up and pack. We have to be out of here in less than twelve hours."

Everyone stood, looking at each other, then scattered to pack. The thing was, we *did* need to pack. We needed to leave as soon as possible so we could put as many miles between here and ourselves whenever Peter made it back to Drake.

I watched as Elliott and Eva headed upstairs, and Peter

slowly got off the couch to join them. He had a huge scowl on his face.

Thorn and I strolled into the hallway...and then his footsteps paused.

Arrow made his move and tapped Peter on the shoulder. This was the plan we were banking on—he was supposed to get Peter outside while we were all "distracted" and tell him to leave so Peter could tell Drake they'd aided him, hoping that Drake would partially forgive them.

But Peter ignored him, turning back toward the stairs as we turned left to head down the hallway. He wasn't going outside to talk to Arrow.

We needed him to go so we could tell the others what was really going on and he could "escape."

If he didn't leave now, our entire plan would be ruined.

CHAPTER TWENTY-TWO

MY BREATH LODGED as I tried to figure out what the hell to do. Thorn and I kept walking down the hallway because we *had* to. Otherwise, Peter would know we were watching.

"Hey," Arrow whispered.

He lowered his voice. It wasn't nearly as quiet as it needed to be for Thorn and me not to hear him; however, he had to be loud enough so Peter would with his human ears.

"What?" Peter snapped. "I've got to pack before my *son-in-law* knocks my ass out for, like, the tenth time."

Thorn's amusement wafted through our bond, and a giggle built in my chest. I swallowed to hold it down, afraid it might be too loud if the noise escaped.

I sort of wish I could go knock his ass out now, Thorn teased and tugged me to his chest. His sky blue irises lightened, almost matching the diamond flecks in the center. His eyes were my favorite thing about him—the color of the cloudless sky—with his plum silvery dragon wings being second, a color I favored when I painted the night sky. Both colors represented details I enjoyed most when painting any scene.

Our connection sprang to life, but I couldn't focus on it. Not with everything going on.

"Outside, *now*," Arrow whispered urgently. "You'll want to hear this."

"Fine." Peter scoffed. "But only for a minute."

Some tension eased from my body, but I wasn't sure I could trust my gut. What if he didn't leave?

When the front door shut, Thorn and I crept into the living room. Though Edna wasn't truly kicking us out, once Peter got loose, Drake would send his warriors here as quickly as possible. I wasn't foolish enough to think that Peter couldn't locate us. Yes, we were on a ton of land, but there was a mailbox with numbers in the front of the house. He could give them precise enough instructions to get here.

"They're busy. You should leave them," Arrow said on the porch outside the door.

He must have been blocking it so Peter couldn't come in.

"I *want* to." Peter huffed. "I've tried, but they caught me sneaking away, and I don't want to piss off that unstable jackass and have him punch me *again*."

My hands fisted. He didn't get to talk like that about Thorn...my *mate*. I reached for the doorknob, my dragon snarling in agreement, our anger blending as one, when Thorn caught my hand.

He beamed, the happiness lighting his face breathtaking. *I love this side of you. I mean...really happy Everly, aroused Everly, and possessive Everly are all three tied as top contenders, but we want him to leave. Remember?*

Next time, I will punch him. Hell, I was getting comfortable with a gun. Maybe I could shoot him in the leg. Nothing that would cause serious injury, just pain, which would only be a small piece of what he'd exposed me to during the past six years.

Let's add badass Everly to that list of top-four contenders. He waggled his brows. *Seriously, all versions of you are my favorite...except when you're mad at me. I don't like that version.*

I rolled my eyes. *Neither do I.* Just like I didn't like it when I hurt him. That was the worst feeling in the entire world.

"Go. Tell Drake that we're not on their team and that we let you go so you can tell him what's going on." Arrow's voice deepened. "Echo will help you get out of here while they're preoccupied with packing. The rest of us can distract them until he returns."

"Seriously?" Peter asked warily.

"How else are we going to get a message to Drake?" Sydney gritted out. "It's not like we can say, 'Hey, we made a mistake.' The only way we can apologize is to get someone he's open to trusting out of here to let him know we're turning against them *and* they have nowhere to go. If Drake's warriors rush here, they should be able to track them."

He paused, and my heart raced. I'd expected him to jump at the opportunity. What the *hell* was going on?

Peter huffed. "This could be a trap."

"We're splitting up from *them*." Rex snorted drily. "We made it clear we don't want to be on the losing side, but whatever. Suit yourself. Go back in like a good little human and get ready. I'm sure your company will be fine without you indefinitely."

I held my breath, waiting for his response. I'd thought

he'd be halfway down the road by now, but he was still standing on the porch.

Crap.

"*Fine.*" Peter's voice grew higher in excitement or fear... maybe a combination. He wasn't out of the woods yet. "I'll tell him. Just get me the hell out of here. They'll be looking for me any second. I can't even go to the bathroom without someone knocking on the door."

As if he had summoned Elliott and Eva, they headed down the stairs, their eyes wide. Their mates were following them, their faces blanched.

"Dad—" Elliott started, but I placed a finger to my lips.

I didn't want Peter to get startled and be too scared to leave. Elliott's brows furrowed as Eva scanned the living room.

"Let's go. You can't get your stuff or tell your kids good-bye." Echo's voice grew louder, as if he were reaching for the door, too.

Eva's head tilted back, her pupils slitting. A snarl came out of her throat, and smoke trickled from her nose. She was angry, and she'd shift if she didn't stop it.

Olive green scales peeked through her pale skin. We had no time. I ran to the threshold of the door and whispered loudly enough so they could hear, "This is what we want. Please, calm down."

"What?" she breathed, a puff of smoke hitting my face. "You *want* him to leave?"

I waved a hand in front of my face, dissipating the smoke. Thank goodness we'd cut all the fire alarms, or they'd be ringing. "Yes, the whole thing is staged."

I'd been worried about Elliott running his mouth when I should've been more concerned with Eva taking action. She was always quiet, making her easy to overlook, but her time as Drake's captive had changed her. She'd been training with vigor, and she'd become a woman of action.

Mom would've been just as proud as I was.

Sol took the last few steps and stood right behind Eva, scratching his head. He asked, "So...we aren't leaving?"

Thorn wrapped an arm around my waist, making it clear we were in this together. He said, "We have to go. Peter can help them find this place. Edna and the others are leaving as well, but the warriors are staying with us."

Sighing, Mindy's body sagged. "Oh, thank gods. I couldn't believe Mom would do that to you after the way you helped Emily and considering that Elliott and I would be split up."

"Unfortunately, you'll still have to choose." Thorn frowned. "We can't all go to the same place—there are too many of us—but you're more than welcome to stay with us if you prefer."

He didn't put pressure on them, and I understood why. Elliott was my brother, but I refused to be like Peter and not allow him to make his own choice. "Or if Elliott wants to leave with your family, that's fine, too. You two are fated, and being apart would be difficult."

"Uh..." Elliott gawked at Eva and me. "It's just, you two are family, and..."

Tears burned my eyes. Before all of this had gone down, he wouldn't have included me in the equation. Now he didn't want to be apart from Eva *and me*. Something finally clicked into place—we truly were family.

"It's fine," Mindy said. "Mom has her entire thunder to look after, and you all need as many people to help as possible. Besides, you guys are my family, too, and I'm learning how to defend myself in ways my body can handle, despite the wreck." Mindy leaned forward and kissed Elliott's cheek. "So don't worry. I won't try to talk you into splitting from our sisters."

Thorn squeezed my side, and a tear fell from my eye. I hadn't realized how badly I needed this moment.

The front door opened, and all the warriors except Echo headed inside. Thorn and I glanced over our shoulders as Fury nodded.

"Echo should be back in a few minutes. He's carrying Peter to the side road." Arrow bent down and grabbed the blankets he'd slept in. "The countdown is on."

"Mindy and Elliott, are you two packed?" Thorn took my hand and tugged me back toward the room we'd been sleeping in.

Elliott pursed his lips. "I've got to get the gaming system and a few other things. When we realized Dad never made it upstairs, we stopped what we were doing."

"Can you finish up and get Mindy to ask Tia, Belinda, Ryu, and Merlin to gather their things?" Thorn opened the door to the bedroom. "They're leaving, too."

Mindy turned back on her heels. "Sure can. They're in their room. I'll go tell them now."

This time, we all dispersed, getting ready to leave the place that had been home for the last few weeks.

Around eight the next morning, our group—minus the older dragon shifters, who'd stayed with Edna—rolled into the place we would call our new home.

We were all exhausted after heartfelt thank-yous and goodbyes and a ten-hour overnight drive. Sleeping in a loaded vehicle while fearing that someone might notice our tag had everyone on edge. We hadn't wanted to risk swapping out the vehicles but planned to do so as soon as we got settled.

Theron led the way in his oversized red truck, while I

rode in the SUV with Cassidy, Reece, Kari, Chandra, Echo, and Fury. The warriors sat in the middle row, with Echo behind my seat and the two women and Reece in the far back. We'd split up in the best way possible for fated-mate communication, so Thorn and I were riding separately again.

My dragon surged forward, making my skin crawl even more. Between retrieving the warriors and now this, we'd been split up a lot during the past twenty-four hours, with only a couple of hours at the house together in between but with everyone around. I needed alone time with him horribly, even if it was just cuddling, and I couldn't fathom how I'd managed to not try to run and escape to get back to him when I'd been separated from him at the château.

His dragon grumbled through our bond, and his voice popped into my head. *When we get there, I'll need you in my arms. It's been ages since I've touched you.*

I chuckled. I shouldn't have been surprised we were going through the same withdrawal. We were so in sync it wasn't even funny, and our connection grew more and more each day. *No one will be able to pry me away from you.*

We'd just passed through Steelville, a small Missouri town, and were following a stream into the woods. Steelville was quaint, with a small downtown area of brick buildings lining both sides of the main street, and I was learning that most dragon shifters preferred to live in these types of isolated places.

Several miles from the center of downtown, we turned onto a dirt road into the thickening trees. After a few more miles, we turned right onto another dirt road that took us closer to huge, rolling mountains. As we rounded a bend, three small cabins surrounding a pond came into view. Each cabin was identical, with hunter green siding that blended in with the trees and a lighter green porch with steps that led to a white wooden front door.

A man close to Thorn's age was leaning against the first one, and we pulled into that driveway. I knew better than to think we were staying with the thunder, since we couldn't risk our enemy seeing us if they dropped in.

We stopped in a line, and soon, each vehicle was unloading.

The man leaning against the stair rail, looking every inch the warrior, pushed off and strolled toward us. His dark auburn hair was styled upward, and his face was clean-shaven, revealing a sun-kissed complexion. His peridot eyes focused on Theron.

"Spike." Theron strolled over to the man and held out a hand.

The younger man took it. "You must be Theron."

"I am." Theron yawned and winced. "I'm so sorry. It's been a long night."

Thorn strode up to me and took my hand as he said, "Thank you for letting us stay here. I know it puts you out."

"If this helps you take down Drake after what he did to my dad, I'm all for it." Spike's jaw clenched. "He should still be in charge of this thunder—he was only three hundred years old—but Drake made sure that didn't happen. Not with his injured talon. Between my dad and the five older dragons that his warriors slaughtered, let's just say it's been a hell of a year for deaths at Drake's hands, and the pain is as fresh as if it had happened yesterday."

His anger and pain broke my heart. "I'm so sorry for what he did to you." Those words weren't enough, I knew. I still missed Mom so much; I'd give anything to hear her voice one more time...to smell her honeysuckle scent I was so damn close to forgetting.

"Me, too. But I'll tell you now, this is your home until you don't need it. We don't have injured or old dragons that need hiding anymore, and I knew one day we might need to help another thunder and shouldn't give up the land." He scanned us, taking in our various conditions. Then his attention landed on Reece as she limped to my other side. "Obviously, I made the right decision. You all need rest. I'll come back later when you're better able to talk, but I want you to know right here and now that my thunder will fight alongside you. We don't have huge numbers, only forty able bodies to fight, but we're yours."

Relief poured from Thorn. "That's forty more than we had just a minute ago. Thank you."

"I know you said you have twenty-seven. Each house will hold nine, but it'll be tight." He patted the wall. "There are two bedrooms in each—a queen bed in one and a double mattress bunk bed in the other. There's also a sofa in the living room that has a queen-size pull-out mattress. Other than that, there's a kitchen and one full bathroom." He gestured between the first and second cabin. "That way, there's a building with four showers and more restrooms. Dad built this place in case we had to take others in, so if there's an emergency, you can use those, too. I went ahead and pulled out the sofa beds in each house, and all the sheets are clean. I haven't been able to run to the store, but I'll do that before I come back later tonight so you'll have plenty to eat."

While on the run, I'd seen more kindness than I ever had before. All these people were taking us in and providing food and electricity. Though I wished Drake wasn't a threat, sometimes the horribleness in one person revealed the goodness in others. Despite Drake hunting us, these dragons had formed a network to support and take care of one another, and it was more beautiful than a painting could ever be.

"Thank you," Reece said softly as she took my hand.

"Doors are unlocked, with the key on the kitchen table." He strolled into the woods, heading toward a motorcycle leaning against a cypress tree. "You know how to get a hold of me if you need anything."

The groups formed pretty easily. The warriors wanted to make sure there were at least two in every house, so our cabin wound up consisting of Thorn, me, Reece, Chandra, Kari, Eva, Sol, Echo, and Fury. Vlad, Cassidy, Theron, Hydra, Saphira, Tyson, Rex, and Opal went to the center cabin, with the rest of the group heading to the third. We wanted to keep a mix of groups in each house so we could all get to know one another.

Owen and Asher took guard duty while the rest of us got some sleep. Like before, we would take shifts to keep watch. Not that we didn't trust Spike, but there was just no telling when a threat might fly overhead since people would be scouting the area for us.

Our cabin was smaller than I'd realized. We entered the living room, and the hide-a-bed was pulled out as promised, the end of the mattress reaching just in front of the white refrigerator. To the left was a stove, a small sink, and a large cabinet that served as the pantry, with a square table that sat four in front of it. To the right of the living room and across from the couch was a door that opened into a bathroom, and a door to the far right opened to one bedroom. I could see a queen-size bed with no other furniture inside. As I peered further left, I could see that the other door opened to the room with the bunk beds. This place was so small that everyone would hear every noise we made.

The group insisted that Thorn and I take the queen

room while Reece and the other two women took the couch, and the rest went to sleep in the bunk beds.

I crawled into the lumpy bed. Thorn shut the door and slipped in next to me, then pulled me into his arms. As the comforting buzz of our connection took over, he pressed a soft kiss on top of my head, and I fell quickly asleep.

A ringing noise went off, stirring me awake. I blinked my eyes open only to be blinded by the morning sun reflecting off the wall. We hadn't been asleep for long.

The ringing kept going, and Thorn mumbled as he pulled me back into his arms.

Thorn, a phone is going off. I sat up, pulling myself from his arms to get my bearings.

It's the burner. He reached under his pillow, removing it. There was a missed call.

As he opened the phone, a text message came through.

Theron's thunder is in trouble. Warriors on the way.

My heart leapt into my throat. Peter knew Theron had been talking to Wyvern, and we'd all forgotten. He must have reached Drake.

CHAPTER TWENTY-THREE

I READ THE TEXT MESSAGE, willing my exhausted brain to catch up. There was so much fog, I couldn't function. All I knew was that I needed to do something.

Finally, on the third read-through, I noted it was from Uther. Adrenaline pounded through my body, fully waking my brain.

Thorn tensed beside me before removing his arm from underneath me and jumping to his feet. He typed out something on the phone as I followed his lead.

Standing beside him, I glanced at his reply: **When did they leave?**

I opened the door to the living room and rushed past the sofa bed, trying not to wake the girls.

We didn't need to wait for Uther's reply. Either way, we needed to get to Theron quickly so he could contact Wyvern. I wanted to kick myself that we hadn't contemplated that Peter would tell Drake *everything*.

As we hurried out the front door, Kari groaned. "What's going on?"

Answering her would take precious time that Wyvern

and the others might not have. *Go. I'll be right behind you*, I connected to Thorn.

He hesitated, then nodded and jogged toward the next cabin over. I turned back to Kari, who was sitting on the bed, her face tense. In all the chaos, Chandra was awake as well, her attention locked on me. The two warriors were standing in the doorway, rifles in hand. I was thankful that Reece was still asleep. The last thing that sweet little girl needed was more turmoil.

"Do we need to get to the vehicles?" Kari tossed the covers off her legs.

"No." I lifted a hand. "Drake is on his way to attack another thunder, and we're sending word to them. We're fine here. Go back to sleep."

Chandra frowned. "Is there anything we can do?"

The reality of the situation sank in. "No, there's not. We all need our rest for training and what comes next. If something changes, I'll wake you and let you know."

Kari yawned. "Thank gods." She covered herself up and lay gently back on the bed, trying not to wake Reece.

"Do you want us to go with you?" Echo asked and stepped into the room, hitting the side of the table. He was huge and took up all the space between the pantry and the table.

"Stay here with them, please, in case something happens here." I scurried to the door and paused as I grabbed the handle. "I'm running next door."

Fury walked onto the porch with me. "I want to stay out here for a bit. I thought something was wrong, and I needed a moment to calm down before going back to bed."

I couldn't blame her. Most of the time lately, I was running on adrenaline. I had a feeling that whenever things calmed for us, I would crash for a month to catch up on sleep and everything I'd neglected physically.

Tapping into my dragon, I ran to the edge of the porch opposite the stairs and jumped over the railing. I dropped, my feet hitting the grass, and took off running.

The hairs on the nape of my neck rose as I considered what might happen next. The front door was open, and I could hear shuffling in the house.

"We've got to *go*," Saphira said loudly as I took the stairs two at a time. "They're going to hurt Wyvern!" The last word took on a hysterical edge.

"Saphira—" Thorn said slowly as I stepped into the doorway.

"No!" Saphira stood in front of the sofa bed, shoving Thorn into the kitchen table behind him. The table groaned across the wood floor and slammed the wall, shaking it. "You don't get to *Saphira* me. We're getting in the car and going *now*."

Vlad and Cassidy stood between the table and the stove. They grabbed the table, trying to hold it in place, blocking Rex and Opal from coming into the room. They were stuck at the door.

Grunting, Saphira grabbed Thorn's arms. Pain prickled through our fated-mate connection, and my dragon roared.

I barreled toward her, grabbed her arm, then yanked her away from my mate. Every cell in me was on fire, wanting to teach her a lesson, but the part that loved her like a sister surged forward and asked me how I'd feel if Thorn were in a similar situation.

I'd done many stupid things in the name of protecting him, and as much as I wanted to rip her head off for hurting my mate, she was going through the same thing trying to get to hers.

Her pupils were slitted, and her hands shook as she kept her hold on Thorn. I'd suspected that Wyvern was her mate by the way they responded to each other, and this confirmed it.

"Saphira, do *not* touch my mate like that again, or you won't be able to walk to the car," I snarled, my dragon leaking through. What I wanted to do to her was way worse than this, so I counted my blessings for the control I had.

Her irises blazed with anger. "It's easy for you to say when everyone you love is here and *safe*."

I'm fine, Thorn connected. *I promise. It's just the stress catching up to all of us. If you were in danger, I would do far worse than what she just did to me.*

With his reassurance and having him back on both feet, some of my anger ebbed. My throat constricted. "Saphira, you're like family to me, and so are Theron, Hydra, and Sol. Their thunder is important to me, just as much as everyone here."

She took in a shaky breath and unclenched her hands. I heard the faint sound of a phone ringing on the other end of a call Theron was making. "You're right. I'm sorry." She hung her head.

I pulled my attention away from Saphira to take in our surroundings. Just like Spike had said, this place was identical to ours, right down to the sheets. Tyson sat on the sofa bed, his hair messy and his mouth open. The vacant spot beside him smelled like Saphira, which meant she had probably opened the door to let Thorn in.

"Hello?" Wyvern's voice replaced the ringing.

My gaze settled on Theron and Hydra. They were standing in the doorway of the bedroom on the right with the queen bed.

"Gather the thunder and get the hell out of there,"

Theron barked, the skin around his eyes tight. "You've been compromised. They know you've been talking to me."

"What?" Wyvern asked in disbelief. "How? We've been so careful."

Rubbing a hand down his face, Theron grimaced. "Someone who's been around us got back to Drake, and I didn't realize he knew you and I were still in touch. I'm sorry. I should've figured that out."

Another phone alert went off, and Thorn glanced at the message. "It's Uther. They're leaving the château, but there are five warriors an hour closer, and they'll be flying. They need to grab some things and leave. He said the warriors are coming from the south, so if the thunder flies north, they should be able to get out undetected."

Theron sighed. "Your best bet is to grab what you need and be ready to leave in ten. I'll reach out and see if anyone else can take you in."

"Okay. I'll call you back soon." Wyvern hung up, and the room filled with silence.

Theron was already typing out a message on what had to be the network system, looking for another location that could provide aid.

We were putting so many thunders at risk, and I feared we might have used every resource available.

"When they leave, they need to separate into groups." Vlad tapped his fingers against his leg.

My dragon stirred, and an uneasy feeling coursed down my spine. I watched Saphira, noting how she was wringing her hands. That was a safer way to work out her concern rather than on my mate, so I stepped outside onto the porch. The wide-open space eased my dragon and me.

Joining me, Thorn led me to the side that overlooked

the pond. Now that we were out of there, more people were able to fit in the front room. We'd left the door open.

"That will make it harder for them to decide who to track." That was Rex. "They won't know who all's involved, and since Wyvern is the acting alpha while you're gone, they'll focus on him. They'll blame him for the breach, even if he didn't make contact."

This had to end. We had about eleven days to get a plan in place, including an army, before Drake officially took control of the dragons. We had to begin thinking offensively and get ahead of them.

Theron joined us on the front porch, his phone in his hands. "There are a few thunders around Memphis that can take in the majority of my people. They're about an hour's flight time apart, but they're close enough. We still need a place for about twenty of them."

I understood the predicament. Once shifted, they needed to know where to head. They couldn't risk stopping and someone seeing them along the way. It was best for them to fly high and stay away from planes and other dragons. "What about here?" Especially for Saphira, it would be best if Wyvern came here, but I didn't want to make that decision. That was Theron's place.

Leaning against the railing, Thorn tugged me so my back pressed against his chest. He wrapped his arms around my waist, the sizzle of his touch nearly taking my breath.

"We have an extra building with bathrooms. We can take turns sleeping outside, or we can make space on the floor," Thorn added.

"It would be nice to have Wyvern here so he can be part of the training and the upcoming attack." Theron stared out at the pond. "Drake will be hunting him since he's been in charge. It's not like we have a ton of options."

"It's settled." Thorn nodded. *And maybe Saphira will calm down.*

I mashed my lips together, trying not to smile. I glanced back inside to find Saphira sitting at the kitchen table with her head in her hands, looking worse than I'd ever seen her...which was saying something since she'd been Drake's prisoner for a while.

When Theron's phone rang, her head snapped up. As Theron told Wyvern everything we'd discussed, I headed to my friend and hugged her. I murmured, "Wyvern will be here soon."

Her breath caught, and she shook. "Thank gods."

I had to believe Theron's thunder would be all right. And there was one thing we could do to distract ourselves until they got here: train.

So that was exactly what Vlad, Tyson, Cassidy, Thorn, Saphira, Theron, Hydra, and I did as we waited for Wyvern and the others to arrive.

* * *

My body was slick with sweat as Cassidy and I sparred. We'd been out here for over three hours, and the hot Missouri sun was beating down on us.

Any time we took a break, restlessness would seep back in.

The others were slowly waking and joining us. The warriors were training Kari, Chandra, Saphira, and Errol on firearms across the pond so they wouldn't risk hitting anyone, while Vlad and Thorn taught Mindy, Eva, Elliott, and Tyson how to shoot with arrows about a hundred yards within the thick trees. The rest of us sparred. Part of the strategy we'd decided on was that we needed to use different tactics on the warriors: dragons, gunfire, arrows, daggers, and whatever else we could get our hands on. That would force them to split their response against different groups, based on how we were fighting, versus them employing a straight strategy across the board.

My stomach growled, eager for the pizzas we'd ordered to get here pronto, but I didn't dare take my eyes off Cassidy to search the road. I would hear the vehicle coming, anyway. Rex and Opal had left thirty minutes ago to get the food, and I was hoping they'd be back any minute.

Cassidy swung her fist at me, and I ducked, avoiding that blow, but her left fist swung upward and nailed me on the chin. My neck jerked back. Pain exploded through my jaw, and I stumbled a few steps.

A loud roar rang in my head, and it wasn't my dragon. It was Thorn's. His concern wafted through me, but I pushed it away.

The last time he'd distracted me, I'd gotten hurt, and I refused to take another blow like that. A groan slipped from me, but I pushed through the pain as I bounded over to Cassidy. She raised her hands, an arrogant smirk on her face, and I almost questioned my next move.

I faked a punch with my right arm, and she went to block it while keeping an eye on my other hand. Making sure my arms didn't move, I placed my weight on my left leg and kicked her in the stomach.

Her eyes widened, and she stumbled back several feet, more than I had. She hunched over and wrapped an arm around her stomach just as Thorn reached my side.

"Are you okay?" he asked, pulling me into his arms. His mesmerizing scent was even better with the musk of his sweat laced through it. My stomach clenched with need.

"I...think..." Cassidy gasped, then chuckled painfully. "She's more than fine."

My eyes flicked to Vlad, who was staring at Cassidy with concern.

"I'm sorry—" I started.

"No, it's my fault." She stood straight. "Vlad has been telling me to come out and train with you instead of cooking all the time. I didn't realize I was quite this rusty."

I moved my jaw from side to side, pain flaring back to life. "You got a good hit in yourself."

Thorn's hands gently touched my jaw as he examined it.

My chest swelled with how much I loved him. *I'm fine. I'll be healed in a few hours.*

He scowled. *That doesn't make me feel better.*

The sound of an engine purred, and my heart quickened. Food!

Should I be jealous that the sound of food arriving has your heart racing more than when I pulled you into my arms? he teased, his eyes lightening.

You have me warm in a whole different way I plan on showing you later, I connected and kissed him.

Theron's red truck appeared with Rex behind the steering wheel. We smiled and waved, but Rex didn't respond, and all Opal did was lift her hand and nod curtly.

When Thorn and I reached the vehicle, Rex climbed out and said, "We shouldn't have let Peter go."

What had my stepdad done now?

CHAPTER TWENTY-FOUR

THORN'S BODY TURNED RIGID, and the world shifted under my feet. With all the bad things that had happened to us, I thought I'd have been used to the anxiety, but I stumbled a step.

A large, warm hand grabbed my arm, anchoring me in more ways than one. Without Thorn, I wouldn't have been able to get through this with my sanity intact. He was my foundation...my home.

"What happened?" Thorn gritted.

"Breaking news came on." Rex smacked his lips like he'd tasted something bad.

Opal leaned against the hood of the truck and crossed her arms. "Next thing we knew, *Peter* was on the screen."

I leaned my head against Thorn's shoulder and winced from the pain that flashed through my jaw. I'd almost forgotten that Cassidy had hurt me—it didn't compare to the agony ripping through my heart. Although I knew Peter had never *loved* me, I'd hoped he wouldn't cause more problems for us, especially with the twins involved.

"He informed the world that he got away from his

kidnappers, but his beloved children and stepdaughter couldn't break free." Opal ran her fingers through the end of her ponytail. "A menacing man by the name of Thorn Wight still has them, and he needs everyone to watch for them since the police didn't find them at the last known place they were being held. Then they showed a recent photo of Thorn they'd somehow obtained."

Not only were Eva's, Elliott's, and my faces plastered all over news outlets for every human and supernatural to see, but Thorn's was, too. It was a smart strategy. "We were being cautious, anyway, so it doesn't change much."

"Other than Peter being a bigger annoyance, which isn't surprising. I only wish I'd punched him a few more times before he left." Thorn exhaled, and his neck corded. "If I didn't love Everly so much, I would've already killed him."

"Oh. *That's* why he's still alive." Rex opened the truck's back door. "We've been wondering. He's worthless. Though he did allude to you traveling north and potentially leaving the country, so at least he's splitting Drake's focus to a larger area, and fewer warriors will be concentrated close by."

The aroma of pizza drifting from the back seat had my stomach gurgling again. I could smell the sausage, pepperoni, and cheesy goodness that needed to be in my stomach *right now*. Although the news they'd revealed was less than stellar, it wasn't detrimental. If we got out of the more immediate danger, we'd deal with the kidnapping charge.

Right now, we were hidden, so Peter's public announcement didn't change our strategy. "For Eva's and Elliott's sakes, I don't want him dead. I know what it's like not to have a living parent—it sucks. Better to have a self-centered one than none at all. He does stuff for them...occasionally." Maybe not as much as I'd thought, but I didn't want Thorn or me to be the reason he died. Regardless of his spitefulness, he was their family.

"Hey, I'm not one to judge." Rex shrugged and reached into the back seat, snatching up ten pizza boxes. We'd put in a gigantic order for the twenty-seven of us, plus the twenty who would be here any second. One hundred pizzas should get us by until Spike brought more supplies.

We headed to the large clearing where everyone had been training. There was a sizable wire table with eight chairs. As we set out the food, the sound of wings beating overhead caught our attention.

Glancing skyward, I tapped into my dragon and spotted numerous dragons descending quickly toward us. My heartbeat picked up a notch. Though we knew Wyvern and the others were coming, I wasn't sure what they looked like in their dragon form, so they could be friends or enemies.

Thorn's trepidation washed over me, then disappeared as the group drew closer. He connected, *Theron, Hydra, and Sol aren't worried. It's them.*

My shoulders relaxed, and I noted the duffel bags hanging from their talons. Relieved that they were here, I turned my attention to organizing the pizzas into ten piles. Each of us would get one whole pizza, and I expected the men to eat at least half of another.

The twenty dragons landed within the tree line. They'd shift and join us soon. Saphira, Hydra, Theron, Sol, and Eva hurried to the thick stands of cypress and oak trees to wait on the new thunder while everyone else hurried to grab their food.

When everyone had gone through the line, Thorn and I grabbed a box each of our own and headed toward Theron and the others. We sat against a tree trunk just as Wyvern and his thunder members came out to join us.

As soon as Saphira saw him, she ran right into his arms. He picked her up and kissed her as if they'd always been together.

We watched as the new arrivals hugged their thunder members and met Eva. The group was mainly comprised of men and a few women who appeared to range in age from their twenties to fifties, all fit and muscular. They must have been selected to come here so they could fight alongside us, and that made me like Wyvern even more.

When the last people hugged, Thorn cleared his throat and smiled. "Please, come eat. Then it's time to discuss what we'll do for several days to prepare for the final battle with Drake while we heal as many injured dragons as possible."

THE NEXT NINE days blurred together. We were on the go nonstop, breaking only for sleep. The fated-mate couples completed their bonds, which wasn't surprising, given the looming threat. Why waste time not being connected when the end could be near, even if we didn't want to admit it?

Spike kept us informed about what was going on with dragon politics since we didn't have access to the internet. Drake appeared on the Dragonnet daily to inform the shifters that we were causing more chaos, trying to pit us against one another and reemphasizing that anyone helping traitors would face death. He didn't allude to the uprising, giving the illusion of control.

But there *was* dissent brewing. Thorn and I had been traveling nonstop, meeting shifters halfway between their thunders and where we were staying in various wooded areas while the warriors watched out for any threats while we were busy.

Thorn had healed over fifty dragon shifters, and word was spreading through the injured dragon network like wildfire. That number alone was three-quarters of the known healable injuries in the U.S. Additionally, he'd changed twenty humans who were in relationships with dragon shifters into dragons.

Even though Thorn couldn't heal dragons who had sustained injuries while in human form, I was able to help with rehab exercises to alleviate some ailments, such as back and neck injuries from car wrecks or other accidents. One thing I'd discovered while working with shifters who couldn't fully recover was that many of them had birth conditions from being born to a human whose body wasn't strong enough to birth them. The result was often permanent injury, if not dying along with the mother.

Errol had heard rumors that dragons were taking humans as mates because our numbers were dwindling, which was how Drake had gotten the idea of having a human breeder. But in every situation we'd found, the dragon shifter said they'd felt an undeniable tug toward the human—like Thorn and I had to each other.

Between ten birth conditions and twenty humans that Thorn had changed, our group had developed a theory. Since dragons were dying out, their destined mates were being born human, and that was why dragons were finding connections with humans.

The same people who had started off wary about helping Thorn and me now supported us. Thorn had shown them the great man he was, giving people hope that there could be a better future if he ruled the dragons.

Uther and the queen had been in constant touch. Since

Theron's and Edna's thunders had scattered and Drake's people had found their safe houses, they believed Peter's information was true. Five warriors had altered their search for us to the north, near the Canadian border, which made it easier for other dragon shifters to visit Thorn for healing, but even those five were heading home to protect Drake during the coronation.

We'd considered attacking ahead of time, but with only five warriors away, we'd determined it would be safer to keep training while Thorn and I helped as many dragon shifters as possible in case the future didn't pan out like we hoped.

Spike and nine of his thunder members were grilling hamburgers, steaks, pork chops, and hot dogs. Vlad, Thorn, Theron, Wyvern, Saphira, Errol, Cassidy, and I had pulled the table next to the grill Spike was manning and sat down to talk strategy.

Scooting his seat closer to mine, Thorn placed an arm around my shoulders despite the sweltering heat. Unease swirled through our connection, and I wanted to climb out of my skin.

Tomorrow morning, we'd make the ten-hour drive to the dragon lands. We planned to leave by eight in the morning so we'd have time to get acclimated before we moved on the château after nightfall. Dragons could see well at night, and it would be easier to cloak ourselves in darkness.

Vlad sighed beside Thorn. "Let's go over numbers."

I flinched. Everyone had been avoiding this part of the conversation. We all knew we would be greatly outnumbered.

Leaning into Thorn, I tried to focus on the sizzle of our bond and the comfort he provided.

"They'll have about three hundred warriors on guard at

the coronation." Errol sat across from me, the faint crow's feet around his eyes deepening. "There'll be a minimum of one hundred on guard already. I assume that half will be on guard tomorrow night with the coronation so close. We'll have a little time before the remaining warriors descend."

A lump formed in my throat, and I couldn't speak.

Thorn jumped in. "The queen told me there are five hundred warriors in total. Drake has been recruiting extensively, offering hefty signing bonuses for people who come work for him as long as they pass the screening."

Which wouldn't be hard. Dragons were fit, and there were over one hundred thousand of us in the U.S. That they'd found an additional two hundred who could reasonably step into warrior shoes wasn't that surprising.

Saphira wrinkled her nose. She took Wyvern's hand and looked at her father, then spat, "Oh, I'm sure there was more than cash involved. Drake likes to have control, so something more caused two hundred dragons to magically come on board less than three weeks after his father's death, especially with how his warriors have been getting around, checking on the thunders."

"They tried talking me into becoming one of them, but I told them no way." Wyvern's face twisted in disgust. "I told them we were already down a leader, and they let it go. I'm sure others weren't so lucky."

Theron tapped a finger on his lips. "Maybe because Uther was involved with your thunder."

"You're probably right. Another warrior approached me first, but Uther intervened after I made that comment."

I was thankful I'd been at the château to meet Uther. Not because of Drake or betraying Thorn but because we wouldn't have any inside allies if it hadn't been for Eva's and my time there.

Biting her bottom lip, Hydra leaned back in her chair and glanced at her mate beside her. "That's almost double the numbers we were expecting."

"What about our side?" Cassidy countered from across Hydra and next to Vlad. "We have fifty-six here, not counting Reece."

Reece had pouted about not being part of the fight, but she was six. We wouldn't risk bringing her with us, and Spike had offered for his thunder to take care of her.

"And twenty from my thunder, including me." Spike lifted his tongs at the grill a few feet away from Errol and me. "From what I'm hearing on the injured network, that's not all."

My heart stopped. "What do you mean?" To hear others that might be willing to fight alongside us was amazing, but we didn't want too many people to know our plan. Though I didn't doubt these people were loyal and wouldn't betray us, secrets had a way of snowballing when too many people were aware.

"Don't worry." Spike flipped a steak over. "They don't know the details. Those weren't mine to share. But in the network, people are asking how they can help Thorn secure the crown. They want Thorn and Everly as their king and queen. Not only do you two want to help everyone, but you also understand the lives we lead. That's something we've never had in any other king and queen."

To hear my name connected with Thorn's as if I could do the same amazing things as he could blew my mind. Thorn had changed lives, whereas I was just doing what I could to help. "He'll make an amazing king." I turned toward my mate, smiling so widely, my cheeks hurt.

"I never would've gotten here if it weren't for you," he

replied, raising my hand to his lips and kissing the top. "You're the real prize they're getting."

Saphira gagged and shook her head. "I thought that once I found my fated mate, they wouldn't gross me out any more. But looky there, I was wrong."

"Oh, stop it." Wyvern chuckled and kissed her cheek. "We're just as bad as they are."

Errol cleared his throat uncomfortably but grinned. "Is there anyone on the network who would be willing to join us and can hold their own?"

Spike shrugged. "A few, but I didn't say anything since we hadn't talked about it."

The more Spike hung around, the more I liked him. He didn't push his own agenda and said over and over that all dragons, regardless of age or ability, were strong in their own right. He wanted a king who understood that.

The rest of our group strolled out of the trees, where they'd been training with the warriors with bows, daggers, and guns. Arrow headed straight to our table and joined the conversation. Vlad quickly filled him in on what we'd discussed.

Arrow nodded. "We need numbers, but not too many unknown variables. It could cause chaos since they haven't trained with us. We also want to surprise Drake. Yes, he may have five hundred warriors, but a third of them won't want to harm anyone. A lot of the warriors don't like Drake and were there for the king. If Drake has forced people to join him, and if they see we're winning or making headway, they won't be out to kill, only to draw blood to cover their asses."

It made sense.

"We don't need to attack them at the château." Vlad rubbed his hands together. "We draw them out so Drake will be less protected and go in through the secret tunnel." Only the king had known of the passage, and with his untimely death, that secret was ours alone. "Wait," said Vlad, pausing with a frown. "I thought you had to wait for him to let you in last time."

"There's a hidden button he pushed when he came and got us. It's low to the ground and blends in with the cement —we would've never found it without him." Some of Thorn's tension eased. "If we can pull the warriors away and slip in via the bedroom undetected, it could work."

"That's our tentative plan, but you should talk to the queen tonight." Cassidy frowned. "See where Drake is staying and where she thinks he might go."

"Do you want me to call in some people to help us?" Spike lifted a brow as he removed the meat from the grill and put it on a large plate.

We glanced at one another, and finally, Thorn said, "Only those you fully trust and know are great fighters. We don't need weak fighters who will result in casualties just for numbers. Give brief details about a possible confrontation and tell them to gather near the royal dragon lands outside of Asheville."

Spike grinned. "I can do that." He glanced at the people working the other grills. "Is everyone finished cooking?"

He didn't need an answer because some were already carrying plates of food to the table, while a few others were removing the meat from the grill.

"Let's eat up." Spike beamed. "Get stuffed. We'll need the calories tomorrow."

"Thank gods!" Elliott groaned as he leaned against his mate. "I'm withering away over here."

Just like that, the tension was gone...at least while we were eating.

THE EVENING WAS ENJOYABLE, with all of us hanging around talking, knowing that tomorrow, everything would change for the better or worse. We took the moment to enjoy one another's presence. Elliott and Tyson complained about missing video games and how they had so much time to make up for, while the rest of us poked fun at one another over little things we'd learned from training.

Thorn and I were leaning against the trunk of a cypress, talking with Saphira, Wyvern, Eva, and Sol, when Spike sauntered over. He patted Thorn on the shoulder and slid what looked like a small box into his hand.

What's that? I asked, more curious about how Spike was trying to be sneaky.

Nothing. Thorn put whatever it was into his pocket with an evil smirk.

I arched a brow, not paying attention to the others. *Uh... are you keeping something from me?*

He laughed, his irises lightening. *Not at all. I just want to ask you something.*

I tilted my head back, my stomach squirming. *What's going on? Just ask.*

"Guys, I need time alone with Everly." Thorn took my hand and led me toward the woods.

Saphira called out, "Wyvern and I will need time for that, too, before the night's over."

I rolled my eyes. "We'll make sure to stay in the area. I don't want to chance smelling your brothel."

"You're just jealous you aren't the only two who smell that way now!" she shouted as we stepped into the thick woods.

I used to think she was horrible, but your brother has

taken over that spot, Thorn connected as we leisurely strolled away from the others. *Now I find her slightly amusing.*

Elliott's large personality has a way of making others' seem less...aggravating. I leaned against his arm and listened to raccoons stirring, now that the sky was darkening. *What's going on?*

Patience, he said, and nervousness trickled between us. My mouth dried.

We hadn't been nervous around each other since we'd formed our mate bond, so this was throwing major red flags around. Wariness weighed on my limbs, and I didn't push any longer. Part of me was afraid of what came next.

We came to a clearing where wildflowers bloomed around a grassy knoll. He turned toward me, taking a deep breath. "I want to apologize for something. Something that was stolen from us that I can't fix."

I took a step back, wanting to retreat, but the intensity of his stare froze me in place. I asked the question because I didn't have any other choice: "What do you mean?"

CHAPTER TWENTY-FIVE

THE NERVES FLOWING into me through our connection had my stomach in knots. Add in the way Thorn's heartbeat increased, and my pulse thundered in my ears.

The battle was tomorrow, but why did I feel as if it might be right now?

"Hey." He smiled sadly and touched my arm. "You're not the one who's supposed to be nervous."

I laughed humorlessly. "Kind of hard when I can sense everything you're going through. What's wrong? Whatever it is, we can figure it out together." I needed him to confide in me, not leave me in the dark. This was worse than fighting an enemy.

"Ugh, I'm doing this all wrong." He dropped his hands, rubbing his palms against his jeans. Then he removed the box from his pocket and got down on one knee right in front of me.

I couldn't breathe. The anxiety coursing through us turned into something else, but I wasn't sure what. My heart squeezed as if it'd tripled in size and was about to explode from my chest.

"I know we're mated and married." He beamed, but sadness darkened his eyes. "We're already as committed as any two people can be, by both human and dragon standards, but our marriage was forced...taken out of our control."

Guilt settled hard. We'd gotten married to keep Drake from claiming me as his wife according to dragon law. I'd been upset, not because I didn't want to be married to Thorn but because someone else had planned the wedding on their timetable. It wasn't something Thorn and I had planned and celebrated ourselves, and we hadn't had a chance to argue about what font to use on the invitation or what Eva and I would pick out as my dress. Someone else had selected everything to their own tastes, and it was nothing we would've selected. "It's fine. I'm not upset about it anymore. You aren't responsible for *any* of that."

"No, but that doesn't mean I don't want to fix what I can—because *you're* worth it." He huffed and settled the box in the palm of one hand. "*We're* worth it."

He opened the box, and I saw three rings nestled inside. One was a diamond engagement ring that was simple and elegant, everything that represented us. It appeared to be a two-carat square-cut diamond with tungsten bands wrapped around one another. The band on top was covered with small diamonds, making it the same width as the central diamond before narrowing into a normal-sized band. The other two rings matched each other, with one slightly smaller that had to be mine. Both bands were tungsten with etchings that resembled dragon scales.

"Thorn," I breathed, a sob lodging in my chest.

"Most dragons don't give each other engagement rings,

only wedding bands, but I wanted to do this for you. Though we'll take it off when we shift, in human form this feels right—to symbolize how we met but also to respect that for most of your life, you were human."

He removed the engagement ring, and I lifted my left hand so he could slip it on. Faint scales appeared as he slipped the ring on my finger, and a tear trickled down my cheek as I realized this ring was perfect for me. I connected, unable to speak, *I love it.*

Thank gods. He sighed and climbed back to his feet, removing the two bands and putting the box back into his pocket. "The wedding bands are to symbolize our dragon sides uniting as one."

My hands shook as he slipped the ring on.

"There. Perfect." He smiled as he came closer, the scales disappearing into his unblemished human skin, and he turned the ring to the side so I could see the engraving.

You Own Me

Unable to hold the sobs in any longer, I let go, my shoulders shaking and more tears trickling down my face. This moment was perfect, and even better, we were alone. No wedding could come close to this.

He'd moved to slip my wedding band on my finger when I croaked out, "Wait."

His alarm slammed into me, and his jaw clenched.

It was his turn to sweat, but only long enough for me to remove the engagement ring. I said, "The wedding band goes on first, then the engagement ring on top." He probably hadn't realized that since he was a dragon...and a man.

Relief flooded him, and he chuckled as he slid the wedding band onto my finger. "I was nervous there for a second."

I put the engagement ring back on, and the two rings

perfectly nestled together. "You shouldn't be. You own me, too. And now it's *my* turn." I snatched his band from him, and my body tingled when I saw he'd put the same engraving on his.

I slid the ring on his finger and connected, *I do.* Dragon law could go fuck itself, for all I cared. I wanted to claim him as mine the same way he'd claimed me at the château.

You don't know how badly I needed to hear you say that. He leaned his forehead against mine, pulling me into his arms. *Hell, I didn't even realize I needed it.*

That was the thing about us. We knew what the other person needed, even if we were clueless. *Thank you for this. This means so much to me, and it's more perfect than any wedding ever could be. You and me alone, together, and having this sacred moment is more precious than any ceremony.*

You deserve it all. Adoration filled his face as he gazed into my eyes. *Every day, I need you to know you're more important to me than anything else. Even if we wind up running the kingdom, your happiness and your safety will always be my priority. Maybe it shouldn't be that way, but I wouldn't change it for the world.*

It might be selfish, but I wouldn't, either. *I feel the same way about you. I will always be on your side...against all odds.*

Oh, I'm clear on that. You wouldn't still be here if that weren't the case. He ran his fingers through my hair. *Tomorrow, when we take the throne, I want it to be clear that we belong to each other in every way possible. That we're a package deal. I'm not just taking over as king, but we're leading together to help our people and make things right in this world.*

My body heated at his touch and his words. I didn't

know what I'd done to deserve Thorn, but I would never give him up. He valued me in all the ways that mattered: heart, body, soul, and mind. *I could be happy anywhere in the world as long as I'm next to you.*

He kissed me, the warmth of his love pouring into me. My tongue brushed his lips, eager to taste him. Groaning, he opened his mouth, and our tongues collided. He matched my every stroke, and his hand fisted the hair at the back of my neck, deepening our kiss.

But it wasn't enough.

I needed all of him.

Slipping my hand under his shirt, I traced the curves of his muscles. With each brush of my fingers, the sizzle between us increased as his abs constricted, driving me wild. The rest of the world disappeared, along with all the anxiety and drama. He was my drug, and I was addicted, needing him more than I'd ever needed anything in my life.

He tore his mouth from mine and kissed down my jawline and neck. I leaned my head back, giving him better access. He paused at the juncture of my throat and collarbone, right where my pulse pounded against my neck, grazing his teeth along it.

My dragon roared as my head spun. Though we'd already claimed each other, solidifying our bond, there was something so possessive in that action that I became a puddle in his arms. Mind fuzzy, I lowered my hands, fumbling to unfasten his jeans, *needing* to touch him.

He chuckled, low and throaty, feeling every ounce of my desperation. He moved me backward a few steps until the thick trunk of a tree pressed against my back, giving me balance.

Finally, I unbuttoned his pants and pushed them and

his boxers down. He sprang free, and I wrapped my hand around him.

Gods, you drive me crazy when you get like this, he purred as he leaned back and removed the shirt from my body.

I moaned in protest until he covered me again. His hand slipped around my back and unfastened my bra in one quick motion. He tossed it so it landed close to my shirt, and I moved my hand, stroking him.

He hissed, his body shivering. My dragon growled in approval as I slowed my pace to drive him wild.

He lowered his head, his mouth capturing my nipple as he grabbed the band of my elastic-waist shorts and pushed them and my panties down. His tongue rolled across my nipple, and I leaned my head back just as his fingers slipped between my legs, circling.

The sizzle of our connection and the way his mouth and hands worked my body had pleasure swirling through me. He teased and tormented me until my stomach clenched, and I quickened the pace of my hand on him, wanting to work him into a frenzy.

He groaned and opened his connection to me further. I reciprocated, and our emotions and sensations merged, becoming one. The friction built in me, bringing me to the edge. His fingers quickened, and ecstasy slammed into me and our bond. My body shook as he didn't slow, freezing me in place and holding me at the mercy of his touch.

When the pleasure ebbed, a more desperate hunger took its place. That wasn't all I needed.

Clutching his shirt, I spun around and slammed him against the tree. I didn't try to be careful, just ripped the shirt off him. As the material revealed his perfectly toned chest, my body demanded another release, but with him.

I climbed him, wrapping my legs around his waist, and he sank right into me.

"You own me, Everly," he whispered, a hand cupping my cheek as he moved inside me. "All of me. Forever."

Rocking against him, I held eye contact. "I love you so much it hurts at times, and I'm so thankful I'm a dragon so I can experience every single one of those emotions."

He pressed his hips into me and rolled, forcing me to lean back, but I wanted to watch him as we made love.

Taking our time, we enjoyed the slow buildup. We'd done it slowly before, but this was extra special. Not only had we claimed each other, but we had rings that signified our bond. A piece to carry with us even when we weren't beside each other.

With locked gazes, we moved in sync, the friction building in us. I wrapped my arms around his neck, and we pressed our foreheads together, keeping our eyes on each other the entire time.

One of his hands cupped my breast as the buildup promised to explode, and when he gently ran a finger over my nipple, the orgasm rocked me. My body shivered as pleasure flooded between us, and the area around his eyes tightened. His mouth opened as his release joined mine.

Our breaths mingled as we watched each other come undone. The pleasure was constant and never-ending. We stayed that way, breathless, until our pulses calmed.

Then he kissed me...and I was ready to go again.

IT WAS close to ten before we managed to stop touching each other. We'd had sex four more times, each time better than the last, but we had to get back and see what else our allies might have learned.

Begrudgingly, I put my clothes and shoes back on, and Thorn found his pants ten feet away in some brush. I wasn't sure how that had happened, but we'd had sex in a different position every time, so...yeah.

Thorn nodded toward the cabins, indicating he was ready to return, but all I could do was growl.

His brows furrowed. "What?"

"You're shirtless." I pouted. I didn't like the idea of anyone else—especially the women—seeing him like that.

Chuckling, he pulled me against his chest and kissed my forehead. "That's your fault. You ripped my shirt apart."

I extended my bottom lip out further, trying to prevent a laugh from escaping. It had been my fault after all. "Seemed like a good idea at the time...now I'm not so sure."

"Oh, it was a very, *very* good idea," he said as he nipped my bottom lip. "And sexy as hell. I like you that desperate."

My face flamed, but I didn't try to hide. Not with him. "Well, you, my dear, have a way of making me that way, and I'm pretty sure it won't ever change."

"Good." He sucked on my lip. "Because I need to work on my endurance. Five times just wasn't enough. I think one night, we need to see how many rounds we can go."

I moaned, already wanting to have sex again. "You'd better stop, or we'll be having another go right now."

His fingers dug into my hips. "Then let's—"

"You know we need to contact the queen," I interjected. If he finished that sentence, I would be naked again in seconds.

"Fine." He released me and took my hand instead. He connected, *Only because we need to make sure we're prepared for tomorrow so we can sex it up again.*

I laughed, knowing this moment of no stress would dissipate the closer we got back to camp. "Deal."

Hand in hand, we headed back, and when we reached the cabin grounds, everyone was still in the same area, but there were no smiles or laughter anymore, only serious and stern faces.

Saphira arched a brow. "You guys were gone longer than any of us, which is sad since you two were the first to leave." Then her eyes landed on my hand. "Oh, my gods. Did you exchange rings?"

Everyone turned to look at Thorn's and my hands, and Eva, Saphira, Cassidy, Hydra, Mindy, Kari, Chandra, and Reece hurried over and gushed. Normally, I wasn't one for attention, but in this instance, it didn't bother me. This was yet another way Thorn and I had claimed each other.

Let me go grab a shirt, Thorn connected as he sneaked away, happiness brightening his face.

When Thorn came back, we got serious.

Thorn informed us that the queen had answered. Drake had taken over the royal bedroom. She was staying in the bedroom all the way down the hall. Theron and Spike alerted us that they had reached out to the thunders they knew had fighting experience in the injured network to see if they would help. Many had said they'd try, but with such short notice, they weren't sure how many could come.

We'd done everything we could for tomorrow. The only thing left to do was get the best night of sleep possible.

We all went to bed, but even though I was cuddled in Thorn's strong, comforting arms, sleep eluded me.

I focused on closing my eyes...and enjoying his touch.

My heart hammered. We were walking through the woods toward the royal dragon lands, having parked about twenty miles from the edge of the property in a public area humans used.

There were a hundred of us. Spike and Theron had hoped for more, but we were running out of time, so they'd messaged their contacts, telling them where we were going in case more could come, though I wasn't hopeful. We had more than I'd expected, so I'd count that as a blessing.

Uther had said three hundred guards were watching the territory at all times and that Drake would be increasing that number by morning. Essentially, the closer to the coronation he got, the more guards he put on duty, but that was a good thing. That meant most of them wouldn't be well rested.

We'd split up to travel to avoid detection and had chosen a meeting place a mile outside of dragon lands. We needed to reach the edge of the property around midnight.

Thorn, Elliott, Mindy, Eva, Sol, Saphira, Tyson, Wyvern, Arrow, and I were traveling together. We walked in silence, trying not to rush. Drake's warriors would be watching for us in dragon form. Arrow had informed us that humans didn't come close to the dragon lands, likely deterred by the dragons' presence, but we had to be careful. These woods weren't technically part of the dragon lands.

As we neared our destination, trepidation surged through our group. Even when I thought about something else or concentrated on the feel of Thorn's hand in mine, my limbs grew heavier. We were heading into a fight against trained people who outnumbered us, but there wasn't a better option.

Though it'd been hours, it felt like we reached the meeting location in minutes. None of us dared to speak.

I laid my head against Thorn's chest, and his arms wrapped around me as we waited for our allies to arrive. Even Elliott didn't speak, his face pale, knowing what we were about to do. Not only that, but their father was likely with Drake.

Opal, Echo, and Fury would lead Kari, Chandra, Hydra, Errol, and Brenton. They'd take the right side of the château. Cassidy, Rex, Blaze, and Owen were in charge of the group that would attack from the left, which included Mindy, Eva, Sol, Elliott, and Tyson. Both groups would use a combination of bows and firearms. It would make it harder for the warriors to counter any of them since they'd have to deal with both bullets and arrows. The rest of us would attack down the center so they could follow and surround the château, hopefully catching Drake's warriors by surprise. We had daggers and would be fighting by hand or in dragon form. The few of us who'd trained regularly with firearms each carried a gun as well, including Vlad, Theron, Spike, a few others in his thunder, and me—just enough to throw Drake's warriors off balance.

Our warriors and Spike's group would be in dragon form to start, while the rest of us would stay in human form until we knew what we were up against. There was one hard rule: Thorn, Vlad, Theron, Saphira, Wyvern, and I would stay in human form to enter the château through the secret passage, which couldn't be done in beast form.

We got organized in silence since, this had all been agreed on before now.

Thorn and I took our position front and center. It had been a point of contention with the others, but we'd stood our ground. How could we expect any of them to participate in this fight if we weren't willing to lead the charge? It didn't seem ethical.

Are you ready? Thorn asked, taking my hand. We each held a dagger in our other hand. His anxiety mixed with mine, and I knew it had more to do with the possibility of me getting injured than the fight itself.

I needed to counter him with confidence. *Let's do this.*

Our group moved quickly and a lot less quietly. The dragons would know we were coming, so we needed to use surprise to our advantage.

We hurried onto the dragon lands, crossing the road that marked the territory. I could hear our people shifting into their dragons behind us, but from what I could tell, this area was clear.

Our group stood in the clearing, waiting for Drake's warriors. That was the plan—lure the warriors out so we could fight them here.

Time ticked by, and Vlad groaned. "They aren't coming," he sneered. "They're making us come to them so they have the upper hand."

My heart sank. Of course Drake wouldn't let his warriors leave his side. He wouldn't want to risk his life, knowing we'd be desperate to get to *him.* But he hadn't accounted for one thing. Something that would bring him to his knees.

I turned around and scanned the group. "Who has a phone I can use to connect to the Dragonnet? I have an idea."

CHAPTER TWENTY-SIX

DRAKE'S EGO was his ultimate weakness, and I planned on using it against him. He had enough advantages over us —we needed to force him to send the warriors here.

"I do." Spike held out his phone. "I'm already logged in."

What are you thinking? Thorn asked and squinted at me like he was trying to see inside my mind.

You're going live on Dragonnet to tell the world we're at the château, about to attack, and that you're going to be king as your father decreed moments before death. I turned to him and looked into his eyes. I'd just called the king his father.

He flinched but recovered quickly enough, so I continued, *Ramble, do whatever it takes, but stick with that story. Make Drake lose his shit and want to shut you up, even if that means the warriors leave him to come here.*

His eyes twinkled. *You're brilliant and downright scary. Remind me never to get on your bad side.*

You'd better not. I arched a brow, enjoying his teasing. *Or you'll have more at risk than losing the crown.*

Before taking the phone from Spike, I lifted a hand.

"This could put your whole thunder at risk. I want to make sure you've considered that."

"My presence here already does that," Spike countered, placing the phone in my hand. "It won't make a difference."

I took the phone, not having a rebuttal. That was true and one reason I didn't blame other dragon shifters for not showing up. If we lost, they, and potentially their thunders, would die for allying with us. They had just as much at stake as Thorn and I did.

I nodded because my throat was thick with too many emotions to express. These people believed in us, and all I could do was hope we didn't let them down. I reached for Mom's bracelet and our rings, none of which, of course, were there. They were all safely back at Spike's cabins so I wouldn't lose them during the battle. One day, I'd be able to wear all my precious jewelry without fearing I'd need to fight or shift.

Thorn took my hand and squeezed it comfortingly. *Let's do this together. If we make it through this, it'll be you and me leading our people.*

Part of me wanted to say no, that he was the one they needed to see, but it would infuriate Drake more if the woman he'd proclaimed as his was standing by his brother's side where she was always meant to be.

"Actually..." I handed the phone right back to Spike. "Will you record us?"

"You've got it." He lifted the phone. "Just tell me when you're ready. I'll use the king announcements hashtag to get the live stream on Drake's radar quickly."

"Use all you need." Thorn placed an arm around my waist, pulling me against his side.

We should've dressed differently for this, but we'd come here assuming the warriors would be eager to attack us. The possibility of us going live hadn't occurred to us, so we were wearing dirty jeans and black shirts to blend in with the shadows.

Even so, Thorn always held an air of power. His dragon was so damn strong, far stronger than Drake's, and that couldn't be ignored, even without being physically in Thorn's presence. His chiseled face was entrancing, and add in the light scruff that emphasized his strong features, and he was a highly arresting man...and all *mine*.

I, however, was a prime example of a hot mess. My hair was pulled into a low ponytail so it wouldn't get in my face when fighting, and I wore no makeup. Why would I for a war?

None of that mattered; this was something we had to do. Otherwise, we'd be walking into a slaughter.

Ready? Thorn connected and looked at me.

I was sure our height difference was comical, with him having almost two feet on me, but I loved how my head fit right at his chest. *As ready as I'll ever be.*

This was your idea. His chest shook. "All right, let's do this."

I inhaled to calm the stampede dancing on my heart. I'd been nervous going into battle, but not *this* badly, and I wasn't sure what that said about me.

"Rolling," Spike said as he pointed at us. All the others who'd followed us there moved back as if making sure they weren't in the frame. Those already in dragon form stayed on the road, waiting for instructions.

Sweat beaded on my forehead, and my heart pounded in my ears. Even deep breathing wasn't helping me.

Luckily, Thorn didn't miss a beat. "Most of you probably don't recognize me in my human form since my bro—" He stopped and connected, *I can't call him that.*

You only need to refer to King Arman and Queen Mira as your parents, I assured him. It didn't matter that he and Drake were related—it mattered that he was Arman and Mira's firstborn son. *And remind everyone that you're older.*

His unease ebbed. He cleared his throat. "Drake has played on repeat the time when I removed some of his warriors' dragons while desperate to save my *fated mate* from being forced to marry *him*." Anger roiled into our connection, and Thorn's breathing turned ragged.

I nestled my head against his arm to show the world I did so without being forced. I stepped in while Thorn recovered. "The only reason Drake wanted to *marry* me was that he knew Thorn and I were fated. He wanted Thorn to try to save me so he could capture and kill him. He wanted to put fear inside *you* so you would be easier to control."

Thorn found his voice again. "All of you thought I was dead. The truth is I went into hiding when I was six because of the fear that surrounded my powers. I stayed in hiding for the past twenty-one years, not bothering anyone until Drake had my adoptive parents kidnapped to force me to return." Thorn paused, letting the meaning of what he'd said settle over everyone. "I believe he did that because he knows I'm older, stronger, and the rightful heir to the dragon throne. I threatened his position."

A dragon roared miles away, from the direction of the château. The tension that had coiled in my stomach unraveled. Drake was watching. Now we had to get the warriors here.

"King Arman realized his error when he witnessed Thorn protecting a thunder that Drake was attacking," I continued. Now that we had Drake's attention, we needed to clinch it. "The king came to stop the attack and found us there. He realized Drake does not have the temperament to take over. He apologized to Thorn for allowing his fear to control him when it came to his own son, and he announced that Thorn was the rightful heir to the throne." I paused. "Drake killed his father on the spot."

More roars came from behind us, and the sound of wings flapping became louder.

The warriors were coming.

Thank gods. I hadn't been sure it would work.

"That's why my *mate* and I are here." Thorn gestured to our surroundings. "We're outside the royal dragon lands, ready to face my brother." An icy feeling of disgust swirled through our bond at that word, but he continued without missing a beat. "I'm here to fight for Everly's and my freedom, and for every single one of you. One of the last things my father said was for me to take the throne, and I will do everything in my power to respect that wish."

Though my back was turned to the approaching dragons, I knew the moment they arrived. There was a shift in the people behind Spike, who tore their gazes away from us and into the sky.

Vlad lifted a dagger as the dragons on our side flapped their wings and ascended.

It was time to fight.

"No matter what happens tonight"—Thorn's jaw clenched—"know that being different doesn't make anyone inferior. Protect one another, stay loyal, and remember to love one another."

Our dragons flew overhead, racing toward the oncoming warriors. Thorn and I turned to see what we were up against.

At least fifty dragons flew toward us. They hadn't bothered to come in human form, which meant more of our people needed to shift. Our arrows and bullets wouldn't severely injure them, although they would annoy them. We'd planned for this, knowing most of us would need to shift at some point.

Come on, Thorn connected to me, tugging me toward the woods. *Let's move.*

I glanced over my shoulder, searching for Vlad, Saphira, Wyvern, and Theron. They were supposed to come with us. Everywhere I looked, I saw humans shifting into dragons, blocking my view.

I can't find our team, I replied as I tried to keep up, despite glancing behind us.

Saphira and Vlad know where the rock is. Thorn kept pushing forward. *They'll be rushing there, the same as us.*

That was one thing we'd agreed on. It was inevitable that the groups would split up, and we were to move forward as planned. I hated the thought of only a handful of us running together in case of an attack, but we needed to take advantage of the smaller warrior numbers.

We jogged through the clearing as a burnt orange–scaled dragon swooped down, going for Thorn. My mate released my hand to battle the dragon, and I noticed four others peel away from the herd and fly toward us.

They'd wasted no time locating Thorn, which was why I'd wanted the others with us.

Get to the secret passage, Thorn connected, as the burnt orange dragon expelled flames at him.

Although I knew the flames wouldn't hurt him, acid churned in my stomach as this asshole went after my mate. *You thinking I'll leave makes me wonder how well you know me.*

With my right hand, I pulled my gun from its holster, and with my left, I gripped my dagger. I didn't hesitate; I aimed the gun at the burnt orange dragon's closer eye and fired. The bullet hit its mark, and the dragon's fire fizzled out immediately as its body dropped to the ground.

Our warriors had taught us three spots to aim for on a dragon: the eyes, the nose, and the small area where its jaw and neck connected. The eyes and nose were a dragon's most vulnerable points, and striking them would cause actual damage. The small area between their mouth and throat would sting but wouldn't take them down. Everywhere else would feel like a bug hitting them—annoying, but it wouldn't hurt.

Thorn moved closer to the dragon, his skin flushed from the flames, but the other four were almost upon us.

I'll take the navy and scarlet dragons. Swinging my gun toward the larger scarlet one, I shot at its nose. Thankfully, my aim was good, and the scarlet dragon let out a horrifying screech as it plummeted.

The oncoming attackers took note, and I knew without a doubt that I wouldn't have such an easy time taking them down.

Gunfire erupted behind us, along with the sound of arrows whistling through the air. As more wings flapped, my jaw clenched more tightly. Both sides were engaged, and we were officially at war.

I kept my eyes locked on the approaching navy dragon, who'd been joined by a mustard dragon and a violet dragon.

I lifted my gun, and the dragons zigzagged so I couldn't get a clear shot. They weaved around each other, making their pattern random. I didn't want to waste bullets and miss my mark, so I held my fire.

The violet dragon cawed—a sound I'd only heard from a bird before—and the three of them straightened and dropped.

All three targeted my mate as if I were of no consequence. I'd show them they shouldn't underestimate me.

Extending its talons, the violet dragon went for Thorn's shoulders, while the other two aimed for opposite sides of him with their huge mouths wide open. Drool dripped from their sharp, jagged teeth as if they were looking at their all-time favorite snack.

I focused on the navy dragon first.

Thorn's magic thrummed through our bond, and his hands glowed. He planned to strip the violet one of his dragon by grabbing its talons. He'd done it before.

Running away from him, I stretched out my arms, keeping them steady. I aimed for the navy dragon's soft spot near the throat, going with my gut and firing. The bullet went into the dragon's mouth and hit the back of its throat. Its mouth clamped shut, and it whimpered. Unlike the other two, it pulled away and flew back toward the château.

Pivoting, I was about to shoot the mustard dragon when a dark brown dragon hurtled in front of me a second before I pulled the trigger, steamrolling the violet dragon deep into the woods.

Thorn forward rolled, his body disappearing a second before the mustard dragon's teeth gnashed right where his torso had been.

That was too damn close for comfort.

An arrow whizzed across the clearing and lodged in that vulnerable spot near the mouth and throat of the mustard dragon. It threw its head back, roaring, but Thorn and I didn't waste time watching to see what would happen.

We took off running.

More dragons would be coming, which was what we wanted, but our people wouldn't last forever. We needed to get to the château, find Drake, and kill him.

As we reached the first stand of thick red cedar and oak trees, Thorn and I turned around.

The fight was brutal, despite our having greater numbers. Obviously, Drake's warriors were better trained, but so far, we were holding our own.

More are coming, Thorn connected, pulling me back to the present.

Now that he mentioned it, I could make out the sound of dragons flying this way. I forced myself to turn around and take off deeper into the woods, with Thorn keeping pace beside me.

Even in the woods, the dragons would sense us, but they wouldn't know who we were until they reached us. Hopefully, most would assume Thorn and I were with the others.

We picked up our pace, and for once, I didn't feel completely winded. All that training was paying off because it didn't use to take much for me to get a cramp in my side. My lungs filled easily, but I wouldn't celebrate my new fitness achievements until this was over.

Two dragons darted toward us from between the treetops. They must have peeled off from the main group to deal with us. The magenta dragon had its gaze on me, but it shifted its attention to Thorn, as did its lavender dragon friend. Why were they ignoring me? The likely reason had a chill running down my spine.

Drake didn't want me hurt. He still wanted me by his side.

Keep running, Thorn connected, taking my arm and pulling me along beside him. *The entrance is just up ahead.*

He was right. With two dragons chasing us, maybe no one else would join them. If we could drive them off, we could safely hide away.

I tapped into my dragon, and she pushed me forward.

In the distance, the hill with the fake rock entrance came into view, and I pushed harder. The sound of the wings was right behind us.

Spinning, I raised my gun and aimed at the dragon's nose, but as soon as I pulled the trigger, the dragon lifted higher, and the bullet hit its neck and bounced off. The dragon scoffed.

The magenta dragon turned its creepy white eyes on me, suddenly deciding to attack. It made a clucking noise, and then the lavender one focused on me as well.

They sped across the last remaining feet toward me, and Thorn snarled at my side. As I readied myself, he jumped in front of me.

No! He didn't have time to fight them off, either.

He was going to die.

CHAPTER TWENTY-SEVEN

THORN'S MAGIC flared through our connection as his hands glowed, but they were on us. He reached for the dragons, and they jerked back out of reach. They darted into the air, preparing to descend on him again.

Wheezing, I gripped my dagger, ready to cut an asshole, when the magenta dragon's head jerked toward where the rest of the fighters were.

The lavender one darted over Thorn's head toward me. I held my dagger close to my side so the dragon wouldn't see it. I would wait until the last possible second to reveal my hand after stumbling and making it think I was frozen in fear.

Unfortunately, I didn't have to act. This entire battle scared the shit out of me. There was so much more to lose than just our lives. The future of our people was at stake.

Thorn snarled as the dragon floated just out of reach of his white-glowing hands and dipped down, its talons extended toward me. Then I realized what was going on.

They were going to take me to Drake.

I'd rather die than be back at his side.

Get down, Thorn connected.

Gunfire pelted the magenta dragon, and rushing footsteps came closer. It had to be someone we were waiting on.

Sharp nails dug into my shoulders, and I swung my dagger, ignoring the agonizing pain. Thorn spun around, but the mark was made. The dragon flapped its wings, jerking me backward.

My dragon roared inside as I slammed my dagger into the top of the lavender dragon's talon. It shrieked but maintained its hold on me with its uninjured talons, lifting me higher. I drew my gun and leaned back, aiming for where the jaw connected with its neck. If it released me and I fell on my back, it might hurt, but I'd be out of its grip.

I fired, hitting the spot, and the dragon screeched.

The dragon and I dropped.

I closed my eyes, bracing for impact, but something hard slammed into me, and soon, I was hugged against a strong, masculine chest as someone ran with me in his arms.

Between the scent and the buzz, I knew without a doubt who my savior was—Thorn.

Something crashed, and over Thorn's shoulder, I saw a large lavender tail barreling toward us.

Watch— I started, but that was all I got out.

The tail slammed into Thorn. His upper body crashed on top of my left side, knocking the wind out of me. My lungs burned as I tried to suck in oxygen.

I'm sorry. He groaned as he rolled off me and onto his feet.

Not your fault, I replied as I sucked in a huge breath. *You caught me. It would've been worse if I'd hit the ground from the fall.*

The thrumming sensation in our bond flared, and his hands glowed as the lavender dragon huffed and whipped its tail at us again. Thorn raised his hands and caught it. Gripping the tail, he clenched his teeth and pulled hard on his magic. *Get out of the way in case I can't hold it for long.*

I climbed to my feet, ignoring the sharp pain in my ribs, and moved several feet back. The dragon whimpered as its body shrank. It was losing its strength, which meant Thorn wouldn't be struggling for much longer.

Glancing toward the magenta dragon, I noted Vlad, Theron, and Wyvern surrounding it with their daggers lifted. Saphira stood several feet away with her gun aimed at the dragon. The dragon hunkered down, blood pouring from one of its eyes.

Saphira had taken a shot. The dragon shook its head, whimpering as it flailed its legs and tail around to protect itself. If Saphira shot at it again, she'd have to aim close to Wyvern. She wouldn't chance hitting her mate.

I had a clear view of its nose, but I didn't want to chance Wyvern or Vlad getting in the way of a bullet, either.

I glanced at the lavender dragon. Its scales were fading to reveal a woman with long orange-red hair. It wouldn't be much longer until her dragon was completely gone, and she'd be permanently human.

I'm going to help the others, I informed Thorn, and took off with one target in mind.

Displeasure washed through our bond, but Thorn replied, *I'll be there in a moment.*

The magenta dragon shook its head from side to side and rolled around to keep Wyvern, Theron, and Vlad from reaching its face. Luckily for me, the eye nearer me was the bloody one, but it would sense me sneaking up on it.

I focused on moving swiftly but quietly. When I got within ten feet of the dragon, it sniffed, and I froze.

It jerked its head to the side so its good eye could see me while smoke trickled from its nose.

I had to move fast before he blasted me with fire. I lowered and tapped into my dragon, then ran toward it as quickly as I could. As soon as I was within striking distance, Thorn yelled, "Everly! No!"

The dragon opened its mouth, and flames encompassed me. My skin heated, and the fire swirled down my throat. Though it didn't feel as if I were being burned alive, the fire rubbed painfully against my skin. The closest sensation I could compare it to was when I was younger and a friend had gripped my arm with both hands and turned them in opposite directions. I hadn't expected it to be this painful— no wonder Thorn had yelled.

Gritting my teeth through the agony, I focused on putting one foot in front of the other. The closer I got to its mouth, the rawer my skin felt. The blast threatened to trip me backward, and I couldn't sense anything other than the flames crackling in my ears and the intense stench of brimstone.

When the roar of the fire and the scorching heat melded together, I had to trust I was at its mouth. I leapt, sweeping my dagger up, the flames burning under my arms, and swung down hard.

The flames vanished, and I was thankful for the fire-proof dragon spray that we'd soaked our clothes in earlier. The wind rushed in the opposite direction, toward the dragon. Then there was an agonized scream.

When the air stilled and my hair blew out of my face, I found that I'd stabbed the dragon's tongue. I yanked the dagger out and swung again to make sure the jackass stayed down for the count. I wouldn't let any of my friends get hurt if I could help it.

Everly, move, please. Thorn's magic swirled through our connection. *I'm taking his dragon, and I don't want to risk affecting you.*

We both knew that likely wouldn't happen. He hadn't been able to remove my dragon when he'd tried to take it back, but I didn't want to take a chance. Not anymore. I wanted to remain a dragon shifter and be with my mate as an equal in all ways.

Stumbling back, I inhaled heavily, the pain still affecting me.

Saphira ran to me and threw her arms around me. I winced from the discomfort.

"What's that for?" I asked through gritted teeth.

"I couldn't shoot at him, and that dragon was getting its bearings." She dropped her arms. "If it weren't for you, one of the guys would've gotten hurt. But..." She paused and put a finger in my face. "Don't ever do that shit again, or you'll be hurting worse than a burn right now. I love you."

"I love you, too, and I wanted to make sure no one got hurt." I glanced at the former lavender dragon, now a girl passed out cold on the ground. Her breathing and heart rate were steady. Her skin was pale with freckles all over her body, so I was certain that was her natural skin tone and not from the trauma.

"That's so freaking crazy to see in person," Wyvern rasped as he joined Saphira.

We needed to get into the tunnel. The magenta dragon was already halfway back into its human form. The scales disappeared, revealing a naked middle-aged man. His eye was still bloody in human form, and my stomach roiled. But he'd attacked us. We'd had to protect ourselves.

I'll take Saphira and Wyvern into the tunnel, I

informed Thorn. *Join us as soon as you can.* Vlad and Theron could keep an eye out until all three of them could come.

Sounds good, he answered, concentrating on his task.

I rushed over the slight rocky incline and went to the boulder that blocked the entrance to the tunnel. I reached around it, searching for a latch.

"Let me," Saphira said as she bent next to me. "I watched Vlad do it when we came to rescue you."

That hadn't been long ago, but it felt like ages. So much had changed between now and then, yet we were back here, right where Thorn's entire existence had started—at the royal château.

She dug her fingers into a small crack between the boulder and the one next to it and gritted her teeth. Something clicked, and when she removed her hand, her fingers were bleeding. She put them in her mouth before she dropped them. "There," she mumbled.

Wyvern growled and lifted the lid a little too roughly, as if to make the entrance pay for injuring his mate. I mashed my lips together, trying not to smile. That would only aggravate him further.

"Go on down." I gestured to the small makeshift ladder cut into the concrete. "I'll get the others."

Nodding, Saphira went down first, with Wyvern following right after.

I scanned the area to make sure no one else was approaching. Glancing at where Theron was standing, I saw the former magenta dragon in human form, lying very still on the ground.

The injuries he'd sustained had taken his life in human form.

Thorn's face was etched in agony. He knew that taking

the man's dragon had led him to that fate, and his regret swirled into me.

We've got to go, I connected, afraid to speak out loud in case others in dragon form were close enough to hear us.

That was enough to snap Thorn out of his daze, and he waved Theron and Vlad toward me. They didn't hesitate.

I kept watch as Theron went down the ladder, but then Vlad pointed to me, then Thorn and the hole. He wanted to go down last, and I wouldn't argue. We'd already had the door open for far too long.

I lowered myself and jumped to the bottom. When I landed, my feet stung, but nothing like the burn still lingering from the dragon's fire. Thorn followed suit, jumping down after me, and a shiver ran along my spine.

I hated being down here. The area was just big enough to walk into upright, about ten feet wide and twelve feet tall, but the cobwebs throughout had me wanting to get out of there. I could hear the rats scurrying away from our feet.

Lovely.

There was no light in the direction we were going, and it was already dark here since the sun had gone down. But that wasn't a problem, as we were all dragons. None of us spoke until Vlad had climbed halfway down the ladder and shut the door. When it snapped closed, dirt trickled down into Vlad's and Thorn's hair.

Part of me relaxed, while another side tensed even more. This was the beginning of the end. We'd made it here, but the next stop was inside the château, where we had to face Drake.

It wasn't that I feared him but more that I couldn't stand the power he had over us. He was cruel, smart, and unpredictable, and he made me feel downright icky. The memory of his onion breath when he'd forced a kiss on me would haunt my nightmares forever, and I hated that he would always have that over me.

"How's everything going with the others?" Saphira whispered as she leaned against Wyvern's arm.

Vlad and Theron were the only two who could tell us, since their mates had stayed behind.

"They're holding on, but only because more people showed up to fight." Vlad's jaw twitched. "We need to move quickly. The new dragons are mostly untrained, and there've been some deaths on our side." He nodded toward the other end of the tunnel.

Theron ran a hand through his hair. "From what Hydra can guess, about fifty more showed up with weapons."

Surprise filtered through Thorn. "Every person helps."

How I wished we could've found more people and trained them, but we'd been on borrowed time. I was thankful more had come to fight alongside us. "That's because they believe in *you*."

No, they believe in us. Thorn took my hand and tugged me to the front of the group, squeezing past Saphira and Wyvern.

We led the way toward the other end at a rigorous pace. The stagnant, dank air had us moving more slowly than normal, even though we were supernatural.

"This is creepy as hell but an effective secret weapon," Wyvern mumbled.

"No one but the king knew about it, so it's safe to assume we've used it more than anyone," Thorn answered without breaking his stride. *When we get there, I need you to promise you won't run into danger if something happens to me.*

My breath caught. *Only if you make the same promise to me.* I looked at him, slowing slightly, raising an eyebrow. *As long as you make that promise, I might consider returning the favor.* I smiled sweetly.

He scowled. *That's different. He wants to take you as his wife.*

And he wants to kill you.

Death is better than the future he wants for you. His jaw clenched as his pupils slitted.

He had me there, but that didn't mean I would agree to his asinine request. *Doesn't matter. Life without you would be agonizing, so I'd rather keep you alive.* Especially a life where he was gone and I was Drake's *wife.* The thought had a cold settling deep into my bones.

The end of the tunnel approached, and with each step we took, Thorn oozed more frustration. He didn't like that I wasn't agreeing, but he shouldn't have expected anything else.

Drake is focused on both of us. I slowed as we reached the end. *And we're a team, right? As long as we work together, he can't touch us. So stop with the overprotective fated-mate act because I want to be the same way. As long as we trust each other to do what's best for ourselves and our people, we'll know we did our best.* I wanted to assure him that everything would work out, but I didn't know that. I'd had the same belief when it came to Mom and her illness, and I'd seen how that had ended.

Of course I trust you. He pivoted and pulled me into his arms. *I just don't want anything to happen to you, but you're right. If either of us made that promise, it would be a lie.*

You own me, forever and always. This almost felt like a goodbye, but I had to say it because the future was so damn uncertain.

His determination soared between us. *You know I feel*

the same way, but I won't say it. This is not how our story ends. I refuse to believe it.

I heard Saphira and Wyvern kissing. We all knew what would happen next.

My skin sizzled from our touch, and Thorn kissed me. The kiss was full of promise...like he was forcing me to believe that everything would be okay.

I swept my tongue into his mouth, needing his minty taste to carry with me, and pulled away.

Vlad cleared his throat, and Theron, Saphira, Wyvern, Thorn, and I turned his way.

"Get your weapons ready." Vlad's entire body tensed. "There's no telling what's on the other side of that door."

The queen had confirmed that Drake was holed up in the royal bedroom. The windows had views of the front and the back of the house, which would make protecting him easy, but he didn't know about the secret passage in the wall.

"How many guards do you think he'll have there?" Theron held a dagger in one hand and a gun in another.

"Around five." Vlad held his weapons in his hands, too. "They'll be positioned everywhere, but we'll need to get him before other guards can get in the room. They'll be close by."

"All right." Wyvern held up his hands, ready to fight. "Let's get this done so we can save our people."

When Thorn noted we were ready to fight, he pushed the button...and the door slid open.

My heart dropped. Drake wasn't the only one surprised.

Thirty warriors turned toward us.

BOTH SIDES BLINKED at one another. We'd severely underestimated how many warriors Drake would have with him, but at least Uther, Jerry, and Gemma were part of the thirty. Hopefully, they wouldn't try to hurt us horribly...or at all. But a warning would've been nice.

The royal bedroom took up the entire side of the house, with three sections of windows that overlooked the backyard, the side yard, and the front. Five warriors were planted at each set of windows, leaving fifteen spread across the center of the room.

"Why didn't I know about that secret passageway?" Drake snarled as he rolled away from us across the gigantic gold-framed bed.

Move, Thorn commanded as he jumped into action, pushing two purple chairs out of our way. Vlad, Wyvern, and Theron were on his heels, springing into action.

Chaos ensued.

Ladon, Falkor, and Jessie hurried to surround Drake, their weapons at the ready. Falkor stood in front of Drake, not quite blocking him with his six-and-a-half-foot tall

MMA fighter frame. His cobalt irises focused on us, and his pupils slitted, revealing his dragon. "Warriors at the windows, stay put but fire at them if able. This could be a diversion. Everyone else, attack *him*." He gestured at my mate.

Nine warriors rushed us from all sides while Uther, Gemma, and Jerry paused near the dark cherrywood double doors.

Four warriors moved straight for Thorn, and the thrum of his magic took hold.

"Don't underestimate the others," Ladon shouted, and narrowed his ice-green eyes at my mate. He stood slightly behind Falkor and was smaller, but not by much.

"Do *not* severely harm the blonde," Jessie added, her short bleach-blonde bangs falling over her cinnamon-brown eyes.

One of the other warriors, a woman, hurried straight at me. She didn't pause as she swung a fist at my face. I ducked, and she hit only air. Grunting, she tried to correct her balance, but not before I slashed her neck with the dagger. Her eyes bulged as she clutched the wound, trying to stop the blood that oozed between her fingers.

My heart pinched in discomfort, but I didn't have time to acknowledge what I'd done.

I spun toward my mate in time to see him grip a warrior's arm. Thorn hadn't brought a gun, only a dagger, knowing he'd need to use his magic. Three other warriors attacked him from the front, back, and left. The one on his left sliced my mate's arm with a knife.

Thorn hissed as his dragon roared through our connection, and he released the man from his right hand, the magic sharply cutting off from inside. Whimpering, the warrior fell to the ground. I kicked him in the head as I jumped over his body to reach my mate. I aimed my gun and shot the warrior behind him in the chest.

The warrior fell back into the passageway from which we'd emerged, and I pivoted toward the warrior in front while Thorn spun around to fight the one who had cut his arm.

Another weapon fired, and Thorn dropped to the floor as a tranq dart whizzed over his head and hit the warrior I'd been about to face.

"Uther, Gemma, and Jerry!" Falkor shouted. "What the hell are you doing? Attack!"

Now that my opponent was down, I spun on my heels to find that the five warriors diagonal from us had turned in our direction, their guns raised. I clenched my teeth when I saw Uther, Gemma, and Jerry fire their weapons at the same five who were focused on us.

The other two warriors jerked toward the trio. They swung their weapons at them as the man on the outer edge screamed in anger or fear.

I fired my weapon at the screamer. My bullet landed right in the center of his eyebrows, and his body dropped.

As I prepared to take out the second one, sharp pain exploded in my right shoulder. I pushed through it, pulling the trigger, needing to help Uther and the others. All I managed to do was strike the second warrior's arm.

My shoulder felt as if it were covered with flames, and I glanced down at my injury. Luckily, it was a bullet wound, not a tranq. I'd be fine, but blood soaked my shirt.

"Do *not* hurt her," Drake screamed, and smacked Falkor in the back of the head. "I need her well so we can marry tomorrow during the coronation."

Falkor flinched, his body turning rigid. "She's killing warriors! I had to do something."

"Tranq them!" Drake spat.

Crazily enough, I was Drake's weakness...or rather, his obsession to have me was. Vlad rushed past me, focused on the warriors at the windows on the left, overlooking the front of the château, now that our warrior allies and I had eliminated the ones watching the backyard. Uther and the others raced to help him. We had thirteen warriors against our eight. Way better odds.

Falkor lifted a radio. "We need backup, *now*. In the king's chambers."

My heart dropped as Vlad said, "End this."

Out of the corner of my eye, I noticed Theron, Saphira, and Wyvern charging at the warriors at the windows past the bed.

We need to go for Jessie, Falkor, and Ladon, I connected with Thorn.

Just as I said that, all three of them lifted their tranq rifles at us.

Take cover under the mattress, Thorn connected.

Following him, I leapt to the side of the mattress and ducked, evading two darts flying over our heads by mere inches. If we hadn't moved, we'd have been knocked out cold in seconds.

"Shit, my gun is jammed," Jessie croaked, her fear leaking through.

"Stay with Drake," Falkor commanded as his footsteps stomped our way.

Then the bed dipped. The two of them were coming at us from both sides since the bed frame abutted the light gray wall.

Roll under the bed and hide. You're hurt. I'll take the two of them, Thorn connected, his own pain, stress, and anxiety swirling through the connection.

You are, too. You were stabbed, remember? Pretty much the same thing, I replied, refusing to budge. Since I was on the side further from Falkor, there was only one thing that made sense. *I'll take Ladon.*

Before he could argue, I jumped to my feet, Thorn's displeasure washing over me. Ladon was at the edge of the bed, and he startled back at my sudden appearance. I swung my dagger and stabbed him in the shoulder. Somehow, I hit the same area on him as the bullet had hit me, so we had almost identical injuries.

He grunted and fell backward as I heard Thorn make his move. As I leapt to the edge of the mattress, Ladon was getting back up. My dagger was still stuck in his shoulder, and I didn't have time to aim before shooting, so I reached up and gripped the bronze chandelier hanging over the bed. As soon as my body weight pulled on my shoulder, sharp, throbbing pain blossomed. My vision darkened at the edges, but I tapped into my dragon, using her strength to swing my feet into Ladon's chest. I made sure my foot hit the dagger protruding from his shoulder so it went deeper.

He stumbled backward, his feet tangling in the white comforter, and fell off the side in front of Jessie and Drake.

The fated-mate bond thrummed to life, informing me that Thorn was using his magic, which gave me some confidence.

I dropped onto the mattress, ready to take on Jessie and Ladon, when the sound of more guards approaching turned my blood cold.

Backup was here, and we hadn't secured Drake.

Grunts, gunfire, and punches echoed around me, but I couldn't lose focus. Not when so much was at stake. I dropped in front of Jessie, my gun aimed at her, but someone caught my legs. I crashed onto my stomach and looked down to see Ladon with his arms wrapped around me.

Drake laughed maniacally as Jessie swiped the gun from me and dragged me to my feet. She was stronger than me and easily forced my hands behind me, my shoulder smarting the entire time. A whimper escaped, despite my best efforts, and my vision blurred. *Jessie has me.*

I blinked, trying to clear my vision, and took in the room. Thorn had Falkor, his hands glowing brightly as the man tried to get away from him. Saphira and Wyvern had been tranqed. She was a lump on the ground, with Wyvern lying over her, protecting her from more darts. Theron had been detained by two warriors gripping his arms, while Vlad, Uther, and Gemma were facing the door. Jerry had been tranqed, along with the other five warriors they'd been fighting.

Releasing Falkor, Thorn turned to me, not worrying about the door. He growled, "Release my *mate.*"

"Don't worry." Drake sneered. "She won't be your mate much longer." He pointed at Thorn. "Someone shoot him."

The bedroom doors burst open as Ladon clambered to his feet. Queen Mira entered the room with ten warriors following close behind her. Her striking baby blue eyes were devoid of the kindness that usually filled them, and her dark chocolate hair had been pulled haphazardly into a bun. She wore a long silk gown, but that was the only semblance of the queen I'd met not too long ago. Her gaze landed on Thorn as Ladon yanked the dagger from his shoulder, then lifted a gun with his uninjured arm. He stood just a foot away from me.

"Do *not* shoot him," Mira commanded, her jaw clenched and anger shining through.

Drake growled, "Get out of here. You have no business here."

"*I* am the *queen*, and you're still a *prince*." Queen Mira lifted her chin in challenge. "Until you're crowned, I'm in charge."

The ten warriors behind her charged into the room, two of them heading to Theron, their guns aimed at the men who'd detained him.

"Ladon, shoot him," Drake seethed. "Don't listen to the mumblings of a stupid *woman*."

That wouldn't happen. *Thorn, get ready.*

Everly, don't do— he started, but it was too late.

I leaned back, my shoulder searing in pain, and kicked Ladon in the side. Thorn roared as he vaulted over the mattress and landed right in front of Ladon, his magic churning as he ripped Ladon's dragon from his body.

Jessie released her hold on me, and I stumbled back and slammed into the wall. I hunched forward, ready to lunge at her as she attacked my mate...but something else happened.

Jessie turned her gun on Drake.

I inhaled sharply, trying to make sense of it. She was loyal to Drake. She was one with Ladon and Falkor. Why would she be helping us now? There had to be a catch.

"What are you doing?" Drake spat. "Take out the *abomination*!"

"No," she gritted. "He's not an abomination. *You* are. You killed the king, and he denounced you as the heir to the throne."

"You work for *me*." Drake smacked his chest, his face reddening. "Turn that gun on Thorn, or I'll make you pay."

Stepping forward, Uther straightened. "Your threats won't work on us any longer."

"What about your little girl?" Drake snarled, evilness etched all over his face and darkening his eyes.

Thorn dropped Ladon, and our connection went back to normal. "You won't harm her. She's hidden, and you won't ever find her."

Drake's nostrils flared even more. "It doesn't matter. I have others I'll take. People will *obey* me."

"Have you always been this way, and Arman and I were too blind to see who you really are?" Queen Mira's bottom lip quivered. "What have we done to instill so much hate in you? If anyone should be like this, it's Thorn, not you."

The hurt wafting from Thorn was worse than my bullet wound. I stumbled to him and took his hand, pushing my love toward him.

"Because I lived in his shadow," Drake hissed. "Everything you did was because of *him*. Even when I made you proud, there was sadness behind your eyes. I'm tired of it, and I deserve to *lead* and be the best king ever known!" Drake's chest heaved, and then he struck Jessie and reached for her gun.

The warrior ducked, countering the move, and when she rose again, she elbowed him in the nose. The pop of bone had Drake gripping his face, and Thorn released my hand, dodged Jessie, and launched himself on top of Drake.

Falling on his back, Drake moaned as Thorn straddled his waist and punched him in the face.

"You will *not* touch my *mate* ever again!" Thorn punched him in a rhythm. "You will *stop* calling her your *wife*!" And he jabbed again. "And *this* is for *kissing her*." With each statement, Thorn hit Drake again and again. "And *this* is for looking at her *naked*."

"Thorn, don't!" Queen Mira cried. She hurried to them and dropped to her knees. "Let him go."

The white-hot rage crackling through my mate was unwavering. All his anger and resentment was coming to a head, and Drake deserved every bit of it. Looking around, I noticed every warrior, along with Theron and Vlad, watching the scene unfold.

I cleared my throat. We needed everyone to get out of here and, more importantly, for the battle outside to end. "Someone tell the warriors outside to halt their attack! Drake has been captured and is no longer in charge."

One of the warriors who'd held Theron down glowered. "I don't have to listen to you."

Theron spun around, kicked the warrior in the face, and gritted, "Yes, you do."

"I'll handle it," Uther said.

I nodded, and he hurried out the door. I turned around and noticed how bloody Drake's face was. If Thorn kept it up, his brother would die.

Queen Mira continued to cry. She'd lost so much, and even though Drake was horrible, she didn't want to lose another son.

Knowing I was the only one who could get through to him, I squatted beside Thorn and touched his arm, hoping that it would be enough to make him pause. *There is a fate for him worse than death.*

He stilled, and his eyes turned to me. I sucked in a startled breath.

They weren't the eyes I was familiar with. They were dark, angry, and malicious...nothing like those of my mate... my husband.

Then I realized I couldn't just *try* to talk him into stopping. I had to succeed, or this might change him forever.

CHAPTER TWENTY-NINE

A COLD CHILL ran down my spine as the significance of this moment hit me. I pushed all my love and support toward Thorn, trying to break through to him the only way I knew how.

We shouldn't kill him.

His nostrils flared, and he shook his head. *That's not an option.* He turned to punch Drake in the face again, and instinct took over.

I leaned over Drake, blocking his face from Thorn's view with my own.

What are you doing? Thorn snarled, his chest heaving. He dropped his hand, and some of that anger faded into concern. *I could've hurt you.*

But I knew you wouldn't. I squeezed his arm softly, needing to take advantage of the moment. *If you kill him, it's the easy way out for him. You need to show our people that you have mercy but not forgiveness. That'll make you different from your grandfather and dad.*

Queen Mira sniffled but didn't say anything. I

suspected she knew what I was doing, especially given the way I was protecting Drake.

What do you mean? The cold, distant part of him remained. He could snap in a second. *He deserves to die. After everything he did to you...to us...*

I know he does. I understood his reasoning, but that didn't make it right. *But he's out for the count and not attacking. Killing him would be no different from what he did to the injured. You'd be killing someone who can't protect himself. The warriors were different. They were attacking us.*

So we just...put him in prison and risk him escaping? Thorn's neck corded. *No fucking way.*

No, you take his dragon. With my free hand, I lifted his chin. *Then we use the story he and Peter gave the media about you kidnapping us. We blame them, find evidence that he has blackmailed and threatened people and killed your father, and expose my stepdad's fraud, landing them both in prison...human prison. Two birds, one stone...kind of. But it takes care of the accusation of you kidnapping us. There's no doubt Eva and Elliott will agree to correct that.*

He sucked in a breath, and his forehead creased.

What's a fate worse than death for Drake? I pressed. *He was determined to be the strongest dragon king imaginable and kill you because you're the rightful heir. That's been his whole goal. If we do this, he'll live as a human in human jail while you and I rule over our people. That's his own personal hell.*

There was silence for a moment, but when his irises lightened closer to their normal sky blue color, my lungs began working again. He was coming back to me.

For the record, I want to kill him. Thorn's jaw twitched. *I want him to die painfully, slowly, and to know it was by my hands. It scares the shit out of me that the desire is so strong. I'm not sure what to think of myself or if I deserve you.*

I know you want to. I do, too. I brushed the hair from his forehead and kissed the center of it. *He's an asshole and a complete waste of air. But we can't let him control us and make us into different people. That would give him power over us. Let's change it so he's miserable and hates himself for the rest of his very short existence. And this just proves that you* do *deserve me. You're this angry because of what he did to me, but you're listening to me when it's the last thing you want to do. If anything, I'm not worthy of you.*

He cupped my cheeks with both hands and kissed me. The all-consuming hate ebbed out of our bond as he connected, *I will always listen to you. You own me.* He pulled back, a twinkle in his now normal, breathtaking eyes. *And you're totally evil. You know that?*

I laughed, feeling completely carefree despite where we were. *Oh, I know. That's one reason you love me.* I straightened and glanced down at Drake.

His face was almost unrecognizable. One of his eyes was swollen shut, while the rest of his face was cut up and bloody. His white button-down shirt had blood spatter all over it, and there was nothing regal about him. He groaned in agony, and he turned his head and winced.

"Thorn?" Queen Mira's voice quivered.

Thorn and I knew what she was asking.

"I won't kill him, even though I *want* to." Thorn glanced at his cut-up knuckles. "But I will be taking his dragon and calling the police. My *mate* is right. He deserves to live out the rest of his life watching Everly and me lead and doing the opposite of what he intended."

"That's fair." The queen nodded and wiped the tears from her face. "Just as long as he lives."

"No," Drake groaned, his unswollen eye opening. "Kill me."

Thorn laughed humorlessly. *You were right, as always. He'd rather die.* Then he turned his head to Queen Mira and asked, "Where was that concern for me when I was six and hadn't done any intentional harm?"

My heart squeezed. "You gave the king his dragon back. It wasn't even a mistake since you didn't know what you were doing." I wouldn't allow her to accuse him of *any* wrongdoing, intended or otherwise, and I was glad Thorn was calling her out on her behavior.

Her mouth dropped open, and then she closed it, swallowing hard. "It was a mistake. Losing you changed me in ways you'll never know."

That I could believe. Thorn was about to experience the same thing. The hurt emanating from him nearly shattered my heart, but now wasn't the time to dwell on it. It was time to step up. *Babe, we need to clean this mess up and check on the others.*

He tore his gaze from his mother and focused on me, our love flowing through the bond and soothing his pain a little.

He held his hands open, and the thrum vibrated through our bond as his palms glowed. He placed his hands on Drake's chest, and the sensation grew stronger, indicating he was pulling the magic from Drake's body.

A few of the warriors behind us gasped. Watching his hands glow had taken me off guard the first time, too, but not anymore. That was part of him, and eventually, no one would fear it.

Drake tried to push Thorn's hands away, but with the state he was in, he barely had the strength to move. Each time Drake did, he flinched, but with Thorn's magic pulling away his dragon, he must have gotten a second wind because he shifted onto his elbows and tried to yank his bottom half out from under Thorn.

My mate didn't budge an inch.

Trusting he had things under control, I stood and assessed the room. All eyes were on Drake and Thorn, but Uther had left to handle the fight outside.

"If anyone has reservations about following Thorn, you need to leave and find another place to live and work." One by one, I locked eyes with everyone in the room.

"What?" one of the men holding on to Theron asked. "You won't imprison us or threaten someone we love?"

The thrumming stopped, and Drake whimpered. Thorn stood and took the spot next to me, and I glanced over my shoulder to find Drake passed out.

Good.

"That isn't how my queen and I will rule." Thorn placed an arm around my waist as he addressed the room. "There will be laws that must be obeyed, but we will not blackmail or force anyone to work for us. However, if you maliciously break the rules or cause problems, we will lock you in prison without hesitation."

"But there will be repercussions if we leave," the same warrior insisted.

My throat constricted, and I leaned against Thorn for support. My shoulder ached from the bullet wound now that my adrenaline was wearing off, but it didn't compare to what all these people had gone through...what we *all* had been through due to Drake.

Thorn's hand tightened. *We need to take care of that. If the bullet is in there, it needs to be removed.*

I know. I'm a premed student, remember? I tried to

tease, but the joke fell flat. The pain hadn't conveyed my humor at all. *Just reassure them, and let's get out of here.*

He nodded. "If you choose to leave your position as a warrior, there will be no repercussions. I want only people who are happy to protect my mate and me and who will find the position rewarding to stay on. There's no catch, but if you'll excuse me, I need to take care of my mate. She's injured and losing blood." He gestured at my shoulder, where my shirt was crimson.

"We'll handle it from here," Vlad assured Thorn. "And we'll find a room for Saphira and Wyvern until they wake."

For a moment, I expected the warriors to band together and prevent us from leaving, but they parted for us, and each bowed as we left.

I BLINKED A FEW TIMES, trying to believe what I saw in the mirror. It was ten minutes before the coronation, and two staff members had finished helping me into my dress, styled my hair, and done my makeup.

Like our wedding, it was a complete makeover. Unlike my wedding dress, however, this dress was elegant but simple and far more my style. It was a flattering white, strapless dress with a sweetheart neckline and a gold wrap at my waist that blended with the gold-fitted skirt that brushed the marble tile. Silvery glitter dusted the gold, giving the fabric a regal sheen.

My blonde hair fell in gentle waves that complemented my features, and the makeup artists had used natural colors that brightened my eyes and complexion. They'd done an amazing job, including adding a slight red tint to my lips that I hadn't wanted, but I was glad I'd gone along with it. It added the right touch. I almost didn't recognize myself.

"You look gorgeous," Thorn murmured as he stepped behind me.

I smiled, my hand running over the ginormous marble sink in our royal bathroom. The very one that had been the king and queen's, then Drake's, before he was carted off to prison early that morning.

I turned from the mirror and scanned my mate. He almost didn't look like himself, either. He wore a fitted black suit with a white button-down shirt, a black vest, and a tie in the purple color of the dragon royal family. His normally messy hair was combed but not gelled into place, much to the hairdresser's chagrin. I wouldn't have liked it gelled, and I was glad he'd put his foot down.

In bed this morning, he and I had agreed that if we were going to do this, we'd do it with our own flair. We understood we had to look the part, but we hadn't been raised regal, and our reign would be about helping our people, not ruling over them. We couldn't lose the part of us that our people would relate to best.

"You don't look so bad yourself." I grinned, my body warming at his presence. "But seriously, this bathroom is so large, it's atrocious." I glanced at the marble tub behind him and the large rain shower to the right of it. The dual sink was as wide as the room, with more than seven feet between the two basins. To the right of the shower was a huge-ass walk-in closet where our clothes would soon be.

He waggled his brows. "We might not be too upset about it tonight when we get back to our room."

He picked me up and set my bottom on the marble counter, and my legs wrapped around him.

It'll be fun to make sure we violate every inch of this room and our new bedroom. His irises twinkled.

Warmth flared throughout my body. My dragon roared, not wanting to waste a minute before we got started. My human and logical side won out, but damn, it was hard...no pun intended.

A knock sounded on the bedroom door right before it opened. "Your *Majesties*," Elliott cackled. "Your fans await, and of course, Mindy, Eva, Sol, and I wanna escort you out in style."

Thorn tilted his head back and rolled his eyes. "You do realize you won't actually be escorting us outside, right?"

"Hey! Why not? My sister is gonna be royalty," he scoffed.

"Yes, Everly is." Mindy chuckled endearingly. "Not *you.*"

I unwrapped my legs and realized the front of my skirt was wrinkled. I cringed. *I'm sorry.*

I'm not. His pupils slitted. *Anytime I have the opportunity to have your legs wrapped around me, they'd better be. I don't care if our clothes get wrinkled.*

My heart expanded. I loved him so damn much, it hurt.

He helped me off the counter, but when I started for the bedroom, he caught my hand.

Wait, he connected and tugged me toward him. *I want to give you this.* He reached into his suit pocket and pulled out the bracelet my mom had given me. I held my shaking arm out, and he fastened the bracelet around my wrist. "I figured we aren't in danger anymore, and since this is a special occasion, you might want to wear it."

My vision blurred. "It doesn't go with the dress." The white-gold bracelet with interchanging small hearts and diamonds and two dangling white-gold hearts—*Everly* engraved on one and *The love between a mother and daughter is forever* on the other—was more humble than dressy.

"It's perfect with your dress." He ran his finger across the hearts. "And fuck it if anyone disagrees. Their opinion doesn't matter."

A tear broke free, trickling down my face, and I truly understood, more than I'd ever thought possible, what he meant every time he told me these words... "You own me."

Hand in hand, we headed into the bedroom and outside to our people, ready to take the throne and crown that was rightfully ours.

THE CORONATION VIDEO played on repeat on the Dragonnet. Thorn, Saphira, Wyvern, Errol, Brenton, and I sat outside on the gray wooden terrace around a round glass table, a laptop open so we could scroll through the latest news as we ate breakfast. Thorn and I had our backs to the sunflower-yellow château, facing the massive backyard where our wedding ceremony and coronation had taken place.

"This was the most attended coronation in dragon history." Errol mashed his lips together and smiled. "I'm so proud of you two."

Every time I saw the video, I got teary. More than five hundred people had crammed onto the château grounds to watch the ceremony. When the news had spread that Thorn and I had taken Drake down and would ascend to the throne, people—especially the ones Thorn and I had helped—had shown up in hordes, driving all night, desperate to get here on time.

Wildflowers had lined the terrace where the ceremony took place. Errol had proclaimed us the new king and queen and crowned us with gold crowns designed in scales that matched our wedding bands. Then we'd stood and turned to our people, and the cries of joy still rang in my ears.

Most warriors had decided to stay on, but a few had left because Drake had forced them to be there. Not blaming them, Thorn and I had gladly seen them off. There were so many things Drake had done that couldn't be undone, but we wouldn't continue that legacy.

Speaking of Drake—he, Peter, Ladon, and Falkor were all in prison for numerous crimes and would be there for the foreseeable future. If the time came to release them, we'd cross that bridge when we got there, though none of them could threaten us anymore because they were no longer dragons.

The only downside of the situation was that Elliott and Eva had left. They'd even split up, each going to live with their fated mate's thunder. It made the most sense since their fated mates had loving, welcoming families, but they visited one week of every month, which was more than enough for us to get our fill of them.

Tyson had found his fated mate, too, one of Spike's thunder members. He'd wanted a fresh start and had left to live with her.

Though Theron, Hydra, Sol, and Eva had returned to their thunder, Wyvern had moved here with Saphira. Wyvern was the commander of the warriors, and Saphira had become my righthand woman. She was helping me locate all the shifters Thorn could heal. And of course, Brenton and Errol had taken positions as Thorn's and my chief advisors around finances and dragon affairs.

All the women we had protected had headed back to their thunders. As such, Jerry, Gemma, and Uther worked from their family homes, helping Wyvern, since Drake had forced them to relocate.

We decided to let Mira stay in what had been the guest house, the very one I'd been forced to stay in when I arrived. Thorn was slowly mending his relationship with his mother, though it would never be parental...more like close friends. I was glad he was trying; I never wanted him to have any regrets.

Cassidy and Vlad left to join Vlad's father's thunder. He'd lost twenty-one years with them, and now that Thorn wasn't in danger, it was time to mend their broken relationship. They didn't go long without visiting us.

"Well, that's one reason we're so busy." Saphira took a sip of her coffee while she scrolled through her notepad. "I'm scheduling a visit next week for a family that needs healing. What day works best for you two?"

I took a bite of eggs, and my stomach fluttered. I'd felt the same sensation last night, and it had caught me off guard. I swore I heard something softly beating in my stomach. I had to be imagining things.

But when Thorn's eyes bulged and he stared at my midsection, I knew I wasn't the only one hearing it.

Everly, when was the last time you had your period? Thorn glanced from my stomach to my eyes.

I pursed my lips. *Uh...over five weeks ago.* I dropped my fork, and it clunked loudly on my plate. I stared at him. *I'm never late.*

There was another flutter, followed by that fast, pounding rhythm. Like every time it fluttered, a heart worked harder...hard enough for us to hear what was growing in me.

He blew out a breath and smiled. *You're pregnant.* He

jumped to his feet and lifted me from my chair, then turned toward the doors that led inside the château.

"Hey!" Saphira snapped. "Where are you two going? We're having a meeting."

"It can wait." He strode through the doors without pause and carried me upstairs.

The world passed in a blur as I locked eyes with him and murmured, "Where are you taking me?"

To our bedroom...to celebrate. He smiled. *Because we can finally be together without danger, and knowing our baby is coming makes me happier than I've ever been. I want to show you how much you own me.*

My body warmed, ready to show him the same thing.

He was right.

Nothing could get better than this.

ABOUT THE AUTHOR

Did you enjoy this book?
Please leave a review for it on Amazon.

Join Jen's newsletter to get exclusive content, enter giveaways, and receive free books and excerpts.

Join Jen's Newsletter here.

Follow Jen L. Grey on Facebook here.

Join Jen L. Grey's Facebook group here.

ALSO BY JEN L. GREY

Twisted Fate Trilogy

Destined Mate

Eclipsed Heart

The Marked Dragon Prince Trilogy

Ruthless Mate

Marked Dragon

Hidden Fate

Shadow City: Silver Wolf Trilogy

Broken Mate

Rising Darkness

Silver Moon

Shadow City: Royal Vampire Trilogy

Cursed Mate

Shadow Bitten

Demon Blood

Shadow City: Demon Wolf Trilogy

Ruined Mate

Shattered Curse

Fated Souls

Shadow City: Dark Angel Trilogy

Fallen Mate

Demon Marked

Dark Prince

Fatal Secrets

Shadow City: Silver Mate

Shattered Wolf

Fated Hearts

Ruthless Moon

The Wolf Born Trilogy

Hidden Mate

Blood Secrets

Awakened Magic

The Hidden King Trilogy

Dragon Mate

Dragon Heir

Dragon Queen

The Marked Wolf Trilogy

Moon Kissed

Chosen Wolf

Broken Curse

Wolf Moon Academy Trilogy

Shadow Mate

Blood Legacy

Rising Fate

The Royal Heir Trilogy

Wolves' Queen

Wolf Unleashed

Wolf's Claim

Bloodshed Academy Trilogy

Year One

Year Two

Year Three

The Half-Breed Prison Duology (Same World As Bloodshed Academy)

Hunted

Cursed

The Artifact Reaper Series

Reaper: The Beginning

Reaper of Earth

Reaper of Wings

Reaper of Flames

Reaper of Water

Stones of Amaria (Shared World)

Kingdom of Storms

Kingdom of Shadows

Kingdom of Ruins

Kingdom of Fire

The Pearson Prophecy

Dawning Ascent

Enlightened Ascent

Reigning Ascent

Stand Alones

Death's Angel

Rising Alpha